A BULLET
BETWEEN US

THE MORETTI CRIME FAMILY
K DOSAL

ALSO BY K. DOSAL

YOUNG ADULT TITLES

What Do You? Standalone Series
What Do You See?
What Do You Regret?
What Do You Want?
Austin – A Short Story

MAFIA TITLES

The Moretti Crime Family Series
A Bullet Between Us
A War Around Us (coming soon)

A BULLET BETWEEN US

First Edition
Publication Date: May 26th, 2021
ISBN: 9781735884523

Cover art: Mitch Green

K D O S A L . C O M
SWEET & DANGEROUS ROMANCE

DAVINA

I'd walked into an alley where death awaited me.
Terrified under the brittle moon, I'd been left behind as blood swept into the pristine snow.
I'd closed my eyes and waited for the afterlife, welcoming it.
Death had never come for me, but it ended the life I once knew.
Now, I lived in fear, running from a world ruled by vicious men.
An organized world where power and violence had no limit.
And I was in the middle of it all.
It'd led me to him, Ilias.
But in this world, my nightmare was etched in the face of every man I stumbled upon.

I didn't trust anyone, but my heart trusted him.
Even while my mind kept a bullet between us.

ILIAS

I was given an assignment, an order.
Failure wasn't an option. Not when it meant her, Davina.
But how could I keep her alive? I was no hero. Just a man dressed as one, with a heart as corrupted as the same men I grew up with.

TRIGGER WARNING:

Coming from the YA genre, I'm not used to giving a reader any warning. So here it is. Some scenes in this story contain graphic sex scenes, violence, and mature language that may discomfort you. But damn, they were fun to write.

Reader discretion is advised.

.

THE FIVE CRIME FAMILIES

Character Ranking Glossary

MIAMI
The Moretti Family
Lucca Moretti: *Boss, eldest brother*
Salvatore Mancini (Sal): *Consigliere, former boss*
Arlo Greco: *Underboss*
Viktor Novak: *Soldier*
Ilias Novak: *Associate*

NEW YORK
The Vitelli Family
Mario Vitelli: *Boss*
Lorenzo Vitelli (Enzo): *Underboss*
Leonardo Vitelli (Leo): *Capo*

LAS VEGAS

CHICAGO

LOS ANGELES

THE MORETTI FAMILY CREST

For *me*.

NEW YORK

PROLOGUE

davina

A GURGLING SOUND HALTED ME FROM MOVING FORWARD. Quickly, I took in my surroundings, but all I saw were the dark streets of New York, with dim overhead lights illuminating my path back to my studio. An icy shiver ran through my body.

It was past midnight, and the moon was hidden under the looming snow storm, which was why I'd been sent home before my night-shift at the diner was over.

No taxis ran through this part of town — not at this time of night, unless called. The bit of change I'd made from three hours of tips couldn't be wasted on a ride. The roof over my head was far more important.

Glimpsing behind me one last time, I pulled my beanie lower over my head, crossing my arms to keep warm as the snow flurries fell. The left-over snow crunched beneath my feathery footfalls, the threatening feeling of danger causing me to keep my eyes focused ahead and my body on alert.

The unusual sound turned to a whimper, followed by a fist meeting skin. I tried to breathe out the nerves that kept climbing, rising with each step I took.

"Please," a voice begged. "I have a family."

I froze, afraid.

I couldn't cross the alleyway where the sounds originated without being seen. I turned back, but was too far to retreat my steps to be out of the view of the street.

I noticed a dark SUV parked one block away from the alley as I pressed my back to the brick, catching my coat on its grainy texture. My eyes stayed on the blacked-out SUV, hoping it was empty; hoping I couldn't be seen.

"Do you have the payment?" a deep voice asked without a trace of emotion.

"I have a family," the man repeated through his whimpers.

"They all do." His sigh was loud, bored, but his threat remained frightening as his voice deepened. "Don't make me repeat myself."

"*He* said I had another week!" the man spluttered.

"Yeah, that was before you called from your warm office, surrounded by your bodyguards, giving you the balls to speak to the *boss* like you did."

Feet shuffled, and I sank to the ground, crawling towards the metal trash cans in the entry of the backstreet, wishing the darkness would cloak my body from view of the SUV as its door opened.

Using my raven black hair as a shield, I lowered my face to the side. A small opening between the black bags and debris allowed me to watch the view before me while remaining hidden. My breathing quickened, and I bit my shaking bottom lip in an attempt to hold in my fear. The piercing sound of a gun cocking as a bullet shifted to the chamber sent my body into a quiver.

My eyes closed as the gun lowered to the kneeling older man with a bowed head.

The feel of warm tears against my cold cheeks forced my eyes shut, trapping them behind my lids. I caught my sniffles, blowing them into the frosty air to mute any sound my emotions tried to make.

Unwillingly, my eyes snapped open, my gaze sliding back to the man in the shadows.

"The payment?"

My heart pounded.

My tears fell.

My body numbed.

The slight head shake of the kneeling man was the answer the shadowed frame needed.

The muffled sound of a lone silent bullet slipping quietly into the air had no match to the sound once it hit its target. My cry found my ears when the hollow sound of bone and flesh ripped through the man's head, causing a wet splatter to stain the snow. I slapped my palm over my mouth as tears rapidly escaped at the sight of the body flopping lifelessly to the ground.

The dreadful feeling of a presence caused my head to turn, my skin to prickle, my panic to rise. My eyes landed on a pair of dark slacks that were mere inches from me, and I couldn't hold in my cries anymore.

With tearful eyes, I lifted my gaze to a man dressed in all black, except for a gray scarf covering his neck from the harsh winter, leaving only his face and black-inked hands exposed. I stared down at the hand, the bold tattooed letters catching my attention—*NYS*. New York Syndicate.

The Mafia.

My chest shook at the realization, and I finally met his black eyes. They were empty. Soulless.

He didn't speak a word. He simply stared down at me.

With a small nod, he ordered me to follow his steps into the alley and my legs shook as I stood. I couldn't help but look to the empty street before turning back to the dark eyes that awaited my next move. Snow flurries landed in his jet-black hair, his clean-cut beard not hiding his locked jaw.

I never thought I would die just months from turning twenty-three, let alone walk knowingly deeper into the alley where I'd just witnessed a man being murdered. Yet each step I took sealed my fate.

My feet faltered as my head slid back one last time toward freedom. But the man turned his body, towering over mine, watching. His eyes seemed to be *always* watching, calculating. There was no escape. I should've fought, not given in. But my fear beat my will. Fear is powerful to the human mind, and I was its victim.

We'd all heard the whispers of the Mafia, how they cast their wrath on those who didn't look for it, following their prey like a shadow.

"Looks like you found a mouse."

My eyes flew to the killer who stepped away from the shadows and into the dim light, unafraid of showing his face. His eyes connected with mine, but they lowered as he looked over me, light illuminating the left side of his face. A thick scar ran through his left brow and down to the corner of his eye, the angry mark managing to intimidate me further. He was my nightmare, and I was afraid I would never wake up again.

His steps circled me, taunting, while the man who'd found me moved away.

The crunching sound of snow stopped behind me before the feel of leather gloves wrapping around my jaw kept my head from straying from the tattooed man in front of me. The body was flush against my back and his grip tightened, leaving me no room to move. My limbs shivered at the touch of cold metal from a sharp knife digging into my collarbone with warning.

The man in front of me raised his palm, giving nothing more than his order.

"No loose ends," was whispered in my ear from behind, almost as a reminder for himself; a mantra.

The tattooed man shook his head faintly, and my eyes lowered to the body slumped before me. *Soon, I'll be joining him too.*

"What's your name?" My eyes popped back to the deep voice in front of me. But my words were trapped and I couldn't help but steer my gaze away, back to the body. The flash of the casing from the lone bullet that took his life mocked me from the ground.

The knife slid up from my collarbone to the side of my neck with a silent demand to answer.

My ability to speak vanished, and all I managed was a small whimper that caused his impatience to grow. He dug the knife deeper, cutting through my skin until it drew blood. The sting jolted me from his hold, a simple reaction of pain.

He moved fluidly in the dark like a shadow.

Before I got the chance to raise my hands to communicate my mistake, the knife pierced the nape of my neck, slicing down its path, burning along the way.

With each pulse, warm blood ran down my neck and into the merciless winter, and my knees wobbled until they hit the ground. Kneeling.

"*Fuck*."

I looked up as my hands tried to apply pressure, though my body was already weakened at the fast speed of the most vital liquid of life slipping through my fingers.

They both looked down at me. *Tattoo* let a grim expression pass through his features as I blinked up at him. When my gaze met the man who would take my life, I noticed their resemblance.

Nightmare grimaced at my bloody hands as they gripped my neck. "I just reacted." He shook his head toward me, but his words were directed to the man who screamed power over him.

"Get him." *Tattoo* ordered with a nod to the dead body while he watched me bleed out in front of him.

"What about her?" *Nightmare* asked the same moment the rest of my body slumped to the ground. My eyes fluttered, and the bullet casing shimmered into my sight.

"After you are done with him, check her pulse then leave her. She's not tied to us. She'll just be another life taken by the streets." He walked away, and I caught his quick look back to me before I was dismissed.

Nightmare took a deep breath and picked up the body next to me without a struggle.

I was left to the bitter winter as the snow fell rapidly from the sky and a pool of blood spread to the casing — my blood.

I inched my hand through the deep-red stained snow until I grasped the cool metal in my fingertips. The only energy I had left was used to tuck the empty shell inside the pocket of my coat.

The last object to hold my life's attention.

My teeth chattered from the frost bite of the night, and my eyes fluttered until my body relaxed and all I saw was darkness, the same color as the eyes which had found me, and the same color of the eyes of my killer.

I had lost too much blood, teetering on the edge of unconsciousness.

I hardly felt the warm fingers applying pressure to my chilled neck.

My last thought was of my mother.

I hoped the pain of being alone would cease once I met her in the afterlife.

ONE

davina

I T WAS THE STONY AIR, THE COLD THAT CREPT INTO MY BONES that caused my eyes to flutter, to awaken, but the beaming fluorescent lights made it hard to fully take in my surroundings. Disoriented, I pushed past the shining glare from above, squinting, as the loud beeping to my right called my attention as it matched my own beating heart.

Its cadence was strong, filled with life with each beat pumping through my body.

The uncomfortable pain triggered by my movement caused me to wince, and my eyes to close. Yet, my arm felt weighted and weak as I tried to reach and find the source of my pain. I did, and memories rushed back the second the soft gauze met my fingertips.

The alley.

The gruesome sound of a bullet penetrating and taking a life.

The crunchy blood-stained white snow.

The dark soulless eyes of *Tattoo*, and the unforgettable scar of *Nightmare*, the killer.

I'm alive? Yet the real question was, *for how long?*

A shiver ran down my body, but it wasn't from the icy room. It was fear.

The beeping grew with my fear while I scanned the empty room I'd awoken in, searching for danger, but I was alone.

The door opened, and my wide eyes flew toward the direction just as an older woman in light green scrubs froze but quickly recovered. Surprise swirled in her marron-colored eyes as she hurried to the monitor.

"Welcome back, dear. Try to relax." She ushered. "I know it's a lot to take in, but just try to breathe. You are safe."

Safe.

Even with her kind eyes glancing down at me as she looked over my vitals, I felt anything but safe. Not here. Not in a hospital. Not in this city. Not anymore.

Her short brown ponytail swayed, returning her full attention to me as I controlled my breathing.

"I will let the doctor know you are awake, and your fiancé...he's been worried sick."

Fiancé?

I had so many questions, but when I tried to voice them, my throat burned, and a dizzy wave plagued my sight, leaving me wilted on the hospital bed.

"Dear?" The nurse prodded. The beaded necklace that hung around her neck held her name tag. Diana. She picked the faded pink pitcher that rested steps away and poured ice water into a clear plastic cup. "Here, drink this. It may help with your voice." I gladly sipped the clear straw as she held the cup in her hands. "It's normal to feel weak, the large amount of blood loss and transfusion is still trying to catch up with your body." She placed the cup back on the table and grabbed a pen-like flashlight from her chest pocket and shined it into my eyes before tucking it back and heading out of the room.

I was ready to close my eyes as she exited the room but I noticed the tall man in a blue uniform. His back was against the wall in the hall. With the door slightly ajar, his head turned toward the door. His shaved head quickly straightened as another officer stepped up to him. They spoke for a quick moment until the new officer slid his eyes through the cracked opening. His cunning gaze caught mine and the small twitch of a frown etched his features before he turned back to his partner as the door shut.

Tears pricked in my eyes as the uneasy feeling of his gaze remained in my mind.

I'm not safe.

THE LIGHTS WERE DIM INSIDE THE ROOM, IT'D MADE IT EASIER TO open my eyes and look out to the city lights of New York from the open blinds of the window. I didn't get the chance to really look out to the city that almost took my life, not with the feel of a presence on my right. Chills puckered my skin as my body tensed.

"I'm Martin," the voice said. His Bronx accent was strong, and I couldn't dare to turn to face him. Not when I feared it could be their faces I would see—*Tattoo's* or *Nightmare's.*

"I'm here to help, Davina." The sound of my name on his lips was the reason I rolled my head to meet his gaze. He looked tired. Dark circles adorned his dark green eyes as they swirled with fright. His features were strong, pronounced, but even his messy light brown hair didn't match his clean and expensive clothing. Yet, he looked sincere, but nothing was ever as it seemed, not anymore. "Are you in pain?"

Yes.

I didn't reply, and he exhaled. "Here, drink some water." He stood and walked my way with a water bottle in his hand. Martin pushed the button for my bed to rise before unscrewing the cap and placing the chilled top to my lips. I sipped and sipped some more while keeping my eyes on him.

Pulling back slightly, I asked, "Why?" It was rough, raw, and it quivered inside the room. One word, but it asked so many questions, and he would choose which to answer.

"I don't know." He frowned when his sight caught the bandage over my neck. Martin sat back on the vinyl chair while his hand ran furiously over his face and up his hair. "I like to think I would always be the person who helped someone, just never thought to this extent. I just did." His eyes fell to the ground. "I thought you were dead. You were so cold, so pale, and there was so much blood. Too much. You should've been dead, nobody carries that much blood, so I knew it had to be someone else's too."

I froze.

"What do you remember?" His eyes questioned me.

The lie flew through my lips just as easily as it would've been the truth. "I don't."

"Good, you can lie," he replied with a ghost smile, but it quickly faded. "When the ambulance arrived, I scrambled for a reason to ride with you in the ambulance. Said the first thing that came to mind. I just couldn't leave you alone, not until I knew someone would be here with you. But no one ever showed, and something tells me no one will. I just wanted to make sure you were going to be okay."

"But?" I asked the silent word that hung from his words.

"But I believe you are still in danger, and now I'm in it with you."

"What makes you say that?" I rasped, hoping he couldn't hear the alarm in my voice.

"Because why would you have around-the-clock police officers? Either they believe you saw something they need, or someone is watching you."

Bile rose and I covered my mouth in hope it would subside.

Martin only wanted to help, but now I was no longer the only one in danger. I had to figure a way to keep him safe, just as he saved me.

"Do you know how long they will keep me here?" I asked.

"I'm a pre-med student, so I understood the doctor when he said they will keep you until they are sure you don't have side effects from the blood plasma transfusion, especially since you went into hypovolemic shock. You were lucky to not have any organ damage due to the massive blood loss." My brows furrowed but he continued, "But don't worry, they gave you medications to increase your heart strength and blood circulation, as well as antibiotics to prevent any infections."

I nodded, trying to wrap my head around everything he'd said. I'd fallen asleep before I had the chance to speak to the doctor, so Martin was my chance to assess my injuries. "What about the wound?"

"It's been two days, and it's healing with no issues. Maybe after five to six days they'll take the stitching out."

"I can't stay here."

"You can't leave, you are too weak. I'd be surprised if you can even walk straight or have the strength to make it out the door."

"Then I better start gaining it. Will you help me?"

"Of course, but why the rush? You will heal with time."

"Time is a luxury I don't have."

I'd asked Martin if I had any belongings with me, he said my purse and phone. I felt relieved knowing I had money. It wasn't much, but enough to buy a bus ticket and leave the city. I checked my phone, it was dead. Martin left in search of a charger after he instructed some exercises for my arms and legs for me to regain some coordination and strength.

Martin was hesitant to leave, and by his worn appearance, I didn't think he ever would. I ushered him to go and rest. He left some time during the night with the promise of coming back early in the morning.

And while I lay in the cold room alone, I read the cryptic text message from an unknown number wishing I hadn't let him go.

I can help.

IT'D BEEN TWO DAYS SINCE I SAW THAT MESSAGE. AND THREE more had made it to my inbox.

I know you are afraid, but I knew your mother.
Call this number, I can help.
It's a safe burner phone.

I'd ignored every text.

For two days, Martin had been helping me walk around the room, or counting as I stretched my muscles.

For two days, I'd learned a lot about Martin. He was a son to a happily married couple. He had a smart and caring younger brother named Jack, who was ten. I'd asked him if his family knew where he was. He'd said he didn't want to involve them.

The night he'd found me, he was on his way home from a Christmas party one of his friends hosted. He stopped at the red light as the taillights of a SUV drove off from the curb. He'd said something about it screamed for him to turn toward the alley as he drove by. My black hair had stood out from the pristine snow. Martin had called the cops and turned his car around, finding me in a pool of blood.

This spoke a lot about him. He didn't measure the danger he could be in, he just wanted to save *me*.

"I can't hold them from coming in any longer," Martin said as he walked inside the room with a coffee cup in his hands. His pants hung low on his hips, and his expensive grey sweater stretched around his broad shoulders. He closed the door behind him and looked up to see me curled on the bed, awakening from a nap. "Sorry," he whispered.

"It's all right," I replied to both comments. I'd known this would happen. I was surprised we'd been able to keep the cops from interviewing me for this long. Each time, Martin had made an excuse for me, and others I would close my eyes when I heard their voices outside, hoping that if they stepped inside and saw me asleep, they wouldn't come inside. So far it'd worked, and as much as I dreaded speaking to them, it was something that had to be done.

"How are you feeling?" he asked, concerned while he looked over my body as I sat up.

"Sore?" I shrugged, "Although I did make it to the bathroom and back without any dizzy spells or nausea."

"That's great!" he replied, relieved, and we both turned when we heard two loud knocks on the door. Martin looked back at me and his head nodded toward the entrance in question. I nodded. His steps were silent, and the knob turned loudly as he pulled the door open.

An officer stepped inside. The same one whose eyes met mine days before. He looked young, with a freshly shaven face, and his full lips widened with a smile.

I've never been afraid of the law, but there was something about him that seemed wrong, forced, like his smile. He had a cap over his head but removed it as he walked deeper into the room, showing his short dark hair.

"Ms. Cohen, I'm glad to see you doing well. I'm Officer Moss," he explained, turning toward his partner and motioning with his hand. "This is Officer Lewis. We are here to ask you some questions." Officer Lewis was not the same officer who had stood by my door and talked to him days before. Officer Lewis stood quietly behind him as they reached the foot of my bed.

Confused by their titles, I wanted to ask if a detective should be here, but I kept my questions to myself.

"If you could please wait outside, we'll be quick." Officer Moss's attention was directed a few steps away from where Martin stood.

Martin's eyes slid to mine, but I didn't want him more involved than he already was. And even with every sense of my body awakened with panic, I said, "It's fine, babe. Do you mind getting me a drink? Something with caffeine, maybe?"

"Of course, I'll double check with the nurses if you are cleared to have caffeine. I'll be right back," he promised. Martin gave the officer a respectful nod before turning one last time as he stepped outside of the room, leaving me alone with two officers who'd never shown their badges when introducing themselves.

"I'm sure this has been very difficult for your fiancé. How long have you both been together?" Moss asked.

"Time with him has been a blur." I grinned. "Two years, in a couple of months."

"Well, congratulations to you both." He looked down to my clasped hands, and asked, "Was your ring stolen that night?"

"Ring?"

His brow rose, and he nodded toward my hands. I looked down, realizing my slip up.

"Oh, sorry. I'm not sure, maybe it was. I haven't even noticed I had it missing." I could feel both of their eyes reading me, my body language, my words. "I'm sorry, I just don't remember that night. The doctors believe it's dissociative amnesia due to the traumatic events."

"How lucky," Officer Lewis spoke up. His voice was calm, but it was the tone. The sharp dig of not believing my words.

"I really am, the last thing I want is to remember anything of that night, and if my body believes it should stay buried, so do I," I replied.

"Well, is there anything at all from that night? Where were you coming from? How did you end up there? The faces of who did this to you, small details?"

"No, nothing at all. I'm sorry, I wish I had more, but I also don't want to find the answers."

Officer Lewis knit his brows with a nod and turned to Officer Moss.

Although Moss kept his eyes on me, calculating. He quickly forged a smile when the door opened, announcing Martin's entry. "Well, we'll be in contact in case you do remember anything." He looked over at Martin then back to me. "We would really like to catch the guys responsible for this, Ms. Cohen. Best wishes." His white teeth shone through his grimace, and they both stepped back before turning to leave the room.

The moment the door clicked shut, I closed my eyes and let out a relieved breath, but as I exhaled, it became shaky.

"Davina?" Martin asked carefully.

"I need to leave," I whispered.

"Now?" he questioned, but the constricting feeling in my chest grew, suffocating me. "Talk to me." He ushered, but I quivered. "Please."

"A detective should've been here, Martin. They should've shown their badge or identification." I opened my eyes to see his paled face, and I continued, "They didn't even leave a card to call back, a case number — nothing!" I seethed through my teeth. "And the worst part, they knew I was lying."

"Are you sure?"

"They weren't cops, Martin," I heaved.

He looked at me as if I was paranoid, but instead he replied, "What's the plan?"

I couldn't believe what I was hearing. He still wanted to help.

"The plan is for me to leave without them knowing. The plan is to put as much distance from you and this city."

"No."

"Yes. You've already put yourself in so much risk. I can't let something happen to you." I shook my head, but he mimicked me.

"No."

"Martin, I'm just a stranger. You have a whole life ahead of you. Family, school, *everything*."

"Let me at least get you a hotel room, get you somewhere safe."

"No."

"It'll be dark soon, Davina." How could he be so stubborn? Couldn't he not see the danger? "I won't take no for an answer."

TWO
d a v i n a

I T TOOK ALL MY STRENGTH TO CHANGE INTO THE CLOTHES Martin had brought me, as all my clothes from that night were ruined. All I had was my small crossover purse and the bullet casing I'd taken before my clothes were confiscated for evidence. *But were they really?*

As I stood in front of the bathroom mirror of my hospital room, I could see how much these past days had taken me away from *me*; they'd dragged me. Dark circles rested under my tired eyes, my skin was pale, clammy, and my cheekbones were pronounced from the weight loss. But in my reflection, all I could focus on was the angry red scar that marked my skin.

Before coming into the bathroom, I'd looked through the cabinets of the room, searching for the items I needed to clean the wound before re-bandaging. I didn't want to risk an infection, and with the unknown ahead, I wanted to assure it was cleaned before leaving, escaping this hospital.

I winced and cursed once the alcohol-drenched cotton ball touched just the surrounding area of my wound.

"Davina?" Martin's voice flew through the cracked door, worried.

"I'm fine," I replied with clenched lips.

"I can help. *Let me help.*"

I closed my eyes and gave in. "Come in."

"You are mad, woman," he said, looking at the tight grip of my hand that held the cotton. "Here, let me wash my hands, and I'll clean it for you."

I did what he asked, and he picked a new and clean cotton ball.

"It's going to sting, but you know that already. Hold me if you need to."

He didn't have to say it twice. I turned to face him and leaned my bottom against the sink, stretching my neck before gripping his soft sweater.

"What's your favorite color?" he asked.

"What?"

"I'm trying to keep your mind somewhere else. Now, answer."

I looked up to his eyes, and said, "Blue," the same moment the cotton ball stung my wound and my jaw shut painfully.

"What kind of blue?"

"The lightest shade," I whimpered. "The kind so rare that almost looks like ice blue when it catches the sky."

"What about your favorite memory?" His voice sounded distant as I thought back to the time my mother was alive.

"I was six the first time I met the ocean." He cleaned the wound as I spoke, but I couldn't feel the pain, not when all my thoughts were consumed by her. "Seagulls squawked all around my mother and me as we fed them. Others gave us dirty looks for bringing the birds so close to them, but she didn't care. Every time a bird took a piece of bread from my fingers, I squeaked, and my mother laughed. She laughed so much that day, and I loved seeing her smile. We ate at the beach, she'd made my favorite. Turkey sandwiches with chips inside. The chips didn't crunch with every bite I took anymore, but it was perfect as she'd cut the crust ends off the bread for me." He was getting closer to the middle of the slash, bringing me back from the memory with pain.

"What else did you do?" he asked quickly, and his breath blew across my neck, flying me back in time.

"She had a small radio, a tape recorder, and her favorite old rock song came on. She stood and danced, and reached her hand for me to take. She twirled me around on the shoreline while waves crashed, seagulls sang, and we danced to the music until the sun faded, ending the day, but never her smile."

I opened my eyes and found his green ones, as his finger ran across the new tape that held the clean piece of gauze onto my neck.

"Thank you," I whispered.

He ran his thumb under my eyes, catching a tear.

"No, thank you for sharing such a memory."

I gripped his sweater tightly with a faint smile. "You are going to be an amazing doctor."

He chuckled. "Thank you, I hope one day I will."

I JOGGED TO THE IDLING CAR WAITING FOR ME ACROSS THE STREET. My legs were beginning to fail me, but I snatched the passenger door handle and climbed inside.

Martin was waiting in the driver's seat, but as the door swung shut, his eyes took in our surroundings before he sped away. His car still held the scent only a new car would, and inside this clean car, I could see more of him. The expensive and put together life he had.

"I'm paying for two nights at the hotel. This should give you enough time to get the bus ticket for you to disappear."

"Thank you." I touched his hand where it rested on the manual shift stick between us, and said it again, "Really, thank you, for *everything*."

He smirked, sliding his gaze back to the road. "What kind of fiancé would I be?" That earned him a small chuckle from me. "Now, rest. I can see how much making it out of the hospital took from you."

He was right, I felt weak. I closed my eyes and rested my head on the cool window.

We quickly made it to the hotel where I would be staying.

Martin rolled the car into a parking space and shut off the engine.

"I thought you were only dropping me off."

"I just want to get the key and walk you inside."

"Okay."

We both stepped out of his car and into the subtle hotel lobby. I'd offered to pay, but Martin only shook his head, looking at me as if I've grown a second head.

"Stop fussing, Davina." The elevator doors closed with only us two inside. "You'll need the money you have once you are on your own."

I didn't know how to accept so much from him—a stranger. I couldn't understand how people like him still existed in this world filled with so much hatred and spite. At least not after watching someone die right before my eyes. Seeing the emptiness of taking someone's life, the fear. Yet, somehow, Martin gave me a ray of hope, and for that, I would forever be grateful for him.

Martin looked around the hallway as we walked, searching for the room number. Seven-two-six was displayed on the side of the door to our left as we inched closer to the entryway. He pushed the key card inside the slot, and a green light flashed as it unlocked the door. Martin pushed the handle down to open the door for me to step inside.

The dark colored carpet hid any stains from past occupants, but the room smelled fresh, clean, and a single queen-sized bed rested in the middle of the room with an adjoined white bathroom. The crisp white sheets poked out from the neatly folded beige comforter, and after sleeping in a hospital bed for days, it invited my feeble body to lay and rest from today's exertion. But it seemed it didn't only call out for me. Martin flopped on top of the bed, his face hitting the fluffy pillow.

He said in a chuckle, "How about I get you another room? This feels too good to get up."

I stood over him with a dim smile and shrugged.

"Just kidding," he joked, sitting up. "Get any drink from the mini-fridge and any food from the hotel's menu. Don't worry about it, okay?" I was already shaking my head when he stopped me from talking. "Yes, *Dee*. Just say, yes, and let it go. Money is not everything in this world, and luckily I have enough to share it."

He'd used a nickname for me, and he didn't even notice, but I did. "Okay, thank you." I smiled.

"Is there anything else you need before I leave?" I shook my head.

"How about some ice?"

"I could use some ice," I muttered, thinking of my sore wound.

"Okay, I'll go get it. I'll be right back."

"Don't be silly, Martin. I can go." I raised my hands up to him with a slight head shake.

"Fine, just be careful. I'll wait for you until you get back, then I'll leave."

I gave him a quick nod and stepped out into the hallway, not bothering to use my energy by leaving my purse behind.

When I made it to the ice maker at the end of the hall, a sign in bold letters was tapped to the sliding black door of the machine.

ICE MAKER BROKEN, USE 2ⁿ FLOOR MACHINE.

I was tired, worn, and the last thing I wanted was to fetch ice, but I did anyway.

I took the elevator down five floors, and walked to the end of the hall. Small plastic pitchers rested above the machine, and I opened the sliding door to scoop the frozen cubes. Once the pitcher was full, I stepped away and walked back toward the elevator. But I stopped when I saw a cleaning cart outside one of the passing rooms. Small clear bags stood on the top rack of the rolling cart, and I peeked to see if the cleaning service was inside the room. I figured they wouldn't miss one bag, and I needed the bag to fill it with ice for my neck. Ripping one of the bags from the roll,

I tucked it inside the front pocket of the hoodie Martin had got me, and continued to make my way to press the up arrow of the elevator.

The elevator was open to the city, and I stared out into the falling sun until the bell dinged, alerting I'd arrived on my floor.

The doors slid open, but I struggled to take the first step forward.

And like a recurring bad dream, or déjà vu, a cold shiver ran down my body.

Unwillingly, I took a step forward, quietly, but I jolted forward at the sound of the elevator closing its doors, leaving me behind in the eerie hall. The pitcher filled with ice shuffled in my hands, and I gripped the sweaty plastic as a few pieces slipped onto the carpet.

I stood still, listening.

My heart raced, and I looked down to my feet and kicked the melting ice cubes away from my path. I turned back to the opposite side of the hall for danger, and even if I felt it, no one else was in the hallway with me.

Just my mind.

Yet, I couldn't shake off the feeling, not when I was still out in the open. My pace quickened, and as my room came into view, relief crawled inside me. And just as quickly, it vanished.

The door to my hotel room was cracked open when I clearly remembered the clicking sound of the heavy door closing after I'd left.

Please, Please, I chanted.

I could feel the way my anxiety gripped inside me, taking the bit of air from my lungs, restricting me.

My hands shook, and the more I tried to regain control, the more they shook, causing rattles from the ice inside the pitcher. The need to get rid of the pitcher made me lower to the ground, and I placed the pitcher in the corner of the doorway.

With my knees close to my chest, I closed my eyes and inched my head closer to the small opening for any sounds. All I was greeted with was silence.

Don't go inside, my mind screamed. But Martin was inside.

I stood and my body swayed from exhaustion, worry, and the unknown that hid behind the door.

I placed my trembling hand to the smooth feel of the barrier that concealed my fear, forced my hand to push the door open, and I took a step forward.

It was the mixed scent of sulfur and metal that hung inside the room. The same scent from the night a bullet fled from the chamber of the gun when the hammer fired, leaving only the smell of gunpowder behind. The same scent that clung to me as my life slipped away, but now it suffocated me with its death perfume.

Tears sprung in my eyes, my breathing shook, and I dared another step forward.

A cry fled at my sight.

I ran to Martin, but it was useless.

"Martin!" A silent yell stayed trapped in my throat, and I placed my index and middle finger to his neck. But as I looked at his opened and lifeless eyes, I knew he was gone.

His body was awkwardly slouched to the side as his back rested against the headboard. His dark sweater continued to discolor as blood rushed out of his body from two bullet wounds in his chest. I pulled his light brown hair back from his face while I quivered.

"I'm s-so sorry." My cries became hiccups, and I lowered my eyes, unable to look at his dark green irises that held no life because of me.

That was when I noticed his hand hanging off the bed, opened. Below, a pen rested on the carpet. My eyes flew to the nightstand next to him. A hotel notepad laid inches away from falling with ink marks of the pen from the floor.

*Run.
And when you are safe,
Call me.
(212)845-2020
Your stranger fiance, Marti*

Martin had left me a note, but he wasn't even able to finish signing his name.

He couldn't have been killed too long ago, not when blood still ran from his body.

I had to move, I had to run.

But, how could I leave him in this room when he was dead because of me?

He died trying to protect me, but if I died too, what would his death mean?

Run.

I ripped the note from the pad, tucked it inside my purse, and walked away. But before I opened the door, I whispered, *"I'm sorry"* one last time and slipped out of the room.

My tears fell as I rushed to the elevator, and I continuously pushed the down button. My heart beat drummed with panic as I waited, keeping my eyes moving from one end of the hall to the other. Finally, the elevator doors opened. I wiped my eyes and turned, only to find a father and daughter watching me with furrowed brows.

When the elevator door closed, I kept my gaze in front of me. The man pulled the young girl closer to him at the corner of my eye.

"Are you okay? You look sad." The innocence of her voice only made me more desperate to get to the main level and leave before they, too, got hurt. I didn't respond, keeping my eyes locked on the obscured reflections of our silhouettes that bounced off the elevator door. I was too afraid to stain her pure mind with a memory of me. "It's okay if you are, I get sad sometimes too."

"Izy," the man warned.

But all I saw was Martin. My emotion bubbling back made me look up to the numbers that lit as we descended the floors. Then the ding prompted the heavy doors to slide open, and I quickly left. I lowered my face, swung the hood over my head, and slowed my steps to match the busy lobby to keep unwanted attention.

I could almost feel the cold New York winter as I neared closer to the entrance and its grand glass doors.

Almost there.

My hands tingled and my heart spiked with each step I took.

Then I saw him.

My feet faltered.

Officer Moss was talking to the receptionist, a sheet of paper between them as his hands moved as he spoke. He reached inside his pocket, pulled out his phone. He raised his hand to the teller to hold before his head spun.

Our eyes met.

And the doors slid open.

I ran.

"Stop her!" he yelled, but I was already out in the harsh cold.

I ran as fast as I could, knowing he wouldn't give up. My eyes stayed forward as I crossed the street hurried by people walking on the sidewalk. I didn't risk turning back, not when I knew all that kept my body going forward was the adrenaline pumping through me.

But I couldn't run for much longer, because even with the rush of survival, my body was weak.

Profanities were cursed my way as I bumped into people, but even as they faded, the commotion wouldn't end there. They were still following me.

You won't outrun them.

Although, maybe I could out-smart them.

I made a quick left and sprinted, trying to put as much distance between us as possible. When I was ready to make another turn, I dared a look back to see how far apart we were, and how much time I had left.

Officer Moss and his partner were still close, but maybe, just maybe I had enough distance to escape.

His eyes were hard and determined while mine held dread, and I took a sharp turn to the next street, and quickly took in all the cabs waiting for the light to turn red.

A BULLET BETWEEN US

I rushed to the first cab with its light off and jumped inside, only to have my head slam against the plastic back-seat.

"Turn the light on," I said breathlessly, and the middle eastern man turned back with wide eyes. "Please, don't look back. He'll find me." The driver returned his eyes to the road.

"Who?" His accent was strong and filled with shock.

"My boyfriend," I lied.

"I call police," he suggested.

"No!" I exclaimed, trying to hold my tremors, my fears, and added, "He *is* the police."

He clicked his tongue a few times as his head shook. "Oh, dear," he whispered, and just as I wondered if he would toss me out in worry of being in the middle of trouble, the car rolled forward. "Stay down."

Even if I wanted to sit up, my body already betrayed me in the back of this cab with the ray of hope and shelter.

"Where to?" he asked.

I placed my chilled hands on my throbbing wound. "The farthest bus station."

MIAMI

THREE
d a v i n a

THE BLINDING LIGHT OF THE SUNRISE STREAMING THROUGH the window and hitting my eyelids woke me. The sound of children growing restless and the smell of bodies sitting for hours blended together, and the constant swaying that'd made me sick told me the ride wasn't over.

Three bus stops, and it seemed as if my destination would never come. Repositioning my body on my seat and far as possible from the guy next to me, I dared a peek at him. His eyes were closed, and his head rested against the cushion, letting his long black hair curtain around him. He appeared to be asleep, but the heavy metal music that blasted into his ears left me wondering if he was. Then his leg twitched. I followed the movement, watching his Vans tapping the floor as his black backpack stayed tucked between his feet.

"Welcome everyone to The Magic City! We'll be arriving at Miami Airport Intermodal Station at seven-fifteen and the heat is already rising at a nice seventy-two degrees," the voice in the intercom said in high tones and cheer bouncing through the speaker and into the cab.

The inside of the bus suddenly spurred to life as people moved in their seats, but I remained still with the hoodie over my head as my blood pumped with nerves.

Now that I was awake, my neck felt warm and the persistent ache in my wound only increased. I'd tried not to move much as pain would follow, but the pain also created a given reminder of why I'd run away and reached out to the unknown number. I was desperate, and now I looked out the window as the station came to view, I would find out if this was a mistake.

I pulled my dated phone out of my pocket to check the last message.

I'll be there when you arrive.

How will I know who he or she was?

All directions pointed at how foolish I'd been to come here. And when the doors opened, I stood with nowhere else to run. I was exhausted, and my muscles ached from the adrenaline and never-ending tension of being followed.

Martin. I closed my eyes, shaking away the vision of how I'd left him behind. Every step I'd made closer to the bus exit was another minute I'd stolen from his life.

As I stepped outside, the sun's rays swept deep into my skin with its warmth. The smell of clean air and sea breeze met my senses while my eyes squinted, looking around.

Some people rushed out to meet the opened arms of loved ones, while others moved along to their next destination.

Not knowing where to go, or who to search for as I looked around the Sunshine State, the thought of walking away on my own crossed my mind.

Then what, Davina?

Panic swarmed around me as I stood in the bus station in a city I had no knowledge of. Nowhere to sleep or even a place to clean the wound that pulsed heavier with every breath I took.

"Ms. Cohen?"

My body recoiled from the touch on my shoulder. Horror swept inside my heart as I turned in place. A middle-aged man with palms outstretched and wide brown eyes stared back at me, stunned.

The sudden movement I'd made sprung tears of pain from the sting of my healing cut. I held the tears in, paralyzed as I watched his next move.

"I'm Chief Pierce, from MPD. I'm the one you are meeting."

Slowly, he moved his hand to his chest, pulled part of his chain bringing what underneath his clothes hid. A badge.

It didn't mean anything to me. After all, I ran away from two said police officers in New York.

But he knew my last name.

What else did he know?

"My apologies for startling you. I shouldn't have touched you." Chief Pierce's tone was soft as he let the badge hang from its chain.

He took a step forward. I took one back.

His palms rose again, mine sweat.

"I just want to help," he explained.

The question, "Why?" hardly left my mouth.

"I knew your mother. We weren't close and yet, I felt like I had to help you." He exhaled deeply and scratched the back of his head.

"Why?" I asked again, needing more than his vague reply.

"Because for years, I'd tried to bring down the same men you are running from." He almost seemed embarrassed. "I too had to run away from the city. It was becoming too dangerous for my daughter. After getting word from a fellow Chief from New York that you were targeted, I thought of your mom. I'm sorry for your loss."

My mouth was dry, and swallowing his words made it all more difficult. I felt as if he was holding more, but he looked, sounded, and acted sincerely.

I believed he meant well.

Or was I becoming delirious?

"How can you help?" I asked as my will tired.

"I started getting everything settled for your safety here since the first text I'd sent you. All in hopes you would reach back." He huffed with a small smile. "There's a safe house ready for you, along with a few guidelines to go over."

"What kind of guidelines?"

"Think of them as our witness protection guidelines, here in Miami. New identity, food to live off, and a place where you won't be easy to find. After some time, we'll find a more permanent place for you."

I watched his clean shaved features looking for anything he would give away, they gave me nothing. Not a reason for him to lie, or the slightest reaction that he was lying. After everything he'd said, and what I'd taken in, it was the idea of having somewhere to rest that claimed me into this new life.

I was just so damn tired.

"HERE WE ARE," CHIEF PIERCE ANNOUNCED AS HIS UNDERCOVER cop car rolled to a stop in front of a quaint home.

At some point in time the house was blue, but after years of sun, rain, and dirt, it was now faded. Big lanterns hung on each side of the dark wood door, and the yard was well kept. Even if the two-story home had seen better days, it still fit the calm neighborhood.

Chief Pierce got out of the car, but I hesitated.

It wasn't until he stood on the front porch I decided to look both ways down the road and exit the car.

I huddled inside my hoodie with each step I took. My chucks made no sound stopping next to him. The wood below our feet creaked when he opened the door, I shivered.

"Come on in," he said when I stood outside.

The thick, stale smell crowded my lungs as it mixed with the cleaning supplies that must have been used recently. All the walls held an old yellow tint, and the few furniture pieces scattered around were in great condition. Even if the home's age showed, it was in pristine shape, better than the studio apartment I had back in New York.

I didn't need to follow Chief Pierce with my gaze, the creaking flooring gave away each stride he made deeper inside. I followed him to the kitchen, where fruit wallpaper surrounded the trim of the room and ruffled sheer curtains stood still over the small window.

"The house has been stocked with food and utensils you may need, as well as your bathroom." He shifted in his spot. "Hopefully it'll last you a few weeks, but when you are ready to make a short trip for necessities, there's a convenience store just around the block." His bushy eyebrows were expressive as he spoke, and I remained quiet until he said, "I'll wait for the medical examiner to get here to check your vitals before…"

"No," I croaked.

I didn't want anyone's hands on me. No one to see my wound or evaluate the exhaustion I knew I was suffering. I didn't want anyone to know who I was, how I looked like, and most importantly, where I would be.

The least people I met, the less dangerous it would be for me and them.

"I refuse any medical assistance."

"Ms. Cohen, it would be best if…" he trailed off as his eyes zeroed in on my neck.

"All I need is a first aid kit." My tone said enough. I wouldn't be seen. His lips twisted downward. "There's one under the bathroom sink."

"Thank you," I replied appreciatively.

"I'll leave you to rest. We can go over the rules and guidelines to follow tomorrow, and the protection you'll be under."

"What kind of protection?" I asked.

"It'll be finalized a few days from now. Once it's done, you'll have around the clock security." I was ready to decline such a thing, but he cut me off. "It's not a request. It's a must."

I let him leave with a nod. There was nothing else to say. Tomorrow he would be back, but for now, I followed the path up the stairs and into the hall. The first door I pushed through was the bathroom.

My eyes could hardly stay opened as I roamed under the sink cabinet. When I found the first aid kit, I cleaned my wound, letting the tears of pain fall in the lone confinement of the room. Once I couldn't take it anymore, I let the wound breathe by not placing a new gauze, and walked out the door.

The next room I encountered had a bed and fluffy bedding. I didn't care to check the other room, I'd found the rest my body craved. I flopped down to the bed and my eyes automatically closed.

I WOKE UP TO PIERCING SCREAMS.

My screams, as the nightmares followed me awake.

My body shivered from the cold sweats and damp clothes.

Tears rolled down my face as I tried to clear the lifeless eyes, the blood, and fear away.

Darkness spilled from the window. My body curled and I covered my ears from the constant creaking of the home.

Maybe they'd found me.

Maybe I was slipping away.

Either way, how long could I live this way?

FOUR

ilias

MY PHONE ALARM WENT OFF RIGHT AT FOUR THIRTY, reminding me it was time to start my day even as the sun stayed hidden under the Florida sky. I laid on the bed for just a while longer, dreading going into the precinct and putting my hero mask on. Boris's wet nose feathered my fingertips before he stretched and jumped down from the foot of the bed and onto the floor. My gaze followed his movements as his nails clacked against the hardwood floors. He stood against the bedroom door, waiting.

"So, needy, Bo." I groaned. His ears twitched while he continued to wait for me, unamused. The shadow covered most of him, and I smirked at his beautiful black coat and merciless appearance. Because deep inside, he was a soft bastard, a loyal one at that. "Fine, give me five minutes and we'll go," I said to my four-legged beast.

His only reply was to lay his head over two paws, but when he didn't see me moving fast enough out of bed for him, he barked. "Hey, now. I said, I'm coming!" I growled back at him, leaving the bed and heading straight to my bathroom.

I splashed water over my face as Boris sat at the bathroom door, waiting for our morning run.

I slipped into my running shorts and tennis shoes, and made my way to him.

The moment I opened my bedroom door, Bo ran down the stairs, and I followed close behind. I reached for the side table next to the door where I kept his muzzle, but I could tell it was going to be a fight I wouldn't win today.

"Fine, but you better behave." I swear he looked smug, but turned to resignation when I took his leash from inside the drawer. "Sorry, Bo. I don't trust your cat obsession." I patted his head and buckled him.

The air was already too humid, too hot, and the sun hadn't even made its appearance, but it didn't matter to my boy, nor me. We set a steady jog, and my body was already reacting to the rising temperatures.

Crowds of party people were still scattered around the streets of Miami, finally calling it a night, although it was the beginning of a new day. They kept their distance away from me. No, not me, Boris. It was always Bo who could make people piss their pants when he got too close. With cropped ears and close to sixty-seven pounds, he was hard not to be intimidated by, but unless threatened, Bo wouldn't do a thing. Hell, even then, he would wait for my command. We had been jogging for thirty minutes before it was time to head back and get ready for my early shift, but Bo decided to kick it up a notch, picking up the speed and keeping me running faster by his side. Damn show-off.

When we stepped inside the house, he took off to the kitchen, and I could hear him slurping water from his bowl. "Take it easy, boy." I chuckled and headed upstairs for a shower.

My phone rang, and my brother's name popped on the screen. Viktor.

"Da." *Yeah*. I answered in our native tongue.

"Kak dila?" Victor asked how things are, but his tone sounded not so merry, but careful.

"Should I be the one asking you that, Vik?" I switched back to English.

I was young when our mother died, and even if I understood Russian when spoken to me, Viktor has always been better speaking the language, although from a young age he made sure I didn't lose our native tongue.

"Niet." *No.* He took a deep breath and continued. "Just calling to check on you, and making sure you are staying out of trouble."

I chuckled at the irony. "Ehh…"

"Don't fucking play, Ilias."

"Shit, someone woke up on the wrong side of the bed," I teased.

"I don't have time for your jokes, just… Nevermind, Ili."

"Spill."

"I can't," he responded, but I knew what he really meant. *I can't over the phone.* But even if he could, he wouldn't.

"Fine. I'll stay out of trouble as always. Now, let me go. I'll be running late if I stay listening to your unsaid words."

Viktor huffed. "Stay in touch."

I ended the call, running my hands over my face and through my short blonde strands. The only thing I got out of our short conversation was the troubled tone of my brother and uncertainty.

And that was never good.

"ILIAS NOVAK, WHAT THE HELL HAVE YOU GOTTEN YOURSELF INTO now?"

With a smug grin, I watched my partner, Allen, sipping on a styrofoam cup as he waited for me. I walked through the entrance of the precinct to where he was standing. He knew I liked keeping a low profile, so I shrugged and greeted him with an arm shake.

"What the hell are you talking about? I just got back from a call," I asked.

Allen's brown hair was freshly cut around the edges and his brown eyes shifted to the corner as his head dipped. He opened his mouth, but his words got stuck when we both heard my name loud and clear.

"Novak, my office please." I hardly got the chance to see the chief before he returned back to his office.

"That," Allen nodded toward the chief's office, "was what I was trying to say."

I looked down at Allen unamused.

"Thanks for the heads up," I said, and made my way to the end of the precinct.

Allen was the only person I'd ever gotten close to in the Academy. Other than him, I hardly spoke to the others, and that was saying a lot. No one minded. To them, I was just the quiet rookie who kept to himself. When really, I was playing a dangerous game with one foot in the law and the other on a dangerous path.

"Officer Novak, please, come in, take a seat," Miami's chief of police said the moment he saw me standing in his doorway. An uneasy feeling crept inside, but I didn't show it. With a nod, I did as he asked. My thoughts tried to go through anything I might've let slip by, but I was extremely careful. Either way, he couldn't be calling me due to my extracurricular activities outside of the precinct. If that was the case, I would be in handcuffs and behind steel bars, not sitting on one of the burgundy leather chairs in front of his desk.

My phone vibrated for the third time since I stepped out of my car, and I took a peek on the caller ID while he looked through a thick file. Viktor's name flashed on my screen, and the call ended, sending him to my generic voicemail. *Three missed calls.* Lucca, Arlo, and now Viktor. I couldn't risk answering while inside the walls of my work, so it had to wait until I was done with Chief Pierce.

The sound of the folder closing before me made my gaze meet his brown eyes and peppered hair.

"You asked to see me, Chief?"

His eyes assessed me for a while longer in silence, and I kept mine on his, waiting. His lips puckered in resignation, looking like he was finally going to talk after all.

"I'm pulling you to a special task."

I was taken aback. I'd never tried to become better than the next officer, always tried to blend with the rest of the men in blue.

Instead of questioning his request, I nodded. There was no point in explaining how there were more officers with the ambition and experience I lacked. Instead, I kept my mouth shut.

"I'm trusting you will keep this information to yourself as it's completely confidential. This includes the rest of the precinct."

"Yes, sir."

"Good, you'll report only to me," he expressed, as if I hadn't understood his orders.

"Yes, sir."

"From now on, you are in protection of a house that needs around the clock security. There will only be two shifts, you will be taking one of them."

"Who am I protecting?"

"A young-girl."

I waited for him to continue, but he gave me no further details. No name, or why was I protecting a child.

"When do I start?"

"Now."

I watched him more carefully and he'd done good so far in hiding any emotion, but the swirl of dread that swam around his eyes grew the longer this short conversation unfolded, slipping through.

This must have been an important task for him to be concerned, maybe his job was on the line. Maybe he was trying to prove he was the right man for the new position he was now filling. But it was a small team. Too small if it was only him and me, and maybe another officer, which only kept me wondering, why *me?* And why were they trying to keep this as tight as possible? The severity of danger the girl was under had to be the reason. I wasn't the most qualified officer for this, but I no longer gave two shits. I would always protect a kid, this was no different. No point in dwelling on the *why*.

"Anything else?" I asked.

"She's been through some trauma, so tread carefully, please."

With a slight nod, I rose from the chair as he grabbed a small piece of paper, holding it out for me to take. The address.

"Low profile," he said as my eyes scanned the paper, memorizing the address. Once I did, I dropped it down on his desk facedown.

He took a deep breath and ran his hand over his scrub. "Don't use your patrol car or your uniform. Keep your badge and gun hidden on you."

This meant they didn't want anyone knowing the house was being guarded. Easier to fool people with a normal next-door neighbor vehicle than waving a red flag—a cop car. The invitation to come right in because they've found what they've been looking for.

"Anything else?" I asked.

"No, you are dismissed to your new task."

With a nod, I shook his hand. "Chief," I said as a farewell before walking out the door, and out of the police station, happy to be able to go home and change out of this stuffy uniform.

My phone vibrated again, and I reached into my pants pocket, gripping it the same moment I unlocked my black Dodge Charger. I answered Viktor as I climbed inside the cab.

"Yeah."

"You didn't answer Lucca's call. Then Arlo's, so now I have to reach *my* baby brother because he can't do something as fucking simple as answer his damn phone." His agitation was not lost through the line. I took a small, calming breath and shifted my car into reverse, driving away from the station.

"Out of us four, *you* should be the one to understand I can't answer when I'm around the men in blue."

"A text will work too."

"What's so important, Vik?" I asked.

"When are you off?"

My eyes steered away from the busy streets of Miami toward my dashboard, it was noon. "I have an hour right now."

"See you soon," Viktor said before the line dropped. The location wasn't needed, I knew where I had to go.

K. DOSAL

There was no time to stop by my place with the change of plans, and I couldn't show up where I was heading in uniform either. I parked my car in an empty lot and grabbed the duffle bag I always kept in the back seat. I slid my seat far enough from the steering wheel to make room as I changed into dark jeans, combat boots, and a white tee.

I sped away from the lot and headed to my eldest brother's house — Lucca's.

Before taking a right turn onto the road that would lead me to the house, I checked my rearview mirror. Once I was sure no one had followed me, I made the sharp turn.

Lucca's house was more than just a house, more than an estate or even a mansion. It was a fortress; a compound with heavy security surrounding the perimeter. Not only were cameras installed without any blind spots, but there were men guarding it at all times, hidden.

My car rolled to a stop, my window lowered, and I pressed the keycode to get access through the gates. Only Lucca, Arlo, Viktor, the head of security, and I had the code, anyone else had to be let in upon arrival. The heavy gates opened, and the armed guy attending the corner post nodded as I continued to drive past him.

I shifted the gear into park behind Viktor's sports car and grabbed the black cap that laid on the passenger seat. Once my cap sat low on my head, I stepped out of the car and made my way into the terracotta roof and stucco mansion.

The door was unlocked; it usually was during the day. With the amount of people that came and went, it would be impossible to stay locked during the day. Lucca didn't bother with the thought of someone breaking-in, no one would get far enough to touch the front door.

"Did they whistle for you?" Ugo mocked. His dark and hard features and tone were something I was used to from the man I often encountered within these walls. A quick glance to his sly smirk was the only acknowledgment he received from me. I wished I hadn't even given that to him. He whistled as I walked past him with a locked jaw, ready to beat the whistle out of him with my fist. Instead, I ignored him.

I couldn't touch him, and he knew it.

My footfalls were loud against the pristine marble floors. I passed the first set of pillars, then the courtyard that sat in the middle of the house with maintained flower beds all around its perimeter. A small iron table and chairs rested untouched on the far-left corner. Once the courtyard was behind me, I turned to my right and lightly knocked before opening the door.

Lucca's office was grand just like the rest of his house. Floor to ceiling bookshelves in dark detailed wood decorated both sides of the room. He stood with his back to me, speaking through his phone and looking out the big double pane windows that overlooked the backyard and pool. With his attention occupied, I looked away from his tailored black slacks and button up.

Viktor sat on one of the brown leather chairs closest to the mahogany desk. He looked up from his phone and pushed his blonde hair away from his blue eyes. Viktor and I were the only ones who shared blood. Well, half. We had the same last name, as we shared the same mother. Even with different fathers, anyone could tell we were related. Same hair color and blue eyes, although mine were a shade lighter. He was broader and an inch taller than me, but his hardened features and the creases on the corner of his eyes showed our five-year age gap.

He smirked up at me, followed by a nod, but otherwise sat quietly as Lucca continued his conversation through the phone. I walked up to him and rubbed his non-receding hair line just to fuck with him about his age. He quickly waved my hand away with a sneer and my lips perked with a side smile. He motioned for me to take a seat on the open chair, but I preferred remaining standing.

Arlo stood with his arms crossed, leaning against the bookcase. His tired hazel eyes looked my way, and he managed a small dip of his head, greeting me. With my second brother was where the resemblance ended. Arlo and Lucca looked more alike with tan, olive skin and dark hair, but other than that, they were too different to even be considered related. But we *are* brothers.

We might not share blood, but blood was nothing compared to bond and loyalty.

K . D O S A L

I swear each time I saw him, he got bigger. I pat my stomach playfully, referring to his weight gain. Unaffected at my jab, Arlo uncrossed his arms and pulled the hem of his gray tee up, showing off his muscles and ink that covered his body. His brow quirked in response, and I shrugged. His attention shifted the moment Lucca ended his call and turned our way.

Lucca rolled his head and walked to the right corner of the room where the crystal bottles filled with liquor stood on the wood bar. He poured two fingers of amber liquid into a cut crystal glass and downed his drink before pouring another. His eyes stayed on the glass for a second before he turned and gestured to us for a drink. We denied the offer.

Lucca sipped on his drink, composed as always, but his tired eyes matched Arlo's. They seemed stressed even. Which I was sure was the reason he'd already downed a drink and worked on his second. The phone call had his mind racing, but he hid it well. We were the only ones who got to see the small glimpses behind the mask he'd now mastered, bits he'd allowed himself to share with us.

If there was a person I would never want to cross, it was him, my oldest brother. Out of us four, he was the most reserved, and only spoke with purpose and nothing more.

His gaze turned to the cap that still rested over my head, and his eyes lowered to my eyes. No words were needed. I took it off and lowered onto the chair, hoping to relax my now tensed muscles.

"Brief me," he said to Viktor as he remained standing, his eyes following the swirling bourbon in his glass.

"I will have to take a step back from coming so often," Viktor replied.

Lucca lowered to his seat behind the desk, and with precise movements, he removed the cufflinks that decorated the cuffs of his dress shirt, and rolled the white sleeves up to his forearms. From his neck to his fingers, he was covered in ink. Only a couple are from the life I was not a part of. A dangerous life. The rest of his tattoos were his way of expressing what he wasn't able to with words.

"I will let you know if anything changes with any shipments, either I'll send you a message to meet or I'll find a way to come and talk to you," Viktor explained.

"That bad?" Lucca's brow quirked.

"New agent. And a tad too nosey for their own good."

"Does Arlo need to take care of *it*?" Lucca sneered, and his demeanor darkened.

"No, I will," Viktor replied too quickly, and I wasn't the only one who'd noticed. "I said *I will*, Lucca," Viktor repeated. He would never speak to Lucca this way outside these walls.

Lucca took a second before he tilted his glass to Viktor.

"Perfect timing, really," Arlo said from the corner, waiting for Lucca to elaborate the details he was willing to share with me inside the room.

"With the hierarchy changes Sal will make soon, things are a bit... *warm* on this side of the law."

Sal was as close as a father figure to Lucca. He was also stepping down, and word was he would be handing the keys to the Kingdom to the closest person he had, his prodigy, Lucca. The Mancini name would end with Sal, the Organization becoming the Moretti Mafia.

I'd kept my distance from this life—the mafioso life. Seeing three of my brothers in the *Cosa Nostra* was enough. Although, I wasn't the hero, or the outstanding abiding officer. No, I was one of the insiders they had in the precinct, but the most trusted. It was the deepest I would go, and the extra cash it brought was better than living with a cop's salary. If that meant I was a crook, I didn't care, as the last thing I wanted to see was my brothers behind bars. So, I did it for them.

"Keep your distance, both of you." Lucca nods to Viktor and me.

Arlo was right, this was the perfect time because with my new assignment, I doubted I would have much time for my extra-curricular activities. Honestly, I was relieved. I could have my full attention in keeping the child safe.

"Everything good with you?" Lucca asked me, and a ghost smile played on his lips. It never turned into more.

With a ten-year difference, Lucca still tried to father me. In his eyes, I would forever be the six-year-old boy with the tear-streaked cheeks, holding on to him as he left behind the Home for Boys at the age of sixteen. He'd come back three years later when Arlo turned sixteen and helped him get emancipated. Two years later, Viktor turned the magic number on his sixteenth birthday, having the chance to leave the childhood hell-hole we'd been in. Viktor had denied Lucca's help. Viktor wouldn't leave me behind — alone. A week later, Lucca had returned with Sal. I never found out what deal they'd made, how they managed to give a sixteen-year-old, who was jobless and homeless, custody of an eleven-year old.

We never spoke of our childhood.

And I'd never brought it up again, even when the questions inside burned to be answered.

"Just laying-low," I said with a smirk, and a small chuckle escaped through Lucca's lips.

"Good, keep it that way. Now, get out of here. The grown-ups need to talk." Lucca's eyes were laced in humor, while his face remained passive.

"*Baciami il culo!*" *Kiss my ass,* I joked in Italian and stood. I wasn't as fluent as the rest, but there wasn't an Italian curse word I didn't know. Lucca shook his head.

"Ilias." Lucca stopped me from opening the door, and I turned to face him. He stayed quiet, and looked over to Arlo. Whatever they silently shared made his lips twist before he shook his head. "Never mind. Just let me know if you hear anything out of the ordinary."

"Always."

"One last thing." His face hardened. "Don't ignore my calls."

With a nod, I placed my cap back on as he dismissed me.

When I slammed my car door shut, I realized I'd taken longer than I planned. Once I was outside the gates, I floored the gas pedal, making my way back into the busy city.

FIVE
ilias

EVERY DAY FOR THE PAST WEEK I'D BEEN BORED OUT OF my mind. Sitting inside my car for hours was not what I had in mind when Chief Pierce had signed me up for this assignment. I still didn't understand how a twenty-six-year-old with no experience in this field was appointed with such a task.

The first day I'd driven around the perimeter, learning as much as possible about the neighbors, searching through our database, and memorizing exit points of the house and where they led to.

I had two hours left until the next private guard, or officer shift, started. I'd never seen him in our precinct, and I didn't care to ask which county he was from. Although, I knew it was him by the description the chief had given me.

The small two-story brick home was always quiet, the windows covered by blinds that never moved, and no one ever left. If I hadn't known any better, I would've thought the house was empty.

I popped the local news from my phone in between glances to the house, but quickly, the news had my undivided attention.

"Over thirty arrested in massive Florida drug bust after months of investigation," read the headline. **"Six-point-three millions worth of cannabis seized by the DEA and FBI."**

My heart stopped when I recognized one of the DEA agents in the picture. Viktor.

Sliding my finger on the screen, I called him. The phone rang and rang, and with each second that passed by, my leg bounced until I heard my brother's voice.

"I guess you just saw it?"

I ignored his question. "Your fucking face is nice and clear even with your fucking DEA hat on!"

"I am DEA, Ilias. Just like you are a police officer."

And it was a dangerous game we played.

"Can't say much, just know it was all set. Everything is fine, right how it was supposed to go."

So, it was planned?

"Not his?" I asked, referring to Lucca.

Viktor had the sense to laugh, "Oh, *brat*."

"Don't *brother* me, Viktor!"

He continued to chuckle, but it settled. "If you would've kept reading, you would've been able to put the pieces together. You know, the headline and subline don't give as much information as it would the rest of the article."

Smart-ass. Yet, he was right. I didn't read the rest.

"Just keeping the streets clean," he said, and I almost chuckled. We do it for Lucca's benefit.

"Got it." I smirked, and my gaze roamed around the street. My attention shifted back to the house when the front door opened ajar. "I got to go, Vik. Stay safe," I muttered, ended the call, and sat, waiting for someone to walk out the door. But, no one did.

I shuffled over my seat, ready to get out and check if this was a cry for help.

When my hand touched the door handle, a girl stepped out.

No, not a girl.

A young woman, and she couldn't be much younger than me.

Her sleek shoulder-length black hair shifted slowly as she looked around the doorway. Her eyes were covered under a dark pair of sunglasses, and with her guarded body language I knew this was her. The girl whose life was at risk. But, she wasn't a girl, nor a teen, and I chuckled at my own stupidity. How could I have believed someone as a child would have been left on their own with no inside supervision?

When she stepped out of the door casing, her body was fully clothed in yoga pants, and a matching jacket. She seemed ready for a run, but the pair of chucks that adorned her feet gave her away. Her feet slid forward, and her chest rose and fell with resignation when she took the first step down on the small covered patio. I watched as she kept her face trained on the last step.

I thought I would never get out of the car as I waited, but then she took that last step and followed the broken paved sidewalk path. I left my car and followed her from afar.

The chief mentioned she was aware she had protection, and I hoped it was the reason she constantly took in her surroundings once we were in a busier street with foot traffic.

Even in January, Miami's heat was still a bitch, and if she wanted to have a low profile, I wouldn't have walked out with a jacket on. Her steps quickened the closer we got to a convenience store. I didn't want to lose her, but the store was small enough that we would cross paths.

I took a chance and followed her inside.

She walked around the stuffy aisles, not wasting time with brands and grabbing the closest items she needed. Mostly, it was all canned and microwavable meals and hygiene products, like toothpaste and shampoo. Even if I wasn't on the same aisle as her, I could still see her in the corner mirror that hung above. When she headed to the cashier, I had already taken a left down the aisle, grabbed a sports drink, and waited until she was out the door before checking out.

Her long, slender legs gave her a bigger head-start than I would've liked when I spotted her back on the sidewalk. Four shopping bags hung from each hand. She shifted them for a better grip when her hands grew tired. Her strides were long, and with the fear of losing her, I picked up my speed.

We were now inching closer to her street, and just as expected, she took the right turn to her final destination. My footfalls slowed to create some distance as I approached the turn.

Yet, she was gone.

I could feel the way my lungs constricted with alarm, because I knew she didn't have enough time to make it home yet.

My eyes roamed the street before me, searching for unfamiliar signs or cars as my feet sped to a light jog. As I passed the back-side entrance of the antique corner shop, my eyes flickered to the shadow on my left, and my hand automatically reached for my concealed gun behind my waistline.

But I stopped once its voice reached my ears, and my body slowly turned toward the shadow.

"Beckett or Novak?" Her voice wanted to sound strong, but all I heard was the uncertainty in her tone. My name had fallen from her parted lips with a question. But why risk her own safety?

The more I took her in, the more agitation crawled inside of me at the absurdity. There she stood in a small back entry of an old shop, back against a door that was most likely locked, trapped with no exit aside from the one I was blocking. With her sunglasses high on her head, fierce dark eyes shimmered with anxiety around her delicate features. Her cheekbones were pronounced slightly over the ordinary, keeping me guessing the reason behind such a thing. Was she eating? Was she sick? Did she need to visit a doctor?

I stayed quiet, taking her in. Her thick dark hair contrasted her fair skin around both sides of her face, hiding every inch it allowed until meeting her torso.

She shuffled one step back.

I was making her nervous, but just as I planned to ease her mind, her right hand caught my attention. It was just a small twitch, but enough to be noticed. Inside her thin fingers was a can of pepper spray. And that agitation no longer crawled over me, instead it snaked around my lungs, causing my breathing to uneven as my eyes blurred with outrage.

Was this her plan? Confront a perp with a can of pepper spray? Emptying the can would only provoke them and their need to stain their hands with her blood. To take her, and do things even she couldn't fathom.

This was no child's play.

And in this world, danger and death were no strangers to those who believed they could beat the odds of the dark underworld by foolish plays.

DAVINA

IT WAS HIS ICY BLUE EYES THAT FIRST GAVE ME FAITH I WASN'T wrong. The same light blue that had always calmed me, the only color I tried to find every day around my new life to keep my fears tucked inside. To keep me living, even if this way was no longer living. Yet as he lingered before me, trapping my only way out of this confinement, my heart rate sped while his eyes darkened. I tried to let my breath silently escape from my parted lips, trying not to move. Trying not to make any sudden movements as the unexpected was never welcomed. The memory of Nightmare's knife slicing into my skin as punishment for moving caused my healing scar to scream, and my blood to boil, reminding me to stay calm. With each breath and second that passed by as his lips twisted with a sneer, I counted the beats of my heart by each time my scar pulsed.

He was tall, too tall to be able to shove past him. Too broad to be able to try to wiggle away from his form. And the way he caught the small tremor from my hand, he was also too quick to try to outsmart.

I was fucked.

All because I was tired of being scared. Because I believed I could tell the good from the bad, and the soul from the soulless.

His square jaw locked and his head tilted slightly to his left, catching his light blond scruff with the sunlight. The sneer never faded, and he clasped his hands together smugly, relaxed, as if he was enjoying the shudders I was sure my body couldn't hide. My eyes quickly lowered to his hands to see if there were any visible markings on them, but there was nothing. Not one drop of ink adorned his skin.

I didn't get the chance to let my mind make anything out of it, not when he finally spoke, causing my skin to shrivel.

"What if I told you I'm not either of them?"

Neither Beckett or Novak. My body froze.

"Huh? What could *you* do?" Even while his tone mocked me, his voice was rich and strong.

The can of spray no longer felt like a weapon as we stared at one another. It seemed I had brought a joke into my own funeral, a sick joke at that.

With a disgusted expression, he looked as if he wished to peer into my mind. All I searched for was an opportunity to flee. Then, he shook his head.

"Grab your bags." He nodded toward the plastic grocery bags that littered around my feet, and ordered, "Let's go."

I didn't move, and neither did he. Unamused, he raised a brow under his black cap, and sighed loudly. "Put your fucking toy away, because unlike you, I would like to get away from the sun's rays."

I still didn't move. Why would I? I didn't trust him.

"I'm Novak, satisfied?"

"What about your first name?"

"You know it?" he asked, surprised, then dismissed my question. "Look, if I wanted to harm you, I would've done that a long time ago."

I played with his words in my mind, but he didn't look like someone I would follow just a few minutes before. Hell, he still didn't. Why fight me in the middle of the street where a bystander could see, instead earn my trust, take me back home. And…

"Seriously? You want to think shit over after you cornered yourself into a death trap, now?"

"What's your first name?" I asked one more time.

"Ilias Novak. MPD badge number, six-nine-four-five-four." His blue eyes returned to their paler color, and his shoulders relaxed. "Now, can we go or do you need my shoe size too?" He didn't wait to see a reaction, he only spun on his heel and walked toward the house.

Picking up my bags, I followed. The walk was short, and Officer Novak would look back past me, his eyes taking in all our surroundings. I was right, he was good, and had a soul.

My eyes stayed trained to the wood front door of the house once we reached the entrance. We stood in silence, and the feel of his stare made mine fall to the faded black welcome home mat. His black combat boots shifted, and as the seconds passed by, the quiet stretched.

"Hey." His tone was soft and asking for my attention. "Do you need help inside?"

Raising my head, I slid my eyes past his dark jeans, up his light crew neck tee, until I met his soft blues as they looked down at the bags I carried before they met mine.

I wasn't ready to be alone with him. "I think it would be best if you didn't." I'd always been polite, caring how I treated others, but lately, I'd been too afraid to care.

"That's fair." Ilias nodded, understanding swarming around his irises, and I fisted the gold doorknob. As I took a step inside, his voice stopped me. "I won't apologize for scaring you. Not when it was the only way to get you to understand your life isn't a game. What you did was foolish."

I didn't face him, not when I could feel tears pricking my eyes as our first encounter settled in, and possibilities of what could have happened played in my head.

With a nod, I walked inside, locked the door, and released a shaky breath while he stayed outside. The small piece of metal inside the zipper pocket of my jacket was hard to ignore. My fingers picked it out along with a beat-up paper note. I looked at the note without the need to read it, not when I'd memorized the words and phone number long ago. My body slid down, pressed on the door, until my bottom hit the hardwood floors, and my silent tears ran from the pain. With my fingers pressed on the metal, the cool feeling soon warmed, and I rolled it around as the first word on the note rolled in my head. *Run*. But there was nowhere to run, not when it felt like this was the last turn.

A sob vibrated deep from my aching chest as the reminder of that night sat on the pads of my fingertips. The empty bullet casing shimmered, and I wondered how long I had before my past would come for me.

SIX
i l i a s

I NEVER CLAIMED TO BE A HERO. THAT TITLE WAS TOO FAR out of my reach. I hadn't cared for it, still didn't. Although, when I was given a task, an order, I'd never failed. This assignment was no different. It would be easier to protect her if I knew who I was protecting her from. The best way to keep her safe was to collect as much intel as I could and put the pieces together.

The sun lowered, the hours passed, and as I sat on the black leather seat of my car, all I could think about was her. Even her name was unknown to me, and after seeing the dread I'd caused, I decided not to chance my luck.

I wanted to frighten her, to scare her enough to make her worry for her life as I was appalled at her decision questioning someone who'd been following her instead of running. Which only contradicted her. How could she be smart enough to notice me but foolish enough to believe I couldn't have been the same people who she feared.

But as I pressed on to teach her a lesson, her panic rose, and I decided now wasn't the time. Not when she seemed on the verge of an anxiety attack. When it seemed like she needed a decent meal to fill in the hollows of her cheeks, and the color that was absent from her face. Or the way she needed to feel protected, safe. But who was I to make her feel that way?

My last hour was up, and I saw the next officer who would be guarding her for the night driving slowly past me with a nod.

I decided Bo would have to wait a bit longer for me to get home as it was time to search for answers, and I took the next turn toward the precinct.

I TOOK EACH STEP TWO AT A TIME UNTIL I MADE IT TO THE entrance of the precinct. The evening shift was just starting to settle in, and the light to Chief Pierce's office was on.

Good, I hadn't missed him yet.

Nodding and waving at a few familiar faces, I made my way to the back of the room, knocked twice, and waited to be let in.

"Come in." The moment the chief saw me, he quickly rose to his feet. "Is she all right?"

"Yes, she is." I cleared my throat the same time his shoulders relaxed as he sat back on his rolling chair. "Excuse me if I'm out of line here, but I need more information about this case so I know what I'm dealing with. I'm afraid I don't know how to guard when I don't know from who."

"Sorry, Novak. It's confidential. Sharing it with you could compromise the operation."

Fuck. As expected, he wasn't going to talk.

"You made me believe it was a child." I stayed standing by the widows of his room, looking straight at him.

"I did no such thing, officer Novak. Sorry for the misinterpretation." His eyes veered to his wristwatch, his reaction annoyed me, and I masked my features from showing it. "I guess you've encountered Davina?"

Davina.

Her name was unique, delicate, and rare. It suited her.

"I did."

"Anything you would like to inform me, Officer Novak?" Pierce asked.

"Actually, one thing." I took one step closer toward his desk and rested my hand on the border. "Is she sick?"

"What makes you think that?" His lips twisted, and his eyes looked away from mine when I replied.

"I can tell she's not at healthy weight, and she may suffer from anxiety. Is she being seen?"

"I'm sure."

How reassuring.

"But, if you think she isn't, shouldn't you be finding out, Officer Novak?"

I refused to let his comment affect me, and I kept my breathing and posture even. "I'm supposed to be looking out for her safety, not babysitting." Well, maybe I didn't hold it in as well as I wished, but things needed to be cleared.

"You are to keep her safe, that extends to her overall well-being, understood?" His fierce tone and response only gave me more questions.

Did she witness a crime? Is she testifying to a crime? What other reason would not only her safety, but her health, also be important?

"Yes, Chief."

"Good, you're dismissed." Pierce waved me off, returning his attention to the paperwork before him.

The drive home was quiet even as the streets of Miami roared with life outside my vehicle. Merely a shade of gold painted the sky as the dark claimed the end of a day.

While I waited under the red light, I watched as people walked by in crowds, groups, or couples. Smiles and laughter bounced around one another, and it mesmerized me how so much light walked around, when all I've experienced and knew was pain, danger, and death.

I'd lived for my brothers, but even when we were together, we weren't able to let go of our demons, or the humans we were becoming, and had become. Always tense, always looking for the next strike coming our way.

Oh, how easy life could be if I walked around oblivious to the world I lived in. Even before I was born, my life was already set for corruption. All mapped out to where I now sat. Looking in from the outside, I like to think this was how it all was supposed to be. Dangerous games and cheating death. Otherwise, I wouldn't have the brother who raised me or my other two who had a hand in my upbringings. We were all just kids trying to survive in a world with no options.

In the end, the world needed balance, good and evil, and I was at the verge of crossing a line I couldn't come back from. I could feel it closing in, creeping with each day that passed by.

But now that Davina had been assigned into my life, the line of evil stalked my every second.

Parking my car in the driveway of my home, I took a deep breath to ease my head, but the thoughts only grew stronger. That was until I opened the front door and was greeted by Bo's nose and paws on my chest.

"I missed you too, asshole," I cooed as my hands ran over his face and sides. "Come on, it's been too long since you've been let out." Boris agreed as he whined and sat before me, waiting to be leashed.

The night brought cooling temperatures as the sea breeze traveled around the city with welcomed chilling winds. Boris sniffed and walked calmly next to me, enjoying the night as I was.

Then she came into my mind like the traveling winds of tonight, without consent. Davina's fearful eyes bore deep inside me, and all I wondered was how she was.

Assignments weren't meant to be taken personal, and that was why I'd tried to stay as far as possible from such tasks. But how could I not, now that I'd met her?

"Let's go, Bo. It's been a long day."

SEVEN

d a v i n a

A S TIME PASSED, AND THE DAYS ROLLED BY WITHOUT A trace, my time in Miami started to blend together. I couldn't tell the difference between the days of the week, nor did I care.

There was no use for my phone. I had no one to call, no family or friends to speak to or check on. I had no work, not one reason to leave the house aside from a quick run to the convenience store. I didn't try to make friends or get too close to anyone. I learned quickly what it could mean for them. Death. So, I stood inside this house, day after day watching how everyday mirrored the next.

One thing I had noticed every morning was the black car parked across the street, sometimes farther, sometimes too close, but never parked the same spot it had the day before. Even the black car became a pattern, the new normal.

He became part of my normal, even from a distance.

Still in bed, I rolled onto my side toward the digital clock with the bold red numbers. It was five till seven. Ilias would be here any minute.

At times, the sun's rays penetrating the sheer curtains from the window would shimmer in different colors and hues. Like a routine, I stared up to the ceiling in search of the light and faded blue color to call me out of bed. But it was later than the usual time it would happen. The sun was now higher in the sky, brighter, and gold had taken over the blue hues.

Closing my eyes, I tried to picture my favorite color, but my mind could never get it right. Nothing compared to that blue hue color that only appeared early in the morning. It may seem silly how a color could affect the rest of my day, but as a creature of habit, it'd become something that helped me hold onto hope after my mother's passing. But hope had left too.

I kicked the covers off my body and sat. The walls of the room were bare, like the bookshelves and every piece of furniture inside this house. An empty journal sat on top of the small, chipped desk that faced the window. Even the bedding was bland and simple in beige tones, and whites.

I lived here, yet, the place looked stripped of life.

The two-story cottage vibrated as the sound of two knocks flew up the stairs and into my room. My eyes widened, wondering if I'd really heard correctly. Then the sound became louder.

My heart beat unsteadily, my mind trying to comfort me with the hope of seeing a familiar face.

No one would knock on your front door to attack you first thing in the morning, right? I shook my head. Anything was possible. Walking toward the window barefoot, I peered out but couldn't find Ilias' black car parked anywhere. I checked the time. It was shortly after seven.

Where was he? He was never late.

The knocks continued, and I slipped a hoodie over my head and quickly slid into my Converse shoes, not caring about socks. Spinning around the room, I headed back to the bed and plucked my abandoned cell phone from under my pillow. The battery life was at ten percent. Great.

The front door knob rattled again, and a creeping chill flooded through my veins. Whoever it was, was trying to come inside.

Run.

The word swirled in my head, and I tried to calm my breathing, judging the best exit points out of the house aside from the front door.

The spare bedroom faced the backyard, a clear path to a narrow road that led to the main street. Without another minute to think my plan through, I walked silently out of my room.

As I walked deeper toward the back of the second floor, I passed the narrow staircase and my gaze lowered to the front door.

I could hardly breathe from the pressure that kept constricting my lungs and the weight of panic dragging my senses.

"I'm going to count to two before I bust this door if you don't answer."

Ilias.

My shoulders shook from the hard exhales of relief that drowned inside me.

"One," he counted, and I rushed down the stairs knowing he would be able to hear me nearing closer. Yet, he didn't stop. "Two."

I opened the door.

His eyes widened and looked me over before his gaze moved past me and inside the house. And all I could center my attention to was his eyes.

"Are you all right?" Ilias's voice lowered, but his body stood alert.

"Yeah, you just..." I dropped my gaze to the ground and noted the large paper bag with fresh food inside.

"I scared you, didn't I?"

I met the feel of his frosty gaze. There was no reason to deny it, not when his icy eyes softened.

"Where's your car?" I asked, but my voice rose, sounding more as a demand.

Ilias's eyes narrowed. "A street over, I couldn't find parking."

Nodding, I took a quick look back to the brown paper bag and wrapped my arms around me, calming my heart. *You're safe.*

"I brought breakfast and lunch," Ilias said carefully, and all I did was look at him in silence, focusing on the right now. Something alive and present to center me back to the world of the living. Him.

It was the first time I saw him without his black cap on. Blond hair waved naturally away from his face back to his head. The scruff over his pronounced jaw was a shade darker, and just as the rest of his large body, his lips were full, inviting. The denim jacket that rested over his broad shoulders highlighted the color of his eyes, as the white tee underneath brought his lightly sun-touched skin to life.

Ilias looked poised, confident with his own body and certainty to protect.

That was true beauty.

My emotions bubbled because of how far I felt from that kind of beauty, that kind of confidence I lacked. My feet took a step back as my eyes veered to the side, trapping the brewing warm tears. I didn't want to look weak, but I was a mess. And all it took was a good look at him to understand how I never left the streets of New York.

"She'll just be another life taken by the streets," Tattoo had said, and he was right. I might be alive, but my life was gone.

"Hey, now." Ilias took a step forward. "Come here," he whispered. Then his arms were wrapped around me, pressing my cheek into his chest.

He smelled like sea breeze and sandalwood, and he felt like a promise—hope. Gripping him and the feel of hope tighter, I didn't care about boundaries.

I stood in his arms until my breathing no longer ached, and the tears that threatened to fall vanished. Even then, I hesitated when my arms dropped to my sides and took a small step back.

"Better?" His slight smile was anxious while his eyes filled with uncertainty and questions.

With a thin smile, I answered.

"Good, now I need to put this food in the refrigerator before it spoils." Ilias twisted his body and headed toward the front door, not waiting for my response.

While his back faced me, I looked down at my body. My appearance couldn't be more un-put together than his. Yoga pants, unlaced Converse, and a hoodie. But I didn't want to leave him alone downstairs, so I settled on my attire. Then I remembered the low, messy ponytail in my hair didn't hide my scar to its best ability, so I slid the hair tie off, ran my fingers through my hair, and let it fall to both sides like a curtain. I fixed the hood around the nape of my neck higher and assured it was snug over my collarbone the same moment he turned around.

"Lock the door for me, would you?" he asked, making his way deeper into the home.

The deadbolt clicked, and I turned as he passed the stairwell, heading toward the kitchen. I followed his steps, and watched as he placed eggs, vegetables, meat, and cheeses inside. Flour and a few other ingredients now lived inside my cabinets, and he turned to face me.

Ilias leaned his back on the edge of the counter, crossed his arms. "Want to ask you a question, and I need an honest answer," he said.

I stayed silent, unable to promise something that I may not be able to answer because there were things— things I knew were death wishes to utter.

"By the way you answered the door, it seemed you felt in danger. Were you planning on doing something?"

It seemed Ilias saw everything, noticed and picked apart it all. And the way his eyes were now watching me, he already knew the answer.

"What was your plan, Davina?"

Davina.

"How do you know my real name?" My shoulders straightened.

"I know it's hard to trust a stranger, but I'm here to keep you safe."

I closed my eyes for a brief moment before I answered. "You would be surprised how much a stranger had gained my trust before."

Ilias's eyes narrowed. "Then trust *me*."

"The guest room," I replied as our eyes locked. He uncrossed his arms, and rolled his shoulders back. "I was going to go out the window."

"The window?" Incredulity rang in his voice. "Have you taken the chance to look out this said window?" He took a step away from the counter top, not stopping until his feet met the first step of the staircase. Ilias looked back, noticing I hadn't moved, and continued going up the stairs.

He was a cop, sworn to protect, but his aura was troubled, mixed in light and the edge of darkness. It was dangerous to follow him up the stairs. Yet, I still did because in some twisted way, Ilias made me feel secure and all it took was a glimpse of his light blue eyes.

When I stepped inside the guest room, it smelled stale from being closed in for so long. A bare bed stood on the far left side with a beat-up nightstand, and a lamp that had seen better days with dust flurries over its yellowed shade hanging sideways. Ilias stood out with his large frame in such a small room as he faced the window.

"The paint is so old it's stuck to the seal. You would've never gotten this open," he said quietly. "Even if you had, the only way you could've escaped is by jumping." Ilias faced me, eyes turned to slits and lips curled on the corner with displeasure. "You wouldn't have made it far. With such height, your body would've been injured. Even a rolled ankle can disable the best runners."

"I never said I thought it through."

"Then tell me." He took one step closer until his body towered over mine. But I felt no fear. "What would you have done next?"

"You ask questions as if I know the answers," I replied honestly. He took a step back, his head slid to the side as his eyes tried to decipher me like a riddle. "The truth is, I have no fucking clue."

Ilias nodded before dismissing me by walking past me, and I stood frozen with my eyes locked on the stupid window.

"You shouldn't curse. You're too pretty for such words."

"Pretty?" I asked with a huff and turned.

Ilias waited by the doorframe.

"Delicate."

"*Delicate?*" A scoff rasped my throat.

"Graceful, gentle, soft," he kept on.

"You mean, weak?" I sneered.

"Not at all. Reckless? Maybe. But never weak." He peered over my body as if he finally solved the riddle. "Truth is, I don't see an ounce of weakness inside of you. Just fear. And fear can get you killed with reckless games and decisions."

Ilias's icy eyes moved around the room before he crossed the doorway and walked into the hall, adding, "So, let's do something about it by starting with a decent meal."

I was left speechless. He didn't just see all of me, he saw through me.

I stayed behind in the room when I found a sharp letter opener in one of the drawers of a dresser and worked on cutting the paint that had sealed the window shut. Clatters from pots and pans came from the kitchen downstairs. Once I got the window to slide open, and the fresh Florida's air swarmed inside the room, I left to start my morning routine.

After a shower, a clean hoodie, socks, and a pair of yoga pants I felt better and more at ease. The smell of a freshly cooked meal made my stomach aware of its state of hunger, and I walked into the hallway. But as I stood on top of the stairs, I looked over the guest room.

I'd left the door and window open to let the stale air out, but now it called for me.

My feet moved forward until the window was before me. I stuck my head out and checked the distance. And I wondered, could I?

But hell, why wonder when my life could well depend on me jumping out of this window. I swung my foot over the opening, then the other, until my ass balanced my weight on the edge. Twisting my body, I lowered until the only thing holding me was the grip of my forearms over the seal, and my feet stayed flat on the siding.

I took a deep breath, looked down, and pushed my feet.

I let go.

My gaze stayed underneath me, and as my feet touched the ground, I bent my knees slightly to catch my weight. A small pang from the force traveled over my legs from the height of the jump, but no pain followed.

I smiled. And when I looked away from the dead grass, the kitchen window became my view. Behind old sheer and ruffled curtains, Ilias's wide eyes caught mine. My smile turned to a smirk and he shook his head, but his lips twitched in the corners with a forming smile. Then he was gone, and the backdoor opened.

"You are fucking mad, *kroshka*." Ilias laughed, keeping the door wide open. "You proved your point, now come inside before breakfast gets cold."

With each step I took, my smile never left. It felt good to know I could get out even from the second floor of the house. It brought back a piece of confidence I'd thought was gone forever.

Two plates sat on the pocket-sized table in the corner. I'd never used it before and always ate standing at the kitchen counter

Without mentioning how we both would barely fit, I took a seat and stared down at the plate.

"I made *syrniki*. Have you ever had them?" Ilias asked before he took the seat in front of me.

"Can't say I have." Picking up my fork, I cut through the small round bread.

A decent amount of jam and an unknown white portion of condiment was also on the plate along with cut strawberries. I dipped each corner of the bread to try both condiments and popped it into my mouth.

My mouth tangled with different flavors, from salty, creamy, to sweet and fluffy. I hummed with appreciation.

Ilias chuckled. "They are a traditional Russian breakfast."

I cut a bigger piece and added a strawberry. "What are they?"

He thought for a second, watching as I stuffed my mouth. The next bite, I made it smaller and he noticed as he smiled.

"A cheesy pancake?" he tried describing. "I ran out of tvorog cheese at home and the only store that carried it was closed, so I substituted it to the closest I could find at the market which was quark."

I nodded, as if I knew cheeses. If it wasn't American or mozzarella cheese, I wouldn't know the difference. But we were now talking about cheese, and my smile returned.

"So, you're Russian?"

"My mother was."

Was. His mother was gone as was mine.

"Sorry for your loss." I gazed over my almost empty plate.

"It's okay. It seems a lifetime ago." He pushed his plate my way. "Here, eat what you want. I actually ate before I got here."

"Then why fix two plates?"

"Something told me you wouldn't have eaten otherwise."

Seeing Ilias inside the house, sitting within arm's reach with eyes that never left me, with eyes that wanted to care and protect me, subsided the emptiness from this morning, bringing warmth to my heart. His body relaxed the longer he spoke.

I trusted a stranger once again, but this time, I didn't want to make the same mistakes. I didn't want to feel weak or useless. I wanted to be able to take care of myself if the past ever caught up with me. Most importantly, I didn't want to see his sky-blue eyes lifeless before mine. But I needed my mind and body ready for the future, and to achieve that, I needed him.

"Novak?" I began, just as a hidden smile formed around his features. "I have a favor to ask."

EIGHT

ilias

THERE IT WAS AGAIN, MY NAME ON HER LIPS, AND HER timid round eyes peered up at me.

At that moment, I knew I would say yes to anything she needed, anything she would ask. All it took was the sound of my last name coming from her mouth.

Davina brought many emotions, too many in such a short time. Impatience for her lack of strategy and reckless thoughts. Her haste plans agitated me, and her denial of the situations she could put herself in annoyed me, but after witnessing her jumping from the second story window, I was shocked at the lengths she'd go. *What was she thinking? She could have hurt herself.* From the other side of the kitchen window, her head had risen with a beaming smile that quickly turned into a smirk when she noticed me watching her. It had made me chuckle, seeing her reaction. Soon, pride had taken over as I knew a jump without adrenaline pumping through your veins wasn't always easy to make, especially to someone who had never done such things. Seeing the glimpse of belief shining back in her eyes, even if it was only for a second as her shoulders rolled with self-confidence, had been plenty to bring me happiness for her.

"Help me fight back on my own," she'd asked.

With so many emotions that had run past me in just one morning, I responded the only way I could — blindly.

She could've asked for anything, but she'd asked for strength. I could help, but her body language would close off time after time as the day passed, skittish from the simple sounds around the house that made her flinch.

I didn't know where to start. I needed help from someone who had the most experience with the subject of fears, and that person was Lucca. Although, Lucca was more like someone who extorted fears, not vanquished them. The thought of calling Viktor quickly left, he would question me non-stop. So, it left me with Arlo, Lucca's right hand, and my second eldest brother. And he was perfect for the job.

I left the house with the promise of returning tomorrow so we could begin working to help her gain the same feeling of strength she felt after her jump.

With her house in my rearview mirror, I called Arlo.

"I'm in the middle of business, Ili. This better be urgent." Arlo's voice was short, but he would have to deal.

"Define urgent?" I smarted off.

"*Stronzo,* are you fucking dying?" he hissed, calling me an asshole, and I chuckled when his Italian accent only strengthened.

"*Niet.*" No, I replied in Russian, and he took a deep breath. The background noise subsided from his end. He was now alone.

"Italian or Russian?" Arlo asked with a smug smile in his voice. I was the least fluent in both languages, while neither him nor Lucca had an inch of Russian in their blood.

Neither.

"English," I said, unamused.

"What do you need?"

"Advice?"

The line went silent until the sound of his deep breath and seagulls squawking filled my ear.

"Fine, I'm at the marina. Be here in twenty, not one minute before."

"You know I can't be seen at the shipyard," I reminded him.

"Thirty minutes. Malvagio's. Back alley." The call ended before I got the chance to tell him Lucca's night club was too far to make it in time with traffic.

I sped through the streets of Miami, knowing one thing my brothers detested was unpunctuality. With each boulevard I crossed, the darker the roads became and the more it attracted the night life to awaken. People and cars swarmed the streets the closer I got to downtown's elite roads. There was no point in finding a parking valet a street over from the club. Most skyscrapers, hotels, and buildings were owned by the Moretti or Mancini last name.

A black Cadillac SUV blocked the back alley of Malvagio's and three figures hid in the shadows as my car rolled past it. Not far, I was lucky to find a parking meter open by the road. Quickly, I left my car behind and checked the time on my phone.

I was already five minutes late, seven by the time I turned into the alley.

"About time, *fratello*." It was impossible for Arlo not to mix his Italian, but the word *brother* was always nice to hear. Another man stood a few feet away from him, who I remembered as Mario. I'd never seen him so close to Arlo. Usually, I would catch glances of him from afar, but maybe he'd moved up to be so near.

"*Brat*," I responded in Russian with a nod and a smile, but both quickly faded once a mocking whistle echoed around us.

Arlo dismissed Mario, and Mario silently walked away, returning to the car.

Ugo smirked in the shadows, a cigarette hanging off the corner of his mouth as he leaned back against the brick wall. My hands fisted by his arrogance before Arlo narrowed his eyes, dismissing him as well.

Ugo finally submitted, flicking his cigarette into the alley before trailing Mario to the parked SUV.

"Staying out of trouble?" Arlo asked when he felt comfortable to be out of listening ears.

"Define trouble."

"Always needing shit spelled out, don't you?" he snickered, stepping out of the shadow. His dark eyes and strong Italian features erased Ugo's whistles from minutes before, and my hands relaxed with the familiarity of my brother.

"What can I say? One question leads to a hundred."

"I'll give you that. What do you need?" Arlo asked, but my eyes wandered around his attire. He wore black slacks and a black dress shirt with buttoned cuffs.

"New wardrobe?" I asked, already missing his dark tees and full inked sleeves.

"Is this what you came here for?" He tilted his head with furrowed brows.

"No."

"Then spit it out, Ili."

"I got a new assignment," I began, and Arlo straightened. "Who may have a damn death wish by their reckless actions, but it's only because they're afraid, and if I can help build their strength and confidence..."

"Why did you come to me with this?" His eyes pried for answers.

"Because something traumatic happened in this person's past."

He cut me off. "Haven't we all?"

"Yes, but we don't let fear or terror consume our daily life, Arlo."

Arlo nodded, understanding, but his words were far from what I was searching for. "Ilias, some of us can just hide it better." I watched as his eyes demanded. "Why do you care?"

"I just do." I shrugged.

"You realize I master fear in others, not the other way around?" Arlo twisted his head as a loud clatter erupted on the opposite corner where his guys stood. Laughter bounced in the alley, a group of people stumbling along the sidewalk and walking around metal cans. "If you insist, all I can advise is seek medical help? God knows, I wouldn't. But it could be a start."

This seemed to be a waste of time.

Annoyed at myself for even meeting him, I shook my head and took a step back to leave.

"Hey, while you are at it, throw in some self-defense? What better way to overcome *normal* people fears than feeling like you have *some* form of power?" He chuckled mockingly.

I ignored him.

"Ilias, wait," Arlo's voice stopped me, and we were too far apart for our conversation to be private. He knew this too.

Arlo walked up to me, assuring only I could hear as he whispered, "The streets are violent, *fratello*. The change is here, and newcomers will arrive soon. Lucca and Viktor wish to keep you in the dark, but I'm the one in the field and see the threats. I mean it. Keep your head down and away from us until Miami's underworld is fully under Moretti's name."

"I will. Plus, I have my hands full at the moment."

I entered the rowdy streets with his words and warning in my head. As I slid inside the quietness of my car, the louder my mind became. I raised the volume of the stereo. Anything, to keep my thoughts distracted. It didn't work. It wasn't until I got home with Boris by my side that I let my mind ease, my tension relax.

Boris!

How could I not have thought about it before?

Boris had the power to bring assurance, protection, maybe even help with a restless night.

"Hey big guy, you up for an interesting task?" I asked Bo and all he gave me was a grunt, uncaring. "Yeah, I knew you would." I chuckled.

AFTER PLACING A PLUSH BLANKET ON THE BACK SEAT OF MY CAR, I patted my leg. "Get in." I ushered, and kept the back door open for Bo. Instead, Boris stood there, watching my hand.

Today was not the day for him to act out, but I did give him a minute to be an asshole. He deserved it because he knew what was coming once we would make it to our destination, and the muzzle in my hands confirmed it.

Bo huffed and jumped inside.

Once I got into the car, I asked, "Want some music, Bo?" Bo whined, and I took it as a *yes*.

The skies threatened rain as the clouds gloom darker by the minute, and with the sun hidden, the temperatures dropped to its lowest of the season. Fifty-eight degrees Fahrenheit.

Bo hated getting wet unless it was a warm bath, so I was glad by the time we got to Davina's safe house, not a drop had fallen yet. I rushed out of the car before the pour began, and opened the back door.

"*Myjesto*," I commanded Bo to stay. He froze in attention knowing play time was over. I placed his muzzle without a struggle and leashed him. Boris might get his way at home, but outside he obeyed without a fault. "*Molodet*." *Good boy*, I praised him, running my hand over his coat. "Come, I want you to meet someone. Be nice, Bo," I warned.

I knocked on the door and waited with Bo on all fours, calmly looking around the street behind us.

"Holy shit!" Davina gasped as she opened the door only to quickly close it.

I smiled, and looked down at Bo, who's head was twisted to the side while his pointy ears moved, listening.

"May I remind you, you were the one who asked for the favor."

"I changed my mind!" she hollered, making me chuckle.

I patted Bo, bringing him closer to me and whispered, "She didn't mean that."

"Yes, I did," she bit back.

"Come on, Davina. He's harmless."

"Is that the reason his mouth is in a basket? Because he is sooo *friendly*?"

"It's called a muzzle, and I only did that so you wouldn't have to be afraid of him hurting you."

The door slid ajar, her head peeked out. Her silk black hair hung in soft waves, framing her gentle features. With lips puckered, her doe eyes only watched Bo.

Boris quickly caught her anxiety, and he sat tilting his head down but kept his eyes on her.

"Why is he watching me as if he wants to eat me?"

"Really?" All I saw was sweet Bo trying to look gentle.

"I've never had a dog," she whispered, and Bo straightened, turning his head toward the street. Following Bo's attention, a car passed by with blasting music. Davina opened the door wider, and the sound brought Bo's interest back to her.

"Place your palm up toward him so he can smell you. I promise, he will not harm you in any way," I reassured her.

With a small nod, she did as I instructed, and Bo stood. She took a step back. I watched her in her black leggings and oversized hoodie as she hid her hand under the cuffs.

This was harder than I'd expected, and I wondered how far those fears of hers ran.

"Have you ever been bitten by a dog?" I asked.

"No."

"A threatening situation with one?"

"No." Her eyes lifted to mine, and as I held her gaze, her eyes eased.

"Then stop over thinking. I would never do something that could cause you harm, Davina."

Her teeth trapped her bottom lip, and with a small nod, she tried again. This time, there was no fear, no sign of panic. Slowly, Bo took a step closer to meet her hand to sniff. Once he did, he gave it a nudge, and naturally she ran her hand over to stroke his face.

"He'll tolerate you. After all, that was quite the first impression you made on him," I joked.

Davina smiled, and soon, she was petting him with both hands as she stood with fuzzy yellow socks on the threshold.

"Come." She snapped her fingers and walked backward inside. Bo followed her, pulling me with the leash. "Does it hurt him?" Davina gestured to the muzzle.

"No, but he's not a fan of it."

"Can I take it off?"

"Are you after his heart?" I questioned; her smile widened.

"Maybe?" Davina shrugged, watching me.

Holding her gaze, I commanded *stay* in Russian, *"Myjesto."* Bo stalled between us.

Davina hunched over Bo, slowly caressing his face as she tried undoing the buckles.

"His name is Boris, but I call him Bo at times. He will respond to both."

"Hey, Bo," she cooed the same moment the muzzle came off and Bo licked her hands. Davina hasn't stopped smiling, and I took that as a good response to Bo, maybe this would workout, maybe this would help ease her anxiety. But before I would let Bo stay the night to guard, they both needed time to get used to one another.

Once Davina straightened, I let Bo explore the house as we now stood feet away from the front door, unsure of what to do next, what to say.

"So, about your favor," I began. "I got some ideas I would like to discuss."

"Sure, would you like some coffee or tea, Novak?"

I kept my smile from forming when it was all I wanted to do once I heard my name. This was the third time she'd said it, but it was never my first name. I looked over her toward the kitchen. The countertops were bare and, if I remembered correctly, she didn't have a coffee machine when I looked inside her cabinets the other morning.

"You don't have a coffee maker," I added.

Her lips twisted with a nod. "It's instant coffee. Not the best, to be honest, but it does its job." Davina tucked her hair behind her ear, and my eyes followed the movement, unable to keep my gaze off her. She lowered her eyes, and I gave her the space she craved to hide away.

Davina was a contradiction to me. Never sure of what I should do, how to act, or how far I was pushing. Her signals always confused me, intrigued me, but mostly, they kept me searching for glimpses of more of her.

"Truthfully, I'm not much of a coffee drinker."

She sighed in relief once the silence was broken. "I love coffee." Her head shook with a snicker, as she turned and headed to the kitchen.

Sitting on the kitchen's bar stool, I watched as she opened the cupboards. She filled a small pot with water and placed it over the stove before picking up the can of instant coffee, another with sugar.

"What's your favorite?" I asked.

Davina turned slightly in place as she scooped ground coffee with a spoon and into a plain white mug. Everything inside the house was outdated, from the dark cabinets to the white and black appliances, to the green wallpaper that decorated the walls. Yellow tint covered the home of where it had once been white. Some would call it charm and character, but I called it old and forgotten with time.

"I like any coffee, but usually prefer it black. The stronger the better, sometimes a dash of sugar. If I'm feeling adventures, sometimes flavored."

Huh, another contradiction.

Once the kettle whistled, she finished her concoction and faced me. "So, what are your ideas?" She took a sip, her hair and mug hiding her features, only her eyes visible over the mug.

Without softening my voice, I blurted, "I think you need to see someone."

Davina almost spit her coffee back into the mug. Her throat bobbed, swallowing the liquid.

With lips twisted, her tone turned defensive as she murmured, "You think I'm crazy?"

"Many people see a therapist, it doesn't mean there's something wrong with you. It means we all need some kind of guidance in our daily lives to cope and understand our own mind."

"Do *you* see someone, Novak?" Her brow lifted, already knowing the answer.

How could I explain my life was more complex and darker than the everyday cop? I was that one bad apple in the precinct that could stain the reputation of the whole force by just the name of my two eldest brothers.

"It's complicated," I replied. Her posture asked for me to continue, to explain, but as I stared into her dark eyes with my mouth sealed, she gave up with a head shake. "But I can take you, I'll make sure you are safe, and there's no record or trace to follow."

With her eyes on her mug, she said, "I noticed you knew my name without me mentioning it before." Her lashes fluttered as her eyes rose to meet mine. "My *real* first name, not the one I was asked to give by your superior. But do you know my last name, Novak?" Our eyes stayed locked, and while hers hardened and aged before me, mine only sought answers I desperately wished to know, but she held them in her lips. "You don't." She placed her mug on the bar, not letting my eyes go. "Then what makes you think I could speak freely to someone about my troubles when I can't even say as much as my last name?"

She left me speechless, immobile to say the least as her gaze trapped me in her despair.

"I still think opening up will help ease the pain you so clearly suffer from."

"It's not an option."

"Why?" I fished for at least a bit of information she may slip, but she's smarter.

"Tell me, Novak. What do you think you know about me? For example, I know you are very perceptive and notice things, details. So, what have you come up with?"

So are you, Davina.

"By the way you are hidden and the information given, I know it's a fact your life is in danger. I don't know anything else, but…"

"But?" she urged on, leaning closer to the bar.

The way you hide with your hair and big clothes are a cry of your insecurity. Every time I'd see you, your eyes are puffy, and I'm sure you cry yourself to sleep, but after a few hours they return to their regular size filled with hope. No, not hope. Despair, as you wait for what you are running from. It makes me want to hug you and tell you it'll all be okay, so once again you can have hope for humankind. You also twist the ends of your hair when you are deep in thought, which happens many times as you often get lost in the past and present. I notice the way your chest quickly rises and falls when I get close to you, but is it due to fear of me? Or fear for me? If so, why? You also take a step back every time I take one closer to you, are you afraid of men? Maybe you are afraid of me.

I could see so much but not the right things. Instead, I replied, "You wear warm clothes, although Florida is not cold during winter, which makes me believe you're not from the north. You use your hair to hide behind, but it's a failure as your face is something to remember. You want to stand up and be strong, but you use reckless and unrealistic tactics to see another day." Davina's posture stiffened and her arms crossed as I continued on, "The dark circles under your eyes talk about your sleepless nights, and the light hollows of your cheeks tell the many meals you've skipped." Her cheeks flushed, and her chest rose with every word. "Maybe nightmares haunt you, maybe you've lost your appetite from what you've experienced. Hell, it could be the anxiety crawling in your bloodstream, making you jump at every sound inside an empty house, or—"

"That's enough," the empty and broken tone whispered through the air.

"What? Am I hitting a nerve?"

"No."

"I think I am," I dig.

"I think you are stepping too far," Davina's voice rose.

"How far? Because I can keep going."

"I said, it's enough," she seethed.

"I am right. Right?"

"No."

"Please, even your broken reply speaks the truth."

"You were right about one thing." Davina lifted her head. "I do hate the cold, but where I'm from, winters are brutal, and snow and ice are best friends."

Huh.

"It doesn't change the fact that you need to open up to someone."

"Let me get one thing straight, Novak." She picked her half empty mug, discarding its contents down the drain before placing it on the sink and turning back to me. "I will not be seeing anyone."

"Fine, I won't ever mention it again." I let go, and she nodded gratefully. "But, only if you answer, why? Why can't you just take the help that's offered to you?"

Davina closed her eyes briefly and walked away. Then, over her shoulder and just a few feet away from me, she gave me one last answer. "Because I'm not willing to risk another's life for my own."

I learned two things. One, she was a northerner. Two, she'd lost someone recently, too recent. Did one of her family members get caught in the midst of the danger? Was it a lover? It seemed no matter how many questions got answered, I would still be left with more to follow, and new ones to brew, leaving me right where I'd started. Nowhere.

Davina walked away, and I let her. I'd pressed on with no limit, but now with the idea of seeking professional help out of the question, I had to start on phase two and build her confidence alone. I knew it wasn't going to be easy, not with the way the rest of the day would slither awkwardly in silence.

NINE
d a v i n a

I WAS UPSET. I'D SHOWN EVERYTHING SO EASILY THAT HE was able to see right through me. He was wrong about how I hated the cold, but it was safer for him to believe the reason I hid behind warm clothes and hair was due to the weather. Ilias was far from the truth, yet, he inched and tested each possibility to understand and make sense of me. Why did he want answers when all they did was burden and kill? Some things were better unsaid than giving them power by making them more real into the world.

Maybe it was my denial. Either way, I would not speak of that night.

For the next three days, Ilias knocked on my door. We didn't exchange any words, and only Bo would walk inside, sniffing each corner of the creaking house until he would find me upstairs in my room. He would lay under my feet as I wrote in my journal. And every day, I grew closer to Bo, and I hated each night he left me alone in the dark. Bo always stood close by me, his silky short hair and body bringing me heat. When he wanted attention, his cold and wet nose would nudge me to play with him, or to be let out for a few short minutes.

"Your dad will be here shortly to pick you up, Bo," I said, turning toward my bed where he spread comfortably. Bo opened one eye with a huff, and closed it back up peacefully. "I wish I could sleep like you." I chuckled.

The knocks at the door sprung Bo out of the bed and quickly out of the room. His heavy paws scratched each fast step he took down the stairs, and I trailed behind him, trying to keep up. His short, cut tail wagged excitedly as he stood by the door.

When I opened the door, alluring ice blue eyes took me in before they lowered. I watched as Ilias's smile widened seeing Bo sitting patiently next to me. It was the first time Bo greeted him this way, and it seemed Ilias had been waiting for it as he cooed, "*Moloder.*" His native tongue made me aware of the sultry tone of the language, and I wanted to hear more from him. I knew he had praised him as Bo puffed his chest, stood, and walked over to him.

Ilias buckled Bo to his leash and looked back at me. This was the time he would leave with just a nod, and I would shut my door and step back into the quiet home. Instead, tonight was different.

"Don't wear something baggy tomorrow," he ordered.

I was baffled, ready to slam the door in his face from his tone and arrogance.

"I meant, don't wear something that would slow down your movements tomorrow." His blues looked apologetic, and I waited for him to continue. "About that favor, I have something in mind if you are up for it." My brow rose. "Self-defense." He shrugged.

My eyes took in his frame, the difference between our bodies and the strength I knew he carried. I barely reached his chest, and he was twice the size of me. He could easily toss me out of his way with just one arm. That was how I knew he would be perfect to teach me such a thing.

I eased my posture and looked into his magnetic blues as a strand of blond fell over them. "Thank you."

"I'll bring some Tylenol." He chuckled, leaving me behind with Bo at his side.

Great.

AFTER ANOTHER SLEEPLESS NIGHT, I WAS ALREADY TIRED BEFORE the day started.

I watched Bo's head crane to the side as he watched Ilias rummaging through the duffle bag he'd brought today. My attention, too, was on him. His body filled the black Adidas sweats, and his shoulders stretched under the white tee. His back muscles were visible, and I caught myself before my gaze was able to wander. I'd already seen how his left hand carried no ring, or how he never mentioned anyone special. It created questions involving his personal life, but the last thing I needed was to fantasize about Ilias. Although, lately, he was all I could think about.

"I brought my laptop. It's secure for you to use, and I've added a mobile hotspot so you'll have internet." He placed the shiny laptop on the sofa and began moving the center table away, creating a large open area in the living room.

"Thank you," I said sincerely. "You didn't have to."

Ilias brushed it off as if it was nothing. "I figured a good movie or TV show could help pass time." He stood, acknowledging me. "You should stretch before we begin."

I stared at him. A small smile appeared when he looked down, and he sat on the hardwood floor with both feet stretched in front of him as he touched his toes. Meeting him, I mimicked his movements and we stretched in silence. Our only audience was Bo, who laid on his side with his head on the edge of the couch, watching our every move.

"First step in self-defense is not to win. Your goal is to escape." Ilias stood, his large frame hovered over me.

Confused with his words I replied, "But–"

"No fight is ever a fair fight, Davina. Sometimes, your only weapon is your body, so you have to use quick thinking and flee to safety. Nothing more. Even the most skilled fighters make mistakes. But your mistakes can cost you your life." Ilias stretched his palm for me to take. It was hard and rough yet gentle against my soft touch. Even as our hands differed in appearance, they molded into one without effort. I didn't want to let go as his touch felt right, nothing seeming out of place. He took my silence for nervousness, and gave my hand a gentle squeeze—one that gripped right through me. "Don't worry, we'll take it easy." Unaffected by our closeness, Ilias let go.

We both took a few steps back.

Ilias transformed, his easy and approachable demeanor changing quickly, and I was left with a side of him I'd only experienced once from the first time I had met him. His smile was gone, and he looked detached from any feelings. Eyes that chilled my body with menace.

It happened so quickly, I could already feel my lungs constricting, my pulse prickling my hands as it ran down to my fingertips, and all it took was to see Ilias in a different way.

To see him in a threatening way.

"You *are* afraid of me." His quiet voice trailed off in shock. But as I looked into his now light blue eyes, I saw it'd affected him.

I shook my head, raising my palms up to explain it wasn't him I was scared of, but oxygen seemed to vanish from my lungs. I wasn't good at confrontation, and I could never find the right words to explain the reason I made bad decisions was because I couldn't think straight when my throat was closing in and my eyes ached with unshed tears. That my mind blocked any rational thoughts, or the way my stomach turned, and I'd feel ill and cold sweats would come and go.

"No." Unable to meet his eyes, my gaze fell to the ground.

"Then what is it, Davina? Please, explain to me so I can help." Ilias's feet slid forward, mine took one back. "Look at me." I complied to his demand. A crease formed between his brows as his lips twisted. "Please."

"You were right the other day," I admitted. "I don't sleep well. The house is too loud at night, and when I do close my eyes, I'm woken by nightmares of blood, pain, and loss. I hardly have the energy to do daily routines or simple tasks. I hate the moment the sun goes down because I know I'll relive it all over again, but at times, the sunlight isn't any better.

Not when I see small reminders of how I survived when others didn't." I chuckled, but there was no humor, only grief for the innocent girl I used to be, the simple life when I'd lived as a waitress. The time when all I'd worried about was to make enough tips for rent, and if I could walk home in the weather. "I know you want to help me. But as you stood there, with a face stripped of emotion, I froze. It's as if you'd triggered something inside me where I feel like it's happening all over again, as if I was taken back in time."

Ilias closed the distance between us while I tried holding the tears that acted on their own. "I can't get it out of my head, Novak. I'm just stuck in this alternate space in time, where my body is trapped in the present, but my mind and soul were left in the past."

I felt his warm touch on my cheek bringing me back to reality. His thumb ran under my eyes, and wetness smeared as he stroked it away. I kept my eyes tranced to his as their color did what I searched for, comfort, grounding.

"I can't believe I missed it," he said, brushing my hair away from my face. Worry came over me, realizing the beginning of my scar could be seen if he just titled my head slightly to the side. Maybe he already did, but as his eyes continued looking over mine, I doubted he had.

"Missed what?"

"You suffer from post-traumatic stress disorder."

What?

"I'm sorry, I would've approached self-defense in a different way than this if I had known. You hardly know me, and we should work on other things like your sleeping patterns and panic attacks before even starting."

Panic attacks?

"Wait, Novak." I pulled back to get a clear look at him. His hand slid slowly off me and went straight to his hair, combing it back and leaving it at the nape of his neck. His biceps jumped with the movements, distracting me, but I managed to continue, "You are not making any sense. Slow down."

"Really? Because I can see everything so clearly." Pity filled his irises, and I detested the sight.

"Don't. Just, don't look at me that way."

"I just pushed you so hard," he murmured.

"Don't!" I shouted. My palm hit his chest with each sentence spoken. "Don't treat me differently. Don't look at me with pity. And don't *ever* feel sorry for me. Just don't, because I don't have PTSD, nor do I suffer from panic attacks."

Ilias covered my hand with his. "*Don't* be in denial." My lips thinned as anger swarmed my veins, burning through its path, ready to lash out. "You do, Davina," he tried again without pity. "You've become numb, yet at times you feel too much to the point something as natural as breathing becomes a hurdle. You are scared every minute you are awake, and even in your sleep. You don't want to think about it, so you suppress it. But no matter how hard you try, it's always there, mocking you to the point of illness."

"So, what?" I sneered.

"So, do you want to cope, or keep hiding and living in fear?" He extended his arms, waiting for an answer.

"I just want to sleep." I closed my eyes, dropping my head backward and letting a loud sigh into the air.

"Then sleep it is." I could hear the smile in his voice. And I wasn't wrong.

"And what exactly do you propose?" Crossing my arms, I raised my brow.

"Bo."

"I THINK YOUR DAD HAS GONE MAD, BO."

Eleven o'clock had long passed, and I refused to check the time on the laptop that streamed *Hercules*. I had steered away from any real-life dramas and categorized Disney safe for the meantime.

Bo stretched, taking most of the bed's space, placed his head on my side and closed his eyes.

"It's about to be over, what do you want to watch next?" He whined.

"Fine, we'll try to sleep."

Closing the laptop and placing it on the nightstand, I pulled the cover high over me. Bo moved and waited until I settled before placing his body next to mine. My hands rested over my chest, and I stared at the dark ceiling, waiting.

Sleep wouldn't come.

The light winds sneaked inside the house, and the sounds the home made at night became louder in the eerie night. I tried to relax when Bo didn't react to any of the sounds that were made.

As time passed, Bo grew impatient and craned closer to my upper half. His nose nudged my hands over my chest, and I pulled them out of the comforter to pet him.

I ran my fingers through his short coat, feeling his warmth and the fast rhythm of his heartbeat. And each time I stopped, he would nudge me again to continue.

Over, and over again.

Until sleep claimed me, and I woke up the next day with my hand wrapped around his neck and the weight of his head on my chest.

The feeling almost made me cry, and I never wanted to let go of Bo.

"You kept *Nightmare* from coming, sweet boy," I whispered. Bo groaned, not ready to get up. I, too, didn't want to leave the comfort of the bed or him just yet. Instead, I turned sideways and cuddled him.

TEN
i l i a s

WHEN DAVINA GREETED ME AT THE DOOR, SHE SEEMED well rested and with sleep still in her eyes. Her hair was tussled, and her face flushed. I couldn't help but admire the peace in her eyes, or the restraint it took not to get closer to her. To reach her cheek and feel its warmth, the softness of her fair skin.

"How attached are you to Bo?" she asked, interrupting my thoughts, and my mind automatically closed up. My muscles became rigid as I stared at her carefully from across the sofa while Boris looked for something to get himself into.

"Are you asking because you care, or because…" I trailed.

"I'm just curious."

I couldn't help but to laugh, really laugh, as I followed Bo with my eyes. That sneaky bastard.

"Wow, Davina. All it took was one night to fall for Boris so quickly?" Bo rushed my way when he heard his name.

Blood rushed across her neck and up her cheeks, and her chocolate eyes asked for mercy while they stayed solely on me. It didn't help my laughter, only made it worse. I hadn't laughed so hard in so long, that I couldn't remember the last time I felt this light-hearted.

"Could you please stop it!" she squeaked, grabbing the closest thing by her and throwing it my way. Thankfully it was just a balled-up napkin she had used during lunch, and I didn't bother swatting it out of my way. It fell to the ground, and she stood embarrassed, leaving me alone in the living room with only my laughter.

After I'd calmed, I searched for her. It didn't take long to spot her sitting on the dead grass of the small backyard, where she threw a ball for Bo to catch.

"Are you done now?" she sassed.

"Not even close." I sat close to her and watched as Bo tried to destroy the ball she'd thrown. "To answer your question, I am *very* attached to Bo."

"I figured." She let out a loud sigh, keeping her attention ahead. "You should laugh more often."

I ignored her comment. "But, if you've grown attached to Bo, I'm not against visitations," I joked. Davina tilted her head with a smile on the corner of her lips, eyes my way. "How about, when all this is over, we try finding you, your own Bo. I'll train him or her."

"There won't be another like Bo."

Her reply made me grin. "Can't say that's not true."

"Wait." She faced me. "You trained Bo, all by yourself?" she nodded toward him.

"I'm good with animals, and training them isn't difficult once you understand each breed and their personalities." Davina grew closer with each word I said. "I actually trained Lucca's, my brother's, two dogs. They are beasts, only friendly and comfortable with few."

"Are they Dobermans too?"

"Oh no, I actually think their breed is harder to control as they are extremely short tempered. His are both Caucasian Shepherds. Mean little suckers those two are. Well, at least not to me."

"Wow, then why would he want such a breed?"

I grew silent and tore my eyes away from her.

"So, did I convert you to a dog lover?" If she noticed her unanswered question, she didn't mention it. Davina only smiled.

"You did."

"I won't be getting Bo back for a while," I stated.

"No, you won't," she admitted with a chuckle. "So, how much time until we try again?"

"Try what again?" I asked.

"Self-defense."

"When the circles under your eyes fade and you've gotten more meals inside of you."

She processed my words for a minute with twisted lips.

"I didn't notice I looked so…"

She didn't finish, instead she brought her knees to her chest and looked ahead. I dusted the grass off me when I stood, my eyes remaining on her.

"Don't think you look anything less than lovely, *kroshka.*"

My thoughts were spoken out loud and my muscles tensed from my admission. I couldn't see her face, and she didn't turn to see mine. We both stood frozen. I shed the shock, turned, and headed back into the house.

This assignment was fucking with me.

No, not the assignment. Because I knew what I had to do, guard and protect. It wasn't the task. It was Davina.

It was unlike me to think about someone other than my family and Bo. I liked to think it was better this way. My life was dangerous in every sense. From my affiliations to the underworld, to putting my life on the line every day. With or without a uniform, danger waited for me each turn I took, and the thought of bringing someone, having someone, in this life seemed selfish. I'd never had an issue until now. I thought of her, wondered of her well-being, hell, even keeping a distance from her had become a problem.

I'd embraced her body once, felt the way it fit snugged against mine and relished the feeling. I'd waved her hair away from her face just to see her features clearly, not only was it subconsciously, but the memory of the feel of her silk black hair wrapped around my hand made me want to do it again, and again. Then there was the masochist in me that wanted to trap the tear that had fallen from her vulnerable eyes, to feel her pain, only to wipe it away from such a delicate creature. With each small trace I felt of her body, the more I wanted. And the more I craved.

It was dangerous.

Because I was known to be a selfish man.

"You know, I googled *kroshka* last night."

My hand stopped on the door latch. "You did?" I could feel a smirk forming, and my reflection on the glass door confirmed it.

"Yeah. Funny how many hours you can waste when all you have is time and a laptop." Her head stayed away from me as I watched her reflection. Then her hair swayed as she twisted to face my back. "I am no *crumb*."

With the smirk, I faced her. "Your research was shit, I see."

"Novak!" she hollered when she saw me retreating inside.

Bo passed by me loudly, making it impossible to hear Davina closing in on me until her hand surprised me as it gripped my arm and body from moving forward. I turned, faced her, aware that her hand stayed on me as her eyes bore into mine. The intensity of her gaze suffocated me, and I welcomed the feeling just as I kept myself from inching closer to her.

"Why won't you just tell me what it's supposed to mean?" In her irises, curiosity spun wildly.

"Why do you always call me by my last name and not my given name?" I asked instead.

Her mouth parted. "Respect?"

With a light huff, I jabbed some more. "Is that really it?"

"I can research it again and find it anyway." We were back with *kroshka*.

"You could. But maybe you should wait to find out until you are able to call me by my first name."

"Why?"

"Because I think you call me Novak as a reminder of the real reason why I'm here."

Her hand fell as her breath hitched.

I saw the moment she understood. We both knew she called me Novak to keep me at an arm's length. A reminder to see me as the cop that was sent to watch over her safety, and that guy should never call her anything but her name. Anything else would be stepping out of boundaries.

"Unless you don't want the reminder, I suggest not letting curiosity win."

ELEVEN

d a v i n a

CURIOSITY WAS A SIMPLE WORD, AN IMPULSIVE FEELING I couldn't evade. The more I tried to suppress the wonder, the more it crept in, becoming impossible to ignore.

That was how I found myself in the middle of the night, laptop resting over the covers as the screen revealed different things *kroshka* meant, or how it could be interpreted.

Crumb.

Baby.

Baby-girl.

Babe.

I smiled at the last one.

Little one.

I put the laptop away and snuggled closer to Bo.

With Ilias on my mind, a smile on my face and eyes closed, I wondered which one was meant for me.

TWELVE

ilias

I STAYED INSIDE MY CAR LONGER INSTEAD OF KNOCKING ON her door and being around her presence. This helped with focusing on my tasks and not the other impulsive behaviors I'd let slip already.

Davina had become a constant in my mind, and I'd tried to make myself believe it was solely due to her safety. When in reality, it was the way her voice called for me, and my thoughts intruded with pictures and images of her skin.

It all felt unreal. My love-life had always been non-existent, aside from meaningless hookups that the only purpose was to find a release and walk away. A means to an end. Maybe the reason I found it so difficult to keep her away from my mind was how she was the one female I couldn't touch, and the one I've interacted with the most without fucking. Perhaps if I could have her underneath me while I ravaged her body, the craving would go away. The interest would disappear, and the void would be filled.

Or maybe it had been too long since I let out all this pent up frustration, and I needed a good lay.

So much sexual frustration clouded my head that I almost missed the car.

It rolled slowly in the intersection. A newer model Honda with all blacked out windows now had my undivided attention. It kept driving, but it left an unsettling feeling behind. I didn't think of the possibility of someone missing a turn, or how it may have been lost. In my life, nothing was a coincidence, and the eerie feelings were always correct.

I'd decided to stay in my car for the remainder of my shift. At least out here, I could keep an eye out in case the car ever returned. It didn't. And when my time was up, I decided to leave a small written note and pushed it under the front door for Davina to have my phone number with an order to call or text if she needed anything.

When I walked down the few steps of her porch, I noticed Beckett's dark Impala. Walking to where he had parked, I heard the door unlocking before I reached the passenger door and hopped in.

Beckett was in his late thirties judging by the gray that decorated his brown hair and the wrinkle lines around his green eyes. He looked me over before returning his gaze ahead. It gave me more time to assess him, and by the looks, he still looked sharp and in shape. It eased my mind knowing he would be here through the night. His attention and posture seemed alert, taking in the streets.

"Novak," he greeted me.

"I know we haven't spoken much, but I thought it would be good to give you an update," I began, and he turned to face me. "I also thought it would be best if we exchanged numbers to keep ourselves up to date with any activity we may need to know."

"I think that's a great idea. I thought about that, but nothing has been out of place to even initiate the conversation. Plus, I was told the less we are seen together the better." Beckett nodded.

"Another reason why it's best over a phone call or text."

"I agree with you. What you got?" His eyes narrowed, catching the reason I made contact with him to begin with.

"Black Honda, blacked-out windows, Florida tag ending with I36. It was too far for me to read the rest. Could be nothing but…"

"But," he replied, knowingly. "We know better."

"Yeah. Anyway, that's it. Here's my card, I've added my personal number." I grabbed the door handle but stopped. "Which precinct are you from?"

Beckett's silence stretched as I waited for his reply. "I can't disclose that information."

Our eyes locked, I'd hit another dead end.

"Night." I said with a nod, exiting the car.

DAVINA

OVER THE PAST FEW NIGHTS, I'D SLEPT BETTER THAN EVER. Nightmares still came and went, but each time, Bo would wake me and pull me back to sleep. He'd never let them last, and I was grateful for him.

We'd set a routine, and with Bo around, I didn't feel as insecure or worried with unwelcomed sounds as before. It wasn't perfect, memories still rushed back and anxiety continued to consume me, but it became more bearable each time Bo's nose nudged me or snuggled closer, searching for my touch. It was soothing, and with each passing day, I could feel bits of my fears fading.

Ilias had grown quieter, but I noticed the way his eyes would follow my every move when he was around. I was okay with his silence, it helped with the knowledge I'd learned nights before and keeping that distance we both wanted in a way.

But today was different. We were going to try, once again, self-defense moves and tactics.

The attraction felt heavy in the air. It didn't matter how little I had shared with him about my personal life, or his to me, the allure kept pulling me into a sick game of temptation, and I was weak and easily drawn to make reckless plays. It didn't help when his fresh scent of sea breeze and sandalwood soaked my senses, penetrating each room his presence stayed in, only to leave them with his enchanting smell. The closer he was, the more I craved for a deeper draw of his scent.

Bo rested on the corner of a plaid cushion he had pulled from the couch while Ilias and I stood in the living room, stretching our muscles. Our eyes connected from time to time until one of us turned away. It usually was me, as I couldn't take much of the intensity of his baby-blues, the color I constantly wished to see, but on him, I'd become obscured with feelings and silly day dreams. The kind that complicated things when fears of my past came knocking.

"We can start with a few basic moves," Ilias said as he rose from the ground.

The sunlight that passed through the blinds was fading, and Ilias moved the blinds away to peer out the window to confirm the day dwindling as night took over. Usually Ilias left around this time, but he is just now wanting to start the day with me. His back straightened and his attention remained out toward the streets.

"It's getting late," I said, waiting for his reaction or anything he would be willing to give. But his gaze stayed glued to the window. "Should I be worried, Novak?" The feel of my heart racing said I already was.

"Oh, no. Just... looking." Ilias moved away from the window with a smile that didn't quite reach his eyes. They were deep in chaos, and his hands lifted behind his shoulders, tugging off his light gray sweatshirt. The action caused the shirt underneath to get caught with the material.

My heart began to race for a different reason as my throat itched with the sight of his body. His abs were defined, and the sides of his core poked with definition, creating a trail down to his sweats. Even the band of his boxers that hugged his waist highlighted every line. I wanted to clear my throat and control the way my beating heart danced with desire. And until now, I'd realized how long it had been since a man had touched me, since my body pleaded for release, and craved attention. But never have I had this reaction from just the sight of a man's body.

Ilias threw the discarded sweatshirt over the couch, pulling his shirt back in place and turned. "You ready?"

All I managed was a longing nod.

"Well, what are you waiting for? Get up." His brows furrowed. "Or are you feeling uncomfortable?"

I wouldn't describe it as uncomfortable, not in the sense he was thinking. Trying to concentrate back on the task ahead, I stood quickly.

"No, I'm ready."

"Great, we'll start with some heel palm and elbow strikes before we finish with groin kicks."

Ilias tried to make himself look less overbearing as his smile stretched widely, but he looked more manic than ever.

"Novak, stop smiling like that."

His possessed smile fell. "A bit much?"

"Just a tad," I lied, holding a chuckle.

"Fine. Now let's start with what you would do in certain scenarios, then go over the right things to do, or what would be best. Ready?"

Oh, hell. Here we go.

Ilias took a step forward, too quick for my mind to process. I stumbled backward until my back hit the wall. I was surrounded by his body. My heart hammered, and once his hands lifted, I tried to think fast. There was a small opening for me to slide under his arms, big enough for my body to slip by and flee. As the only option my thoughts gave me, my body obeyed my mind. In a fluid movement, my head lowered with my body, and my feet slid through the opening. I wanted to cheer the moment I succeeded, but it was short lived. His strong arm wrapped around my middle, easily lifting me an inch above with our momentums crashing. A surprised shriek ripped from my throat, and my hands gripped his arm.

It all happened so fast. Bo was barking, whining just inches away from us. My feet touched the ground on the same spot I once was and Ilias's heavy hand rested with pressure above my chest keeping me from moving as he turned his attention to Bo.

Bo was clearly in distress as his head bounced with a bark, looking at Ilias then me. Bo's head shook, his stride quickly forming a C around us.

Ilias closed his eyes briefly before his command echoed in Russian. "Boris, *Lyezhat!*"

Bo obeyed as he lowered to the ground, laying his head above his paws, but he continued to whine and my heart broke to see him so torn watching us. "*Tiho.*" Bo silenced.

Ilias drew a deep breath and his eyes were deep blue when they caught mine.

"You good?" he asked calmly.

"Is *he* okay?" I asked instead.

Ilias tilted his head and watched me. His eyes moved over my face and lowered before returning back to my gaze. Then his hand slowly slid up until his palm settled on the crook of my neck and his thumb feathered below my ear.

I froze, knowing the thin turtleneck I wore could easily stretch from his touch to find my hidden scar. Another part of me was captivated with his presence, body, and hard demeanor. I was drawn into the trap of him, his touch and closeness. My blood thumped and my breath rushed at the same pace of my quick beating heart.

Ilias tilted my head up, and his eyes slid over my parted lips before returning once again to mine.

"Answer me, Davina. Are you good?" His voice was deep.

"Yes."

"Did I scare you?" He cleared his throat.

"No," I whispered, and his thumb slipped over my cheek and to the corner of my mouth. With pressure, his thumb ran over my lips before pulling them down in the end.

"Now, to answer your question. Boris is okay," he assured me, and with a quick look at Bo, he was now relaxed and calmly watching us. "But it seems he is not a fan of our approach to self-defense classes."

"Should we stop?"

"Do you want to stop?" he asked.

I shook my head. "I want to learn."

"Then no, we should continue. Bo will soon catch up, but I suggest assuring him you are okay. Something tells me he isn't just worried about my well-being this time." His hand fell away from my face, and I missed his warm and heavy touch on me.

"I can do that."

Bo sat patiently as I made my way to him with Ilias following behind.

"See, Bo. We are just practicing. She's safe and sound," Ilias said as I petted Bo's head.

An hour later, I couldn't even manage to smile.

I ached!

I could only imagine what I looked like while Ilias hardly seemed affected. He wasn't sweating, only his hair was wildly tussled, but it didn't take away from his appeal. Not a bit, on the contrary.

"I need a break." Out of breath, I dropped to the floor and laid my back flat on the carpet.

With light chuckles, Ilias lowered until he mimicked me and laid a few inches away. "We didn't even start groin kicks, Davina."

Closing my eyes, I took a deep breath. "I'm terrible at this."

Ilias stayed quiet, and I almost laughed at his silence. I was glad he didn't try to correct how bad my self-defense techniques or stamina was. Ilias just kept himself from lying, he knew better.

"We'll keep working on it. Don't give up just yet. Who knows, maybe you'll surprise us both."

This time, I did laugh.

"Anyway." He stood, picked up his sweatshirt from the couch, and stretched his arm out for me to take. Reluctantly, I raised my arm with a groan and our hands connected. Ilias pulled me up, but before I had the chance to inch closer, he took a step back and said, "It's getting late. Best if I leave you now."

"Would you like to stay for dinner before you leave?" I asked, and the question sounded like I was questioning myself. What was I doing?

Ilias raised a brow with a head shake. "You need to rest, plus I packed dinner."

"Packed dinner?"

He headed to the kitchen, and when he reached the back door, he looked back at me with a side smile. "I forgot to mention, Beckett and I switched times. I am now here during nights."

"Wait, why? And why are you leaving through the back door?"

"Why not? Now lock up."

Ilias didn't give me the chance to speak, he was already out the door leaving me and Boris behind with many questions.

After eating the leftover soup he had dropped off on my front steps the night before, I took a lukewarm shower and snuggled with Bo under the sheets.

With heavy eyes and the reminder of seeing his car just outside relaxed my body with peace. But Ilias stayed on my mind, and the thought of him staying up all night while I slept comfortably in my bed seemed unfair. I slid my hand under my pillow, bringing my phone out and squinted when the bright light blinded me. It didn't take me long to find his name in my contacts. I'd saved it the night he slipped it through the front door. He had written to call or text him when I needed him, and even as I lie warm and tucked in bed safely, in some way, I needed just a bit of him.

I decided to say something simple, a question of neutral meaning, so neutral it almost seemed silly.

How was dinner? I typed before hitting send.

At first, I wondered if I had the right number for the amount of time it took to get a response. But when I saw the name I'd saved him as on my screen, I bit my smile.

Blue: Why are you not sleeping yet? It's past eleven.

D: Did you know you always answer with a question?

Blue: Yes, I've been told.

Blue: And dinner was great. Now, are you going to answer me?

Now it was my time to take a minute to reply as I thought of what to write.

D: I'm running low on supplies, and I thought you may want to know I'll be going tomorrow to the convenience store. Great, now I'd made myself go outside.

Blue: What time were you planning?

D: After lunch?

Blue: Can it wait until six?

After I read his text, I felt guilty. Ilias wanted to be here when I did, probably even go with me. And here I was making a bogus run to the store.

D: I thought your shift starts at seven?

Blue: I'll pick you up at six. Now go to sleep.

Leave it to Ilias to ignore my question, I chuckled.

D: Are you good with staying up all night?

Blue: you are still not asleep?

This time I laughed, damn him for making me want to keep messaging him.

D: Night, Novak.

Blue: Goodnight, Davina.

THIRTEEN

d a v i n a

AS A RITUAL, I WOKE UP AND LOOKED OUT THE WINDOW, only to feel disappointment when Ilias's car wasn't there. I had an urge to text him, but as the digital clock on my nightstand read fourteen minutes past eight, the last thing I wanted was to disturb him while he rested, or worry him.

Bo barked as he sat by the closed bedroom door, ready to be let out.

"Sorry, Bo," I grumbled, wiping sleep away from my face and I smiled as we made our way down the stairs and into the backyard.

I'd slept through the entire night. A wave of relief knowing there was a possibility I could move on, a possibility of healing from the wounds of the past.

It was a start, and I was okay with that. I felt hope once again, and I knew the person who had helped make it happen, Ilias. I was becoming attached to him. I could feel it in the way my mind would constantly veer to thoughts of him, the way my eyes always searched for him, but what was more dangerous was the way my body began reacting to his presence. Daydreams created an ache with visions of his touch on my body had my legs squirming.

The memory of the way he held me into place with his rough hand firmly applying pressure on my chest yesterday filled me with unspoken promises. I craved the idea of being with a man that could control my body, having power with a single touch.

The future of what could be tortured me, the unknown of what would or wouldn't happen after this was over. Would I always be running? Would I end up dead and be taken to the unknown? Or would I be fully safe to roam the streets without worry? And if so, would Ilias only be a part of the past?

I was never one to have meaningless sexual encounters. I developed feelings, attachments, and even thought of the possibilities of a future with my partners. Not that there had been many. Two to be exact. My first was Theo, my high school best friend who soon became more than a friend, until he went away to college and I stayed behind to take care of a sick mother. After my mother passed away from heart failure, I was quick to find someone to fill at least an inch of the void of being alone. Ricky. We were good together, at least in the bedroom, because we hardly spent time together during the day. After two years, we realized it was best to say our goodbyes.

I'd grown attached to them, but I couldn't say it was love. It was more of exploring and finding myself with each relationship. Maybe this was what was happening with Ilias.

Was I growing attached to him due to the situation? The insecurity and fear?

Maybe I was unable to form a normal relationship, but was anything really ever normal? All I had was a definition created by society, and I'd adjusted through my circumstances.

As the day went by, and time reminded me Ilias would be here soon, I paid closer attention to my appearance and gave away how this was more than adjusting to the circumstances.

With the threat of dying looming every day, my mind threw its hands in the air and said, *live in the moment, it may be all you have.*

I opened my front door, and Ilias's messy wet hair and fresh scent greeted me. I became mute and frozen by his presence. His black and red flannel shirt was open and loose around his waist, and his strong forearms were visible with the rolled-up cuffs. The black shirt underneath stretched over his torso.

My hands wanted to explore the muscles underneath, and I envisioned them lowering until they met the waistline of his dark jeans. Ilias caught my attention with his icy blues. The intensity brought chills over my body. I wanted to learn more about him, read, and explore more of his life.

And that made this pull more real, more than just fascination. It allured feelings that held more than physical attraction.

"Are you ready?" Ilias asked, his brows raised. Straightening my mid-thigh flowy black dress, I nodded. "We'll be back shortly, Bo." He ran his hand over Bo's head when he whined, and turned his attention back to me. "You look all dressed up," Ilias joked, waving his hand ahead for me to step out of the house.

I grasped my thin pillar bar necklace with a smile as I waited for Ilias to lock up. "Thank you, the weather is nice, and I know it may get cooler soon."

Ilias looked over the sleeves and the high neckline of my dress in suspicion. "Yeah, I believe it may."

Dropping my hand from the bar pendant, I looked away from Ilias's watchful eyes and walked down the front steps. He matched my strides, staying close by as he steered us toward the street and crossing until meeting his car.

"The store is only a few blocks down," I said, confused.

"I figured a real store with a larger selection would be better. Plus, I'm hungry." Ilias opened the passenger door for me, I slid over the black leather cushions. His rich scent spiked inside the small confinement of his car, leaving only him to invade my mind.

Without glancing my way, he slid inside the car. His eyes remained ahead as he shifted the gear to reverse and sped out of the driveway. I admired his hard jaw lines with the dusted scruff, the small faded scar by his chin. It was faint but visible, adding another question about his past, about who he was. His nose set in a straight angular line, and another dull scar sat just above the corner of his right eye. It could easily pass as a crease made from a smile, but with our close proximity, it was hard not to notice the small blemish that added to his rough exterior.

Temptation taunted with the desire to run my finger over it. I clasped my hands together.

Ilias had scars out in the open, while I kept mine hidden under clothes.

Do you have hidden scars, Ilias?

Do you have scars that keep bleeding inside?

"Do I have something on my face?" His blue eyes briefly met mine before they returned to the streets.

I looked away. "Sorry, I was staring." With a grin, I peered out the window. Streets passed by in a blur as the sun retreated, parting hues of orange that mixed with the dark violets of the night.

"Hmm," he murmured, but I could see his lips fighting a grin. "Then you should stop, Ms. Davina. You make it hard to concentrate with just your stare."

I wanted to tell him my last name. I trusted him, but the word still sat at the edge of my tongue. It wouldn't come out. I turned away, allowing the scenery to distract me.

I'd been in Florida for over two months now. Until now, I hadn't had the pleasure to appreciate the pool of diversity and life that poured across every vibrant inch.

"Miami really is beautiful," I murmured as we passed by a colorful mural that had been painted on a beachfront brick wall.

"Don't let it obscure the hidden dangers of the city," Ilias replied with a deep chuckle.

"You don't think it is?"

"I think I've just seen too much to think of it as beautiful."

"Well, that's sad," I murmured.

"Is it though?" he challenged, and I faced him.

"It is. Look at all the smiles, the culture, the life that walks by. It's painted in every corner." My hand extended toward the window.

"When *you* see a pretty mural, all *I* see are landmarks for a homicide, an overdose, a robbery. Take your pick."

"You are right, that's not sad. It's depressing." I shuddered at the thought.

"It is."

"I meant the way you don't notice past the hard exterior to appreciate its meaning."

"Or maybe I lived through too much to see it for what it truly is."

"You hate Miami," I stated in a whisper.

"No. Not at all. I love the city, it's all I've known." The car stopped and I was trapped in his gaze. "It just means that beautiful things can't replace the threatening danger." Ilias removed his gaze as I thought about his words. "Anyway, I hope you are hungry."

"Wait!" I stopped him from opening the door, and his attention turned back to me. "Wouldn't it be dangerous to go inside?"

"It looks pretty quiet, Davina." I looked through the window of the small restaurant where only a lone woman was eating in the corner. "Plus, mostly only Russians and Romanians come here." He sat straight in his seat. "Are you hiding from either?"

Before I had the chance to think, I blurted, "No," and closed my eyes at the admission that I'd, once again, given him something that could bring him closer to the truth.

"Good. I was thinking of ordering it to-go, and we can eat it in the car. Sounds good?"

"Perfect."

We walked in side by side, and in anyone's eyes we looked like a couple. The place was quaint, only two people worked behind the counter and two more were in the kitchen.

One of the guys from the back poked his head out when Ilias ordered a *Kulebyaka* after I shrugged at the menu.

"Ilias!" The older man said in a heavy Slavic accent, dusting his hands on his white apron. A wide smile proudly showcased his age around his eyes while his shoulder-length hair was tied in a low ponytail. "I read an order for a meat filled *Kulebyaka*, and I knew it had to be you or your brother. How's Viktor?"

Viktor?

"Ah Dima, good to see you are still kicking. Viktor is working as he should be," Ilias joked, and his demeanor had relaxed since walking inside the deli.

"How rude of me, and this is?" The older man Ilias called Dima looked my way. His platinum hair was trapped under a mesh cap, but his smile remained as he waited for a response.

I looked over Ilias as he was ready to reply, but I quickly cut him off from speaking, afraid he may have said my real name, and not the one I was told to give. "Morgan, nice meeting you."

"The pleasure is all mine, hope you like authentic Russian cuisine," Dima said enthusiastically.

"I do, *syrniki* is my favorite dish." I quickly replied. Dima's eyes lit up and they looked over Ilias. I couldn't yet find the courage to see Ilias's reaction after mentioning the *syrniki* he had made for me. It was the only Russian meal I'd ever had. And here I was, acting as if I knew about the Russian culture, and cuisine.

"Ahh, she's a good one, Ilias," Dima murmured, and his name was called from the kitchen. "We'll bring it out to your car, okay? Oh, and say hi to your brother!"

"Of course, and thank you. It was great seeing you, Dima," Ilias replied, and Dima waved before he retreated to the same door he poked his head out.

Looking up to Ilias, his eyes watched me from the side with a smirk. "Damn, if I didn't know any better, you could have fooled me," he whispered through his side grin. "Let's go and wait in the car, *Morgan*." His smile was wide.

"Oh my God, stop it!" I hissed and followed him to the door.

The feeling of someone watching made me flick my eyes to the corner of the small deli. I met the gaze of a young woman, who couldn't be much older than me, with long straight ash-blonde hair, perfect symmetrical face and large dark eyes. She was beautiful, and her attention slid to Ilias, then back to me before she continued wrapping silverware with napkins.

I shouldn't be surprised. Ilias wasn't a man who would be left unnoticed. The way he carried himself spoke volumes, and if you were to add his looks, he was a threat to any woman.

"*Morgan.*" Ilias smirked while his eyes watched the street, one hand keeping the passenger door open for me.

With the moon now shining outside, minimal light filtered through the obscure windows of Ilias's car. Low classic rock music played in the background, filling the silence of our hidden smiles as we waited for our food. By Dima's reaction, it wasn't Ilias's first time coming here to eat. I would even call him a regular.

"So..." I broke the silence. "I'm guessing Lucca is not your only brother?"

"You caught that, huh?"

"Kind of hard not to when it's very loudly spoken."

Ilias laughed and rubbed his hand over his face.

"I have three brothers. All older than me."

"You are the baby?" I cooed playfully, earning a side look to drop it. Instead, I pressed for a bit more of him. "So, is Viktor the eldest?"

With a loud exhale he replied, "No, Lucca is. Then Arlo, Viktor, and I." Ilias's eyes searched mine. "How about you? Any siblings?"

I'd opened up the door for questions, and now I had no idea how to shut it.

"So, I tell you something about myself but you won't reply to the same question?" he asked humorlessly.

"I'm an only child." I replied quietly.

"That sounds lonely." The simple tone of his voice touched a nerve.

"I don't know the difference, so I wouldn't know. Plus, not everyone is lucky enough to have a full family."

He chuckled darkly. "Of that, I can agree." A gasp slipped through my lips when knocks on my window caught me by surprise. "It's just Dima," Ilias assured me even when my eyes took in Dima's stance. But I couldn't shudder the feeling of shock.

The *kulebyaka* was already cut in smaller portions to share between us, and I dived into the warm outer breading. The inside was mixed with many flavors from the white rice, meat, and fresh spices and melting cheese.

"What do you think?" Ilias asked before he took another bite with one hand on the wheel as we headed toward the grocery store.

"It reminds of a Hot Pocket, but homemade and real food, so this one is delicious."

The upcoming intersection light turned red, and Ilias cut off the music and turned to face me.

The car grew quiet.

"Did you just compare a *kulebyaka* to a frozen and cheap Hot Pocket? This is a real meat pie, with home-made bread and baked to perfection!" I think I'd hit a nerve. "How dare you, Davina." *I definitely did.*

"I said it *reminds* me of… not that it tasted anything like it."

Ilias shook his head and remained quiet.

I almost laughed—almost.

132

FOURTEEN

ilias

THE LONGER AND FARTHER WE WERE AWAY FROM THE house, the more Davina shed the captivity she'd been forced into for protection. She was comfortable, and a bright light spun around her irises with freedom. It was risky to take her away, but any outcome would have been the same if we went to a convenience store near her place.

As the night continued, I'd learned a bit more about her, and with each bit she shared the more I wanted to know of her. Dima was smitten by her in just a matter of seconds. How couldn't he be? She was unique and even as she hid behind her clothing, it was hard not to miss her beautiful and striking features. The more I thought about it, the more I knew Dima wasn't the only one smitten by her. But the word smitten sounded too innocent, and there wasn't a bone inside me that held such a thing.

She'd knocked me speechless by her insult when she called one of my favorite meals a fucking Hot Pocket. No stuttering or sweet talk could ever take that away, so I turned the music up higher and listened to the lyrics to keep my mind occupied as we neared the grocery store.

During this hour, the store was quiet aside from the humming of the fluorescent lights. Davina didn't seem to need much and it didn't take her long to pick a few things. I threw a few snacks inside the metal cart while I watched Davina looking through the aisles deep in thought.

"Why do I get the feeling you didn't need to come to the store?" I watched her back and kept pushing the buggy.

"I did too," she fired back.

"Fine, did you get what you needed or are you going to keep strolling through the store?"

Davina let out a snort. "I'm ready to go."

It didn't take long to checkout and place the few grocery bags in my trunk. Davina remained quiet, and as we pulled out of the parking building, I finally asked, "What's troubling you?"

She removed her gaze from the window and glanced my way, but lights in my rearview mirror kept getting closer.

"I might have lied."

"Might?" I asked, watching the road ahead and flickering my eyes back to the headlights from behind.

"Well, what if I said I really didn't need to come to the store?"

"I believed your lie. Your fridge is near empty." I looked at my side mirror as we rolled to a stop under a red traffic light and thought about Davina's words. She once mentioned not being the best cook, and come to think of it, her freezer was packed with microwavable meals. "But now you have me wondering? Why lie?" I asked tapping my thumb on the steering wheel as I waited for the traffic light to change.

"I guess I thought I needed a reason to text you. Telling you I needed to go to the store sounded like a good excuse at the time."

The traffic light changed as my smile formed at the corner of my mouth. I took a right to a less busy street, and the car followed me into the quiet suburb neighborhood. My smile fled, my body tensed.

"Where are we going?" Davina asked, looking out into the streets.

The large black sedan knew I was onto them, and they inched closer and closer with my increasing speed.

I needed to get out of the suburbs, and fast.

Fuck.

"Is someone following us?" Davina asked, her voice rising with each word as she turned to look back.

"Sit back." Keeping my eyes ahead, I took a sharp left turn. "Hold on. I need to get us on the highway."

A quick peek at Davina showed her eyes tightly shut, her hands on either side of her legs, gripping the seat. Every one of her deep breaths echoed inside the cab, and my attention returned to the rearview mirror.

"Are you all right?" I asked, unable to ignore her well-being.

"Mm-hm," she hummed.

"Words, Davina," I pressed, speeding through the intersection the moment we were out of the suburbs.

"I am," she whispered. "Just keeping my breathing calm."

"Good, keep doing that. I'll lose them soon." I weaved through the slow traffic and kept making turns and gaining speed.

"It's them, right?" She already knew the answer. "I'll never be safe, Novak."

"You will tonight." My hand found hers without judging the reasons why, and gave her soft fingers a gentle squeeze.

The sedan reduced their speed, purposely throwing me off my game. What were they doing? Whatever it was, I was fine with it. It gave me the chance to escape and take Davina to safety.

And the only place in the meantime was mine. The safe house was compromised, and I had to call Chief Pierce to make other arrangements, but first, there was one other call I had to make before returning home.

With a quick squeeze, I let go of Davina's hand, hating the loss of contact, and picked my phone from the console to call Viktor.

It rang three times before I heard my brother's voice.

"I need a favor," I began. "But please don't ask too many fucking questions."

"Well, there goes you staying out of trouble," Viktor joked darkly. "What is it?"

"You are the only one Boris will leave with."

"No," he uttered, dreading my next words.

"I need you to pick him up and keep him for the night."

"Fuck. This better be life or death."

I ignored his comment and glanced over only to find Davina's large eyes watching me.

"I'll text you the address, once you receive it, get Bo."

"Ilias," my brother warned.

"Make sure you take someone, preferably one of your guys, and —"

"*Ilias!*" Viktor's voice grew. "Tell me what the fuck is going on."

"Only if I knew, brother, but I don't. Be careful," I said before disconnecting the call.

The only noise inside the car was the engine shifting and humming with the speed. The street lights flew by in a blur and my eyes never stopped glancing at the mirrors. The beating of my heart couldn't seem to return back to normal, and even if I was used to the adrenaline, this time the danger felt too real, too raw, with Davina being the target.

I knew she was in danger, this was bound to happen, but I'd just hoped this day wouldn't come so soon and that I would have had more time to strengthen her, to help her, to be with her. Because I was sure once I called Chief Pierce, Davina would be moved somewhere else, possibly outside of Florida. It would be the best thing for her safety, but the self-absorbed part of me didn't want for her to be relocated. I didn't trust anyone else to keep her safe. I should've paid attention to her fears, the depth they ran. These people weren't your everyday criminals, they had to be well organized to be able to find her in the short amount of time she'd been in hiding.

And now I was supposed to let her go? Knowing all of this? Knowing if I did, I would most likely never see her again, and maybe I would, but it would most likely be in the news.

This bizarre feeling deep inside gripped my heart in disarray, in chaos of understanding what that one phone call would do. I tried to grasp it all, to convince myself that it would be for the best, but the more I tried, the more I realized why I felt this way.

It was personal.

It was Davina.

I couldn't let her go.

At least not tonight. I needed one night to wrap my head around this. To build the courage to call the chief, to build the courage to watch her leave.

And now, every moment, every glimpse I caught of her, became so much more. For too long, I'd hidden the pull and my will had no chance to fight.

"Where are we?" her small voice asked as the car stopped in my driveway.

I pushed the button to the garage door and parked the car inside. Davina's hand slid to the handle before the garage door started to fall.

"Don't," I rasped. Her hand quickly fell, and my eyes moved back to the door waiting. Once it was fully shut, I let out an exhale. "Now, you can get out," I said, but my body didn't move an inch.

Neither did hers.

DAVINA

THE ATMOSPHERE INSIDE THE CAR CHANGED WITH A LOOMING ghost of time. Whether it was time taken, or time left, it bounced silently with its presence.

Tattoo and *Nightmare* didn't give up on me. It had been foolish of me to consider such a thing. And now that they'd found me, I knew it was time to run again.

I'd felt the panic, the anxiety that ran through my body, as we sped through Miami's streets, but I held it together. I'd breathed in and out, calmed my heart and pushed the fear away. But now that I had the time to think in this echoing silence, I couldn't help the lone tear that escaped.

I had to leave, and that meant away from Ilias too, and it pained me to have to keep running to shield others from the danger.

But it was too late, I had already created a connection with Ilias, and the pain I felt wasn't from running, it was for not having the chance to treasure what it could've been.

Time mocked me.

But I'd danced around it.

"Ilias."

He took a deep breath through his teeth as his jaw shut, and the air grew thick. I turned to face him, but Ilias stayed facing forward and stared into the dark garage. A vein popped in his neck as the silence grew, and his hands gripped the steering wheel.

"You weren't supposed to call me that." He closed his eyes.

"But I don't want the reminder anymore."

"You should."

"Either I'll be gone or dead soon. But right now, I am here with you..." I stopped, and waited until his ice-blue eyes shone past the darkness and inside me. Once our eyes locked, I tried to finish my sentence, "Ili—"

His name sealed between us as his lips collided with mine. Ilias's hands grabbed my head as our mouths danced in a crazed rhythm that matched the fast speed of my heartbeat. I relished on the feeling of his lips, soft yet firm against mine, the way they took, the way they nipped, the way they brought me to life.

The roughness of his scruff scratched my sensitive skin, mixing the burning sensation with hunger, and as his mouth parted and lowered to the nape of my neck, I gasped at the blissful plea of my body.

My hands couldn't stay still anymore, and they reached for his hair and gripped his soft, full locks as they entwined around my fingers. His mouth continued to nip and awaken a thrilling buzz on my neck, and my lips parted each time it became oversensitive. I couldn't take it anymore, and a hushed moan slipped.

His hand moved to the back of my head, tilting it as his lips came back for another taste and meeting my eager lips.

Ilias tasted like pleasure, his lips felt like a promise, and his tongue… His tongue held the edge of wicked ecstasy.

And I was falling into the abyss with only a kiss. It strengthened my need for him, my want to have him, and the stir of feelings crashed, evolved into not wanting to let go.

I wasn't the only one who could feel the change. If anything, I'd learned Ilias was not good with words. He showed me with the way his kiss swirled with yearn and held me as if he couldn't resist to be apart.

With one hand wrapped around the nape of my neck, the other fell on my waist. His heavy palm easily held my side, and with a jerk motion, he tried pulling forward. I was tugged back in place by the seat-belt.

Ilias pulled back from my lips, our heads resting on one another while our breaths mingled in haste.

"You are high with the adrenaline of the chase," he rasped, and I was already shaking my head at his next words. "And I understand, but I'm greedy, selfish. I am not a gentleman, Davina. And this is when you can walk away, sleep in the bedroom with a closed door until the sun rises."

I stared into his eyes, and a breathless snicker tumbled out before feathering his lips with mine.

"I've been in this high since the first day I stared into your eyes."

"Davina," he warned.

"And you are wrong, you can be a gentleman, but I hope not in the bedroom."

His Adam's apple bobbed and the edge of his eyes darkened while whites and light aquas speckled around his pupils.

While we stayed with no space in between, he gritted, "And where would that be, Davina?"

Trapping my lip with my teeth, I mustered the courage to say the words, to bring my thoughts to life by giving them power to be heard without shame.

"Above your sheets and underneath your body."

His breath stilled. "Get out."

The tone of his voice left no hesitation for my hand to reach the door handle, but Ilias was already out of the car. Climbing out, I followed his trail inside the house and closed the same door he stepped through. The lighting was low with only a glowing light illuminating the clean and masculine interior of the house, but Ilias wasn't in sight. I continued walking as my chest heaved with anticipation because I knew Ilias hadn't changed his mind. After all, he warned me, and I happily didn't listen.

I found his back facing me as he pushed a code into a small square by the front door, "*alarm-stay.*" The home alarm echoed inside the walls of the house, and a chill ran over my body.

Ilias's footfalls ricocheted against his hardwood flooring as he headed to the dark staircase. He stopped briefly on the first step and lowered his head, his face tilted to the side. I was sure he could see me standing, watching, even if his eyes weren't on me. It was the only acknowledgment he gave me before he continued his way up. But it was enough. It said it all.

He wasn't pushing, and he was not denying me.

It was my choice.

And I followed the trail of temptation. With each foot step I took up the dim stairs, the more my blood rushed, causing the tips of my fingers to go numb and my teeth to trap my lower lip.

There were four doors in total, but only one was cracked open, where light penetrated out into the hall.

I closed my eyes, took a deep breath, and with a smile playing on my lips, I headed toward the door.

The door silently slid open, and I leaned over the frame, taking a deep breath. His room was tidy, nothing stood out of place. There were no picture frames or books. The only thing that made this room his was the lingering scent of sandalwood.

Ilias was in the far corner by the window, shirt discarded on top of a basket, eyes out on the road. The street lights and moonlight shone over his sun-kissed skin, while the bedside lamp illuminated the black furniture and the rest of the room. Taking my time to watch him, I remembered the first time I met him, and the way I looked over his skin for any ink markings on his body. I had done it to know if I could trust him, if I would find the same markings I was running from, the same people I was hiding from. But with his back toward me, he was still clean of such things. And the sight of his back muscles and clean skin only heightened my attraction.

"You don't have any tattoos." My statement was true even if I hadn't seen the rest of him. With his jeans hanging low on his hips, his body twisted slowly in place, confirming it.

"I'm guessing you don't like tattoos?" he replied leaning against the window sill.

We were far apart, relaxed with each other's presence yet filled with a craving. The air thinned inside the room, making it impossible to ignore.

My eyes roamed over his defined body. "I didn't mind before, I thought of them as a way of expressing feelings."

"And now?" His hair fell over his eyes.

"Now they remind me of a time I would like to forget."

He nodded, processing my words with a wicked smile. "Then, I'll thank my brothers for keeping me from getting any."

I grinned, and he pushed away from the wall. Just that small step was enough for my heart to falter and my gaze to fall from his piercing cool blues.

His body was inches away from mine.

"Without any shame in your voice, you said what you wanted. You walked up the stairs and opened this door searching for it. So now…" he rasped, his scent robbing my senses. His palm held my jaw, and our eyes met once again. "Don't drop your eyes away from me again."

My breath staggered and his gaze fell on my lips. Ilias ran the tip of his thumb over my bottom lip and applied pressure. My lip lowered from the force as his thumb caught its moisture, he spread it over my mouth, leaving my body on fire.

His lips slammed into mine, silencing my gasp. I curled my fingers around his biceps for something to hold onto, my body flush with his heated skin. Ilias hummed with approval, and his tongue explored my mouth, taking away the sting of his nips. His large hands held both sides of my head, keeping me caged against the doorframe and his wild lips.

I couldn't remember to catch a stable breath, my panting becoming enough to fill my lungs with his scent, alive with our hunger. My pelvis jerked forward with the urge of friction, but he was too tall. I didn't care if he would see my desire for him as easy, fast, or slutty. I wouldn't be ashamed for my lust or for my need as a woman. If anything, it made me aware of the intensity of how much I craved him. Ilias had unlocked a part of my body that urged and pleaded for release, that craved for more.

His hands lowered and gripped the back of my thighs, and my dress rose. My feet were swept from the floor and quickly wrapped around his middle. When my core met the hard bulge that hid under his jeans, my mouth parted with a pleasure-filled gasp. I entwined my fingers into his hair, pulling his head back, rubbing against him once more. My body shivered, and he shook his head away from my hands and ran his jaw over the nape of my neck.

"I know *kroshka*," he rasped. "I feel it too."

"Please," I pleaded.

"'*Above your sheets and underneath your body*', you said," Ilias repeated my words, and his body inched back. I quickly grabbed the corner of the door frame, keeping him from taking us anywhere else.

His eyes snapped back to mine when he noticed my reluctance to leave this spot. The corner of his lips lifted as his head craned to the side to watch me. "But you don't want a gentleman."

Ilias pushed my back to the wall, and I shivered from his words as his hand ran over my thigh bunching the rest of my dress until he found the thin material of my underwear on his way.

Gripping the material, he kissed my mouth, tugging on my bottom lip, when the sound of my thong ripping in two filled the silence. He didn't kiss away the sting of his bite this time, instead I felt his smile on my lips. My heart stilled with anticipation.

With my ruined underwear between us, he balled them up and applied pressure onto my clit. I moaned as the raspy lace rubbed circles around me. Unable to stop twisting above him, my fingers curled into his shoulders.

"Ilias," I whimpered.

Ilias discarded my underwear onto the floor and his hand snaked back between us. His thumb circled my clit before sliding down and dipping his fingers inside me.

My eyes shut and my back curled with a breathless sigh.

"Yeah, a gentleman is not what you want," Ilias said, pulling his fingers out and spreading the proof of my needy body over my pussy. He shook his head and continued pleasing me to the brink of release.

I couldn't breathe. Ilias played with me as if he knew each spot, each trigger that hadn't yet been found by another aside from myself. But his hands and heat push the feeling to ecstasy as my body tightened in full pleasure. My body shook and my eyes opened, catching his on me.

With a smile, he stopped.

ILIAS

DAVINA'S EYES WIDENED, AND HER HANDS TWISTED AROUND MY skin, desperate and confused.

Fuck if I didn't love seeing her so needy for me without shame.

With her mouth parted, breathing erratic, and chest heaving, the constricted material of my jeans became painful as my dick throbbed to be freed and deep inside of her.

I took a second to watch her, to admire her delicate features and savor this moment I may never have again. I memorized the color of her flushed skin, the shine of her tousled black hair, her natural deep pink lips that begged for attention. The one time I'd been asked to be myself in the bedroom, to unleash my selfishness and use her body, was the one time I cared for that person. I wanted to take my time, please her in ways she hadn't been pleased before, to ravish every inch of her body and treat her like she deserved.

But our bodies couldn't wait, and my mind and soul had no say when compared to my hunger. I had to be patient. I would take my time soon, but for now, I was going to fuck her until her legs gave out, and her voice

A BULLET BETWEEN US

turned hoarse from screaming my name—the name she'd withheld from calling me, and now that she had, she'd claimed me when it had fallen from her lips.

I was hers for as long as she desired, and I was hers for as long as time gave us.

If she wanted me to take her here, pressed upon the wall while I pounded inside of her, that was what I would give her.

I lifted her higher until her heat hit my abdomen, took her lips, and pressed my weight against her. Keeping her still, I quickly unbuttoned my jeans and pushed them down my thighs. My palms gripped her ass, and I bounced her down until I was plunged deep into her warmth.

Davina's cry was muffled between my lips, and I tried to contain my own sounds of pleasure as her nails dug into my back.

Her slick walls squeezed me; she felt too good, she looked too gorgeous, and I felt too much inside of her. I let go, pounding inside of her with no restraint. Her head fell back with shut eyes, teeth trapping her bottom lip, holding her moans.

I didn't want her to hold them back. I wanted to hear her. And the harder and deeper I fucked her, the more her tits bounced, causing her mouth to split open, her whimpers echoing around the room in a carnal tune.

With one hand holding tightly onto her hip, I snaked the other upward, meeting her full breast. The small pebble of her nipple was hard against her bra, begging for attention, begging for my fingers. I pinched hard, and her body trembled as she cried out.

I fucking smiled.

Because she was close, so close that her walls squeezed my dick so hard I had to control myself from busting inside her before she did.

I buried my face in the crook of her neck, running my jaw against the skin in the way I knew would make her body shiver.

"Fuck, Davina." She was making me crazy, holding me on the edge of addiction.

She was so close and wild to find her release.

K. DOSAL

My *kroshka* was begging for me to make her come. I couldn't deny her. My hand lowered from her chest to her clit and my thumb applied pressure, moving swiftly around with her juices.

"Come, *kroshka*."

That's all she needed for her body to tense, for her back to push away from the wall and onto my body. I didn't stop searching for my own release. I sped up, and with both hands on her ass, I bounced her above me.

Then I heard it again, my name in a plea.

And deep inside her I emptied my release and let our bodies mix in each other's ecstasy.

I held her for a minute longer as we controlled our breathing before letting her unwrap her legs from my hips. Davina's legs buckled, but my hand reached for her pussy making her stand up right from her over-sensitivity. My hand was soaked as it held her heat, and I rubbed it around her core making her legs squirm.

I grinned looking into her satisfied and heavy dark eyes. Pulling my hand away, I took a step back, then another, watching how her legs shook while her eyes followed my retreating body.

Her legs gave out and her body slid down the wall until her bottom met the hardwood flooring.

With tangled hair, swollen lips, and droopy eyes, I smiled down at the beautiful sight of her satisfaction.

I was wrong. Davina didn't hold me on the edge of addiction. I was already obsessed.

"I'm going to leave you right there, Davina. I can't risk having you get too comfortable in the bed. I still have plans for more."

Her eyes widened with my words, and I walked away.

The bathroom tiles were cool under my feet, and when I reached my tub, I turned the valves to fill it up. Once the temperature was warm, I squirted a few drops of my body wash and left the bathroom in search of her.

She was still in the same position I had left her. Her breathing was now even, and she was relaxed with her head leaning against the wall.

Bending down, I picked her up and carried her to my bathroom. It was bright inside, white tiles and walls only made it too intense coming from the dim lit bedroom. Davina squinted, and I turned back to the entrance and toward the light switch to dim the lights. Once we were next to the tub, I let her feet down and grabbed the skirt of her dress.

Davina's eyes stayed on me, and it almost seemed as if they hesitated. I waited, and she nodded. I pulled the black dress over her body slowly, appreciating her milky skin and curves. When my eyes reached her neck, she cocked her head, letting her hair fall back.

A deep red scar marked her neck, the tissue indicating it was still fresh. By the placement it stood on her neck and down her collarbone, I was shocked she was here; alive, and before me. My jaw locked as I tried not to react. My eyes slid up to hers, and we stood in silence.

Davina was the first to make a move as she turned, dipping one foot inside the tub to test the water before submerging herself underwater. I mimicked her movements, and slid her body forward to sit behind her. Bringing her back to my chest, I let her head rest on my torso.

"You are quiet," she murmured.

A few bubbles floated over the water, touching her breasts while the ends of her wet black hair stuck to her shoulders. Bubbles glided over the water with the movements of our bodies.

"I'm afraid of what I will say," I replied, letting my fingertips run over her arms.

"Does it bother you?"

"Bother me?" Was she really asking if it bothered me? Of course, it fucking did. Now more than ever I wanted to stay by her, protect her, and find the bastard that could do something like this to her.

"Yeah, I mean. It's not pretty to look at."

What?

"Wait. Are you worried that I see you differently?" I asked, shocked. I took her chin, turning her head to face me.

Her insecurity appeared again, but what pained me to see the most was the fear. Though, it wasn't the same fear I'd seen in her eyes the first time I'd met her. It was fear of me seeing her undesirable.

It was painted all on her face for me to tell.

"No." I shook my head, and this time I turned her body. Our knees were out of the water as we faced each other, and I took her face with both hands. "Don't do that. Don't think about something I've never said." Running my thumb over her lips, I continued, "Davina, nothing will make me see you differently."

Grabbing one of her hands, I placed it over my shoulder. Her fingertips ran across the welt I, too, had. It had been years since I received the wound, so it was no match to hers. It'd marked my skin, but after time, it faded and held no importance.

"See? I have a scar as well." Her eyes inspected my shoulder more closely. "Now, do you see me differently?" I asked. Her head shook. "Then why should yours do that for me?"

"What happened?" she asked.

"First year in the force. I was young, naïve, and still had a sliver of hope for humanity." I chuckled. "I got shot, well, more of a graze. But it was enough to remember where I stood."

"Where?"

"In a dangerous world."

SLEEP WOULDN'T COME, AND EVEN WITH DAVINA'S BARE BODY pressed on mine in a peaceful sleep, my mind raced. I thought about all the scenarios of how I could help keep her safe. Each solution always held the same answer—I couldn't.

While the moon shone over her half-covered silhouette, I watched her face, watched the scar that was still too sensitive to touch. It'll fade, eventually, but for now, the long and bulgy tissue still did its damage.

She'd wondered if I saw her differently, and I lied when I said I didn't, because it wasn't the way she thought I would.

I saw her strength. But mostly, I saw my way of growing more devoted to her.

The faint sound of wood creaking downstairs put my body in full alert.

This house was not meant to make a sound unless someone was here. It didn't settle in the middle of the night or during the day like Davina's did. No, my house was meant to tell when someone was here uninvited.

I sat up quickly. Quietly, I dressed in a pair of loose shorts, a tee, and picked up two guns and a knife from the dresser.

"Davina!" I whisper-shouted her name, causing her to stir. The sound downstairs grew and it had to be more than one person inside as doors creaked open in opposite parts of the house.

Shit.

"Davina!" I shook her body gently and traced my fingertips over her face to calmly wake her without bringing her in a state of panic. The whites of her eyes had let me know she caught on quickly to my rigid body next to the bed and over hers. "Listen to me very quickly. You need to hide inside the closet for a while. Do not come out, and if you hear someone is about to open it... you shoot," I rushed out, placing a gun next to her hands. "It's loaded, cocked, and ready. All you have to do is pull the trigger. Don't think."

Davina rose from the bed, and the sheets fell. Reaching to the nightstand drawer, I grabbed a pair of boxers and a white tee for her to wear.

"Here, hurry."

"But..." Her chest began to heave with the clothes in her hands.

"We don't have time. Change in the closet and hold tightly to the gun."

I could hear whispers at the bottom of the staircase before it went silent.

Davina tip-toed toward the closet, lines on her forehead and fright in her face. She stepped inside, and quickly dressed. She stared down at the gun that shook in her hand, and her horror-filled eyes brimmed with unshed tears.

"Call Viktor. Be short and quiet," I ordered and handed her my phone. Tears spilled from her doe eyes, and I hated to see the panic and fear inside.

I kissed her, hard and deep, before my forehead met hers.

"Don't be afraid, I'll be back for you shortly. But, if you hear footsteps and not my voice," I covered my hands over her shaking fingers that held my gun, "Don't think."

"Don't go," she pleaded.

"If you see death coming your way, tip the scales. Look at it right in the eye, smile, strike, and run until we meet again." With a kiss on her head, I left her.

FIFTEEN

d a v i n a

THE DARKNESS CONSUMED MY HEART INSIDE THE CLOSET. I was surrounded by his scent, surrounded by dread, knowing Ilias out was on his own with the monsters that wouldn't let me escape.

How could I let him walk away?

My fingers shook, and the weight of the gun burned with awareness of what this one weapon could do. I huddled my body in the corner, dropped the gun, and swiped the screen of the phone in search of Viktor's name. It was the last outgoing call on the phone's log, and I pressed the green button.

Viktor answered before the first ring finished.

"Boris is safe, if that's why you are calling."

I choked on my cry when I heard the faint and familiar accent Viktor had.

"Where's my brother?" Viktor asked quickly.

The house was silent, but my heart drummed loudly.

"He said to call. Someone's inside his house."

"Fuck!" he yelled, and I could hear him moving rapidly through the phone. "Who are you?"

"Davina." I sniveled, not caring if I'd given him my real name. I owed it to him.

"Where are you?" Viktor asked at the same time a loud car door shut on his end.

"Inside the closet."

"Don't get out. I'll be there shortly," Viktor assured me, grunts and shuffling coming from outside of the room.

"Hurry," I whispered before ending the call.

How many people were outside?

The air in my lungs rattled in my chest, constricting the flow with each breath I tried taking. The thought of any harm happening to Ilias while I sat in a dark corner like a rat, hiding from danger as his life was at stake made me ill. My stomach rolled, bile rose, and hives crawled over my skin.

I closed my eyes, tuned out the sounds to background noise, and calmed my breathing.

The fog cleared, and I'd made up my mind.

I gripped the gun and stood on my feet.

Viktor had said he would be here shortly, but I knew a life could be taken in just a matter of seconds. Ilias wasn't going to be the one whose life would be wasted tonight.

Like Martin, he shouldn't be the one to take a bullet or death when it was meant for me.

Silent tears ran down my cheeks, but they felt hollow. I numbed the fears for my life, and they now shouted for Ilias's. I shook the trembles away from my hand to place it firmly on the knob.

I walked silently out of the closet.

His struggles were loud, and I wondered if the neighbors could hear, if they would call for help. But even if they had heard, I was all he had at this moment inside this house.

I denied the terror with each step, deprived my feelings to only the ones I had for him, and rejected any sense of humanity.

I cleared my head, hearing sounds coming down the hall. As my hand twisted the knob, pulling it ajar, I wondered If I could even pull the trigger. If I would hesitate.

A body with eyes wide open stared up to the ceiling in a pool of blood. His hand laid awkwardly over his chest where a wound bled close to the one that took his life. A knife was etched onto his shoulder blade, straight and deep into his skin.

The sight halted my movements, and I trapped my gasp with the palm of my hand. Tears blurred my sight, and before I hid back into safety with the screams in my head, I looked past it.

Ilias, Ilias, Ilias, I chanted in my head to keep me from thinking.

The house was pitch black compared to before, and I had no doubt it was their doing.

I urged my feet to move past the dead body, but before I got the chance, two large frames tumbled out of the opposite bedroom. I hid back in the shadows, wanting the element of surprise if given.

Fists met flesh, and cries that weren't Ilias's roared in the hall.

I took that as a good sign, a sign that maybe we had a chance.

But how many were here?

I peeked around the door frame, and Ilias pounded on the guy's stomach. The figure tried blocking him, but he was no match to the ire Ilias was under. His eyes were dark and not a glimpse of mercy showed in their depths.

His blows kept coming, his face was bloody, and his hair was wet from sweat and blood as it dripped down his neck.

Then his eyes looked up. They locked on mine, and he hesitated his next punch.

It was a mistake. Ilias had wanted me away, not only to keep me safe, but from the distraction I could cause.

And I'd failed.

His opponent took his halt for his own gain, and I watched as it was too late for Ilias to react to the jab of the guy's fists before connecting to his chin. The force took Ilias by surprise, and his head shot backward with a loud thud vibrating in my ears. His head hit the wall, his body slumping down.

I kept my cry deep in my throat as I watched the guy stand before him.

My heart screamed in agony at the sight.

The dark frame whistled mockingly. My brows furrowed at the sound, how could he find such joy?

My palm sweat with the tight grip on the gun. If I had wondered if I had the guts to shoot someone in cold blood, at this moment, I had the answer.

I would when it meant Ilias was in danger.

With both hands, I raised the weapon straight out in front of me.

My index finger hooked around the trigger, and tears escaped my eyes in a rush.

"This was way too easy."

I shivered as I heard the English spoken had an Italian accent.

"You are as good as dead," Ilias muttered as his head shifted upright. Blood stained his teeth through his grin.

"No one will know, pet." The guy spat onto the ground, his hand snaking around his back to grasp the concealed gun.

I peered down to Ilias, who's eyes were wide, watching me holding the gun.

"No," he uttered so silently I was shocked I had heard him.

And when I returned my gaze to the intruder standing above him, the concealed gun was pointed at me.

The man smirked under the shadows. "I found you," he taunted. "You can put the weapon down now, sweetie. We both know you won't pull the trigger."

His lips pursed before his whistles began again, and his body twisted back to Ilias.

I pulled the trigger.

The smell of sulfur and gunpowder hit my nostrils, and I took a step back from the shock and kick of the gun.

But he was still standing, watching the hole on the wall just inches away from his head.

I sucked in a gasp as I was now facing a vicious man. My gun-holding hand shook at my side as the man charged my way.

"Ugo!" Ilias shouted.

They knew each other.

I had no time to react.

In a blur, his gun raised before it struck my face.

A blinding pain shot through my temple, and I doubled over onto the ground, holding my face with my free hand. Wetness spilled through my fingers as I blinked away the dizziness and darkness that wanted to take over, but the throbbing pain on my head wouldn't subside. I looked up.

The man named Ugo stood over me with his gun on my head. His large brown eyes cut over me in slits, and his mouth twisted with distaste.

"That was stupid of you," he spat. "If they are going through so much trouble finding you, I'm sure they won't care if you are dead instead."

He was all I could see, but I wished it were Ilias's blues one last time to put me at peace.

"Davina!" Ilias yelled, distracting Ugo.

And the thing was, I didn't want to only see Ilias's eyes for one last time. I wanted to see them for as long as I could, and in the morning with his arms wrapped around me.

"If you see death coming your way, tip the scales. Look at it right in the eye, smile, strike, and run until we meet again."

I could see death at the end of Ugo's barrel, and I looked at it, smiled, raised the heavy gun, and struck.

Ugo twisted as the first bullet hit his stomach, shocked, with raged hatred in his eyes.

I shot again, again, and again. And with each time I pulled the trigger, I rose higher off the ground until Ugo's body laid next to the lifeless body and the gun clicked and clicked without any bullets left.

I couldn't stop pulling the trigger. The only sound inside the room was the hammer clicking over and over as tears and shouts fled out of my bleak soul.

My name was called, but I was too far gone to be pulled from the haze.

"*Kroshka.*"

I stopped, and the gun fell to the ground in a loud thump. My gaze remained on the man below, the man I had just shot. Blood was everywhere, smearing the pristine hardwoods and his clothes. Even in death, his eyes were restless, without peace, searching out to the open.

Ilias's warmth pulled my face away, but not my gaze. It was still trapped to the life I'd just taken. He covered my eyes and burrowed my head in his chest, holding me tightly to him.

Even in his hold, I couldn't muster any feelings.

I was numbed.

I'd killed a man, and I didn't feel anything. Not a ray of sorrow or remorse for taking something that wasn't mine or within my power to do.

"I'm so sorry, Davina," Ilias murmured.

What was he sorry for?

Downstairs, a door was pushed open, and I closed my eyes at the thought of others coming. But Ilias held me tighter, not worried of who'd walked in.

"*Brat?*" The same voice I'd spoken to on the phone sounded troubled as he shouted.

Viktor.

Ilias pulled my face away but only to bring his inches from mine. Blood stained his features, but all I focused on was his sky-blue eyes.

"Listen to me very carefully. Things are about to change, and you will know a part of me even I'd tried to stay away from. But there are two made men dead inside my house, and you must not say you'd killed one of them. Do you understand?" His eyes bored into mine.

Then I remembered. "But you knew one, you called him…"

"Don't," Ilias hushed me with a small kiss and pulled back. His movements were quick, worried even.

I could tell.

The real danger had just begun.

SIXTEEN
ilias

"FUCK," VIKTOR WHISPERED WHEN HE ENTERED THE hallway with eyes wide, quickly taking in the surroundings. When he noticed me standing inches away from the door with Davina behind me, his shoulders relaxed, his eyes calmed. "Are you okay?"

I nodded, not mentioning the open wound I'd received from the first guy I didn't have the name of. His accent, clothing, and the way he portrayed himself, it all screamed mafioso.

My first thought was Lucca. Arlo had mentioned heat on the streets, the hierarchy change, and the tensions within the famiglia. Maybe they were trying to make Lucca seem weak before fully sitting on the throne of Miami. But then I'd seen Ugo.

It was personal

Ugo had spoken of *finding her*.

The pieces connected, and I was in bigger trouble than I could've ever imagined.

He'd gone as far as going against orders by coming inside my home.

"Ili." My brother was troubled with the scene, the bodies, me, Davina, and what it meant.

Unlike me, Viktor *was* a made man. He couldn't work side by side with Lucca or Arlo with the DEA position he had been molded to hold. He understood first-hand the wrath the family could inflict when one of their own was killed.

I had two made men, from two different families, dead in my hallway.

It was a death sentence, and the way my brother couldn't stop looking around the filthy hallway, he knew it too.

"I called Arlo," he whispered. "I didn't know how much trouble or what you were up against." He wished it hadn't been this.

Viktor's phone rang, and reluctantly, he looked away from me to answer the call. "I'm here." He nodded. "He's alive." He nodded once again. "The front door is open."

Just as he ended the call, the front door opened and shut with a bang. Arlo.

"Ilias." Viktor looked over Davina, who continued to stare off, before sliding his gaze back to me. "You know I'll always have your back. You know that, right, *brat*?"

Even if Viktor did, there was nothing he could do.

"*Cazzo*." *Fuck*, Arlo muttered as he stood on the last step. "Fuck!" he shouted this time, running his hands over his face. Davina twitched from his outburst and stood closer behind me. "And who the fuck is she, and why is she left alive?"

My body tensed at his words, and Davina's gaze fell.

"Arlo—"

He cut me off quickly, eyes blazing. "Don't!" Arlo began. "Don't fucking try to *Arlo* me when there's two dead bodies on the floor. Not any fucking regular citizens, but two of ours. With a witness right behind you." Arlo pulled out his gun.

I didn't flinch. Arlo was a master of fear, but he wasn't trying to inflict it on me, his victim was Davina. And it was working.

"Are you done?" I asked.

Arlo shook his head frustrated and nudged Ugo's dead body with his black boot. "You better start talking, because this," he pointed his gun toward the body, "This will be worse than death, *fratello*. There's an empty clip on his body. You can't even argue self-defense when you could've stopped at the first bullet." His eyes twisted, trying to look behind me.

Thankfully, Davina didn't twitch at his words.

Viktor cut the silence. "We can't trust a cleaner with this. We'll have to do it ourselves."

"It'll have to wait," Arlo said, taking a deep breath as his fingers pinched the bridge of his nose. He looked over at Viktor and nodded my way. "By the way he is leaning to his left and the fresh blood staining his shirt, he needs to be stitched up."

Viktor's gaze shot to my abdomen, and Davina moved away from her hiding spot to stand before me.

They both took her in; Viktor with curiosity, Arlo with distaste.

Davina tugged on my shirt and hissed when she saw the opened wound. We all stood still as Davina walked toward the dresser. With a shirt in her hands, my brows furrowed in confusion until she pressed the material against the cut, adding pressure. Her fingers grabbed my hand, placing it over the shirt.

"Keep applying pressure." Davina looked up to me, her eyes roaming around my hair.

What the fuck was she looking for now?

She took a couple of steps around me until her delicate fingers brushed my hair away from the back of my head. I pulled away from her touch as it caused discomfort from the hit I'd received, then she was back in front of me.

"Look at me," she demanded.

I did, seeing pale skin and dark circles that adorned her eyes. She squinted, and dried blood creased in the corners from the blow of Ugo's pistol. Then I understood. My heart constricted at her attention to assure I was okay. I dared to glance over at my brothers. They too looked baffled as the scene had played out before them. Viktor's lips lifted on the corners, amused, and Arlo's head craned to the side.

"Davina, I'm fine," I uttered holding her face with my free hand.

"I think you have a mild concussion," she judged.

"Concussions are for pussies. Now, if you are done playing nurse, we need to leave and get him patched up," Arlo said, taking a step back.

Davina turned to face him. "Any concussion is to be treated carefully. He needs to go to a hospital and get checked out," she said with strength and balled fists.

"Have you taken a look around, *ragazza*?" Arlo chuckled darkly, and I knew after calling her *girl*, his patience was running thin.

"Stop," I said in Russian.

Arlo's attention snapped to me, and in perfect Russian, "Russian it is then, dumbass." Viktor shook his head, knowing where this was headed.

"It seems I'm the only one aware of the fucking bloodbath in your hallway. Or the death warrant you now have on your goddamn blond head," Arlo shouted. "And if it was anyone else, brother—anyone fucking else, Ilias—you would have been killed the moment Viktor or I walked in because *we* would've taken you straight to your execution."

"You are not involved, nothing will happen to you."

"You think I give a shit about that? I'm worried about *you*, about how can Lucca possibly fix this, aside from killing you, and your..."

"Arlo," Viktor warned.

"You both have no idea." Arlo's lip twisted. "Lucca is now the boss, Sal stepped down to *Consigliere* while things settled. I'm standing as the *underboss*. And here I have our brother bringing the one thing that can get us all killed when our famiglia is hanging by a thread at the new changes. A war with the New York family."

Davina reacted to the one thing she would have understood. *New York Family*.

Speaking in English, Arlo said to Davina, "That's who you've been hiding from, right? You are Davina."

My muscles tensed as my heart rattled inside its cage. *This can't be true.*

Sadly, her eyes replied with the truth.

DAVINA

"PIECE OF SHIT, THEY KILLED IT," VIKTOR SAID WHEN HE PUSHED the buttons of the dead alarm system.

"For not listening about getting a better system," Arlo muttered as he walked past us toward the front door.

"That's enough, Arlo. Last I remembered, I was pushed to live a normal life," Ilias bit back.

I watched them face each other. Ilias had called Arlo *brother*, but they didn't share any characteristics. Arlo was a few inches taller, broad, and intimidating. He wore all black, from the boots on his feet to the stretched tee over his shoulders. Hazel eyes that inflicted tremors, full lips, and a strong jaw only an Italian descent could have. Arlo was someone I would be running from. His dark hair was cut short, adding more of his edge, and with the few tattoos that sprinkled around his forearms, he couldn't look more different than Ilias or Viktor.

"Yeah? Look at how well that worked out," Arlo sneered. His eyes peered over me before dismissing us both by walking out.

Viktor shook his head. "Come on, your face is losing color the longer we stay. Hop in my car, I'm sure Arlo left his somewhere safe."

"I can drive," Ilias muttered.

Viktor lowered his eyes for a second before the corner of his mouth twisted. "I think it's best if you just come with us, man."

"You think I'm going to run?" Ilias asked, but I heard the small surprise and hurt in his voice.

Viktor shook his head with a snicker.

"Please, *brother*." Then his deep blue eyes slid my way. "Just making sure you are safe."

I wondered if Ilias understood, it was me they didn't trust, but that was alright. I didn't trust them either. Not when Ilias's life was at stake.

Viktor wasn't surprised to find Arlo behind the wheel of his car, and thankfully I didn't require much space as Arlo's seat was far back, touching my knees when I hopped inside. Ilias sat next to me in the back of the car. He let out a groan when he rested his head back on the leather headrest with his arm wrapped around his middle.

I was worried about him, but I was sure once he would see a doctor, he would be okay. I stared out the small window to drown my worries, watching as the night stretched in a never-ending twist.

There were so many questions that burned inside of me, and none had been answered. On the contrary, more burst through my mind the longer we sat in silence. The numbness began to disappear, bringing my anxiety and panic to rush back.

Taking a deep breath, I turned to Ilias. His eyes were shut tightly from pain, but he didn't make a sound. His clothes were stained red and his body was smeared with dried blood, red hands gripping his side. My heart rushed with many mixed feelings, from relief to see him next to me alive, to terrified of what he'd done.

What he was capable of.

My subconscious came knocking back, fear settled, and I woke from the trance I had currently been under.

He was a cop! So why are we not going to the police?

"Where are we going?" my voice cracked in the end, but no one answered.

My eyes looked ahead to the men sitting in the front. Something caught my eye as it hung from the visor mirror. A DEA hat. My gaze slid to Viktor. He was a DEA agent.

Nothing made sense, not when I felt the burning gaze of Arlo watching me.

Arlo knew about the New York family.

Arlo knew the dead man that laid at Ilias's house.

Arlo knew my name without anyone telling him.

They were brothers.

And they all spoke about Lucca with respect.

I was sitting in a car with dangerous men, and one of them who I'd grown to care for, but was I now in more danger than before?

My body shivered, and I jolted when I felt Ilias's hand over my thigh. He was trying to calm my thoughts with his gentle touch, and it worked — for a short second. Because as I stared down at his red stained hand, I got the chance to look at my body.

The air seemed to fade as a deep ache filled my lungs. Trembles took over my fingertips as I traced the dried red droplets that corrupted the white and pure tee I wore. The droplets weren't only on my chest or shirt, they covered me. My face bunched in terror, the crinkling sensation cracking over my face. My hands lifted to touch the creases created by dried liquid.

You've taken a life, point blank, my subconscious added as bile rose in my throat and tears hurried to be released from the body of a murderer.

"Stop the car!" I shrieked, my body heaving.

"Davina?" Ilias's concern was lost on me.

"Stop!" I cried, wiping the tears away, but when I stared down at my hands, blood was mixing with their moisture, bringing it back to life. I couldn't take the sight any more, and I covered my mouth.

Tires squealed, and the sudden stop turned my stomach. Arlo jumped out of the car, moved the seat forward, and I escaped the back seat in a rush.

I didn't make it too far before emptying my stomach. My body shook with force as I stayed crunched on the loose paved road.

"I'd wondered how long it would take before this would happen," Viktor said.

Ilias was next to me, moving my hair away from my face and bringing me to his chest protectively. Crying silently, I grasped tightly to him.

"The shock will pass. Here," Arlo demanded, eyeing me carefully with a water bottle hanging from his hands.

I didn't trust my stomach to hold anything, let alone water. Instead, I poured the liquid on my face and hands until the water no longer held a shade of pink and ran clear onto the ground.

I was wrong. I was not inside a car filled with dangerous men.

The car was filled with dangerous people.

And when we arrived at what could only be called a fortress, we were now in the lair and home of the dangerous life.

SEVENTEEN
ilias

DAVINA HAD CLOSED OFF. I SHOULD HAVE SEEN THIS coming. Her body tensed underneath my hand as we pulled up to Lucca's place, and her chest rose rapidly when the car rolled to a stop.

I would be lying if I wasn't worried for our futures. My brothers loved me, but before us four, it had always been the family. After hearing the change of hierarchy, it made sense. The small comments, the rumors, the last time I saw Lucca's stressed demeanor, and the way they'd been trying to protect me for a while. It also angered me because I still didn't know what was happening. How Arlo knew of Davina, and how it all connected.

It seemed that Davina ran from the New York Syndicate, only to be trapped by another. And I was no hero. If anything, I was her downfall.

When we got out of the car, Arlo walked behind us and Viktor ahead. Davina stayed close, but I could see the way she was hesitant to get too close even to me. It hurt. And the more she would learn, the more she would want to keep her distance.

Usually, the house was scattered by soldiers, but it was the quietest it had ever been.

That alone was a bad sign.

Fuck.

"I'll be back with Lucca shortly," Arlo announced as we stepped inside Lucca's grand study, and he looked over Viktor. "Get the kit and patch him up."

"Patch him up?" The room stilled with Davina's tone.

Arlo's lips curled, and when he took a step forward, so did I.

"Arlo," I warned.

He didn't acknowledge me, instead he stared at Davina with punishing eyes. I stepped between his gaze, bringing his eyes to mine. He shook his head with a sneer and walked away.

Davina's hands curled tightly to her sides, and they didn't relax until the door clicked closed.

"You need a doctor!"

"It's a scratch," I said, dropping onto the leather cushion.

"This can't be real." She pushed her hands over her face and paced.

I watched her as she muttered to herself, and I almost laughed at how flustered she was.

"Here." Viktor brought my attention to him and the medical kit in his hands. I hadn't noticed he had left. "You know I can't sew you."

"Yeah." I did. Viktor couldn't stand to even see me get a paper cut.

"Wait?" Davina turned to face us. Her blood-stained shirt covered half of her thighs, and I relished the sight of how sick and sexy she looked with wild eyes, crazy hair, and an untamed tongue. "Then who the fuck is going to do it?" Damn, and now she was cursing.

"Me?" I responded.

"I'll be outside," Viktor announced, making a quick exit.

Davina let out a breath, dropping her head back before returning her gaze to me.

"Have you ever done this before?" She nodded toward my wound and kit.

"Yeah, just not on myself," I replied, and her lips twisted.

"We hid so much from each other."

Yes, we did.

"Come here," I said, but she hesitated her first step, and I closed my eyes at the pain I felt from that small movement. "Are you really okay?"

Her eyes began to water.

Ugo.

"No. But not in the way you believe," she rasped.

Davina made her way back to me, but wouldn't meet my eyes. She busied herself with the medical kit, grabbing cleaning supplies for the wound. Her hand reached for my shirt, but I stopped her hands.

"*Kroshka.*"

"Don't."

I let go of her hand to hold her neck instead. My grip wasn't gentle, but now that we had a minute alone, I wanted to feel her heartbeat underneath my palm, to feel the way her body heated with life and the way she was safe before me. My thumb ran over her lips, pressing down and watching as they turned a deep red.

I clenched her jaw tighter, and her eyes widened before I pulled her arm toward me, and her body followed. I didn't let go of my grasp until I felt her quick breathing running over my lips as her mouth parted.

"I've never been so scared of losing someone," I admitted to her shining dark eyes before pressing her lips to mine deeply to assure she's here, with me, alive.

"So was I," she whispered through our kiss, then pulled away to rest her forehead against mine. She straightened and began cleaning the wound in silence while I got the right materials for the stitches.

"Can you answer a question?" she asked with her eyes focusing on what her hands were doing.

"Depends."

"How are you all related?" That was an easy answer. "You all look so different."

As she finished cleaning, I took a second to think of my next words, and busied myself, withdrawing the needle closer to my skin to begin the few stitches I needed.

"Sometimes, bonds grow deeper than blood. Bonds of honor, loyalty, and respect that with time, differences are not seen, all there is, is family." Her lashes fluttered with eyes that gave me their full attention. I grimaced with the stabbing pain and sensitivity of the wound as I pierced through the angry skin, and continued talking to think of anything other than the way I wanted to scream from the pain.

"I was too young to remember the day I was placed in a home for boys. But Viktor was by my side. Our mother overdosed after taking one too many beatings from my father. We don't know what happened to him, and I don't care to find out. I remember one day at the home for boys, I wet the bed. Victor stood up for me." I chuckled dryly, remembering the time I was scared of my own shadow. "It grew to a fight with the other boys, and all of a sudden, everything stilled and Arlo and Lucca walked into the main bedroom." I wished I could remember that day clearly, but only obscured scenes my mind had captured played out. "Even then, they walked around with power, and everyone could see it. No one could tell them anything. Even the adults let them do as they wished. So, when they stopped the fight and told us to come with them to their smaller grouped room, we followed them. The rest was history, and we became inseparable. They all had a part in me growing up, and by the time, I was six. When Lucca left, things began to change once again and we were not ones to mess with." I drew a deep breath as I inched closer to the last two stitches left, and continued through my teeth, "We didn't see much of Lucca after, then Arlo left, and he too distanced himself. But they weren't just being distanced, Lucca was already thinking of the future for us four."

"What future?" Davina whispered.

"One with people he trusts in the law, as he was molded into a life before creating an empire."

The door ripped open as I finished the last stitch. Lucca walked in with purpose and murder in his eyes, jaw locked as he took in my presence.

"Are you done bleeding in my chair?" His voice was controlled, but his stance and the way he walked over to the bar said more about his wild thoughts than his tone. He poured two fingers of amber liquid into a crystal cut glass before downing his drink and pouring a second. When he turned, his eyes looked over Davina. "And why the fuck is a woman in here?"

DAVINA

THE BLOOD IN MY BODY DRAINED AS A MAN WALKED INTO THE room dressed in a full black suit, filled with power and poise with each step he took deeper into the space. Tattoos covered his neck and hands all the way down to his fingers. His dark eyes looked over Ilias with violence before harshly taking a drink.

Arlo and Viktor stood in each corner in the back of the room, and my heart beat brutally inside when my mind registered *who* Lucca was. It was impossible not to. The way he moved with authority, the way the room seemed to quiet with his presence and the same eerie way he carried himself reminded me of the night I'd met *Tattoo*.

Lucca was a mafioso—they all were—but he was the head of them all. And I stood in his home, inside his study. In his presence.

Like *Tattoo*, Lucca had the same Italian appearance.

"And why the fuck is a woman in here?"

My eyes grew when his cold eyes watched and acknowledged me as if I were a pebble under his feet. I tried to straighten my posture, but it was useless not to show my fear because with him around, all I could envision was the men that had invaded my nightmares and the ones I'd been hiding from.

"Well?" Lucca raised his brow, waiting.

Ilias shuffled in his seat, ready to speak, but I cleared my throat. Even if dread chilled my bones, and fear pricked my fingertips, I was tired of being pushed to the side. And if I were to die, I could at least have a voice. I was a woman in the middle of a man's world, but damn if I was going to be weak in front of their eyes.

"I'm Davina Cohen." It took them all by surprise. It was the first time Ilias heard my full name

"You're from New York," Lucca said without a question.

"Yes."

"And who sent you?"

That took me by surprise. "Sent me?"

"The time for games is over. Start speaking," Lucca demanded with a cold voice, but it held so much more. A threat. "You think I'll believe it was all a coincidence? How you just happen to be led straight to my brother?"

"Lucca, she's not—"

Lucca cut off Ilias from speaking. "Don't, Ilias!" Lucca roared, losing all his composure. "The moment you shot Ugo, you were a dead man walking. I am trying to fucking understand how she comes in the middle of it all!"

"It was self-defense. He came into my home," Ilias spat back.

"Because he had orders to find a stray who just happened to be in *your* bed," Lucca's tone was filled with disgust. "And now, not only will you have New York looking for your head for the death of one of their own, but *me*." Lucca took a threatening step toward Ilias, who sat calmly in his chair.

How could he not see the danger he was in because of me?

"I killed Ugo," I rasped.

Ilias tensed but tried to hide his reaction, and the room silenced with Lucca's sinister smile.

"As much as I wouldn't blink for your life, that's sweet of you, really," Lucca mocked. "But don't utter words that will earn another target on your head, child."

"Ugo had Ilias on his knees after I distracted him by not following the only order he gave me." I looked straight into Lucca's eyes as I continued, "To stay hidden."

"Don't lie, Davina," Ilias said through his teeth.

"I couldn't imagine someone else taking a bullet that was meant for me. So, I raised the gun Ilias had given me. Ugo mocked me, said I couldn't. I pulled the trigger." Viktor shuffled in the corner and all eyes were on me. "I missed, and he charged my way." Raising my fingertips, I touched my temple for him to see the evidence of Ugo's blow. "And while he stood over me with his gun against my head, Ilias called out for him. Ugo looked away, and the heavy gun in my hand lifted once again, and I pulled the trigger. That time, I didn't miss, he was too close. He looked at me with surprise and venom in his eyes. I snapped." While our eyes stayed on one another, my voice lowered. "I just let the smell of gunpowder fill my lungs as I emptied the magazine, and all I could hear was the clicking of the empty chamber in a haze."

"Davina," Ilias whispered for me to stop.

"And the sick part of it all, I would do it again if it meant Ilias would be safe." I shrugged and looked into Lucca's eyes as I said, "So, what's one more Syndicate over my head? I doubt I would come out alive from the first anyway."

"Arlo?" Lucca murmured without releasing me from his stare.

"She's telling the truth," Arlo cleared his throat, "It was too sloppy, Ilias doesn't react that way."

"You can't believe her!" Ilias raised his voice, but it was too late.

"Oh, I can, *fratello*." Lucca finally removed his eyes away from me to Ilias. "It's the way she speaks of your name. I just wanted Arlo to confirm it."

"Lucca." Ilias stood rapidly, holding his side, but bringing me close to his frame.

"Clean up all evidence left, and bring anything that ties her to Ugo's life."

Arlo took a step forward, taking in Lucca's instructions, while my body froze with each word. Then his merciless eyes took me in.

"The Moretti Family now owns you. Until everything is cleared, and I find a way to assure my brother's safety, you are bound to stay here with a target on your head." Lucca placed his glass down onto his desk, and continued, "The only reason you are still breathing is because you saved his life, and unless I find a way out of it, Ugo's life will need to be justified."

"For fuck's sake, Lucca. You cannot do this!" Ilias roared, but I held him back from moving forward.

"You gave me no fucking choice, Ilias! You want to know when the famiglia is at its weakest?" Lucca took a seat, emotion now stripped away. "When a new boss has been named. And now, I have New York in my backyard and older members breathing down my neck as I change the old ways." His lips pursed, and I saw the moment his eyes held a question. "There's just one thing," Lucca added, "How were you protecting her in the first place?"

"I was assigned to watch and protect her," Ilias replied, confused.

"By who?"

Ilias took a second to reply. His brows pinched together deep in thought, and I could tell by the way his mind raced wildly.

"Chief Pierce."

"Fuck," Viktor whispered from the back with his gaze on the ground, but when he looked up, all eyes were on him. "Chief Pierce hasn't been in the precinct for long, and once he arrived, I checked his records. I don't think it's a coincidence he worked for the NYPD before moving here."

"It's not," Lucca said through a locked jaw. "Viktor, bring him in. Arlo, retrieve what I've asked and assure nothing is left. And you two," His eyes moved to Ilias and me. "Don't leave the compound, clean up, bag your clothing, and burn it all, Ilias."

I couldn't understand what was happening. Why were they going after Chief Pierce? What could he possibly be associated with when all he'd done was be assigned to my case?

I watched as they all followed orders without question. They just nodded and left. I felt as if I was stuck in another dimension. A dimension where souls were trapped and bodies moved around like vessels with no empathy or regard for human life. But it wasn't a dimension. It was real. It had already taken a part of my humanity the moment I held a gun in my hands—when I felt its power—and it tore my heart open when I raised it. But, after I'd shot and took the life of a living being, it was me who bled. I bled the innocence and hope I still held for the world.

EIGHTEEN
ilias

LUCCA OFFERED ONE OF THE BEDROOMS FROM THE EAST wing to clean up. As I looked around, I tried not to grimace by being placed on the *east* wing. It was where the untrusted guests stayed. The most secured section of the house with cameras in every corner aside from the bedrooms, and also the farthest to any exit, not to mention upstairs.

He wanted to fuck with her head, but really, he was fucking with mine.

Davina stood in the middle of the large room, taking in all the details. I'd seen every room of this house, but I tried to see it with new eyes. The elegant hand-crafted wood that molded every piece of furniture to accommodate specifically to the size of the room. The warm tones of the beige bedding, clean walls, and chestnut wood made the room inviting, relaxing. You could get lost in the small areas of the room, like the small bookcase, the lounge chair in the corner, and outside on the two-person balcony.

Yet, inside a room where everything was set perfectly in place, Davina stood out. Her eyes shimmered as she held her feelings together, and her arms were wrapped around her body, making her look small. The clothes she was wearing were ruined, and even when she'd tried to rinse her face and hands earlier, there were still traces of blood left behind.

My hand held the back of her head as my fingers wrapped around her thick hair.

"I'm going to go and find you some clean clothes that will fit you better, okay?"

Her hand grabbed my forearm. Her sulky eyes watched mine, wanting to speak. But, instead, she remained quiet.

"I won't be long. You should start a bath."

With a small smile, she left my arms and walked inside the adjoined bathroom, closing the door behind her. I had a feeling like I should be going after her, a feeling that I wasn't used to experiencing. It was uncomfortable, and it pained me the more the time passed and I saw the pain in her eyes.

I'd wanted to give her a minute to herself. But as I placed the clean clothes that one of the house keepers was kind enough to find for me on the bed, I heard small snivels and the shower running. It only took a short second before I was walking inside the bathroom. The ruined shirt and boxers I had given her were littered on the white marble flooring. Steam slipped from the large glass shower, obscuring her from view.

The room grew quiet with me inside, but my heart panged for her. So much happened today, and there was only so much a human mind could take before cracking into darkness.

Undressing, I piled our clothing in the corner, and I opened the glass door. "Davina."

"Please give me a minute," her broken voice begged, but this time, I couldn't walk away when she clearly needed me.

Steam rushed out of the shower as I stepped under the hot spray of water. Davina sat on the white tiles with her knees drawn to her chest.

K. DOSAL

She raised her head and her eyes broke me. Bloodshot, puffy, and filled with agony.

Yet, she still found a way to worry about me. "Your stitches."

"Oh, *kroshka*. You are what matters right now." I lowered and brought her to me.

I moved her hair away to see her delicate features. Her cheeks were pink from the heat of the running water, and I caressed her skin and nuzzled my face against the nape of her neck. In silence, I moved her under the shower spray, and once her hair was saturated in water, I grabbed the shampoo from the corner and began washing her.

Davina closed her eyes, and her body swayed under my hands. My eyes couldn't stay away from her, mesmerized by her beauty, her body, and her broken soul. I knew it was something I could amend. I had done it once. I could do it again.

"I can't lose you," I admitted with our lips tasting the clean water that ran between us and the truth of my words.

Davina's lips collided with mine. Her hands held onto me as if I was all she needed, for everything to disappear. Then they lowered until she held my hardened dick in her hands, and I exhaled from her touch. I wanted to explore her body, and this bathroom wasn't the place I could ravish her and let go until we were spent. But Davina had other plans as her core shifted forward in search for friction.

She needed a release. Her body begged for it, and I couldn't refuse her. I was going to give her what she asked, and then, I was going to make her cry out for me as I had my way.

When she moved her pelvis forward again, I gripped her hips, brought her core against mine, and caged her against the tiled wall.

"You are awfully quiet, *kroshka*," I said against her ear and heard a whimper on mine. "Tell me what you want. Tell me, so I know you are here with me."

"Please."

I parted her legs with my thigh and let my hand run down her body until I felt her heat.

"Please, what?" I taunted, inching my fingertips closer to her mound.

"Please, make me beg your name!"

Fuck. I wasn't expecting that response, or her pleading eyes.

I watched as her eyes closed, and her head stretched upward when my hand covered her completely, applying pressure to her core. Two fingers slid over her warmth until meeting wetness. Her hips bucked under my palm, but they stilled as my digits entered her, and her hands gripped my shoulders. I pumped slowly at first, causing her to wriggle away from the tile and onto me. But as my fingers sped, her hands and body became uncontrollable. Her hands found my hair, then slid down my back as her nails scratched my skin. As our breathing fastened, I couldn't stray my eyes away from her face. She was so close, so needy, so ready, and all it took was for my thumb to slide over her mound as my fingers were deep inside her. Her legs tensed, her toes curled, and her front squirmed forward as she rode her orgasm.

Davina closed her eyes before placing her head on my chest. I smiled. If she thought this was over, she had another thing coming.

My hands grabbed her ass, lifting her feet from the ground. She gasped and quickly wrapped her legs around my waist, careful not to touch my side. With a quick twist of my hands, the water stopped, and we were out of the steaming shower where we met the chilling air coming from the room.

Picking up a hanging towel, I wrapped her body for just a second before placing Davina on the bed. Her eyes grew with lust, and her body inched away to fully lie in the middle with legs slightly apart.

When her eyes lowered, she took a worried breath through her teeth. "Ilias, you're bleeding."

Any blood that swept through my closed wound was something I was not worried about. I ignored every tug of the stitches as my knees fell onto the bed, crawling toward the call of her body.

"It's nothing," I rasped over her lips and took away her next words by getting another taste of her swollen mouth.

In case my kiss still gave her a reason to think, my lips dropped to her jaw, nipping her sensitive neck as they continued to sink down her body. I kissed every part as I descended to her collarbone, her scar, shoulders, until I caught her nipples between my teeth. Davina's body bucked as she moaned. Her tits were so sensitive and responsive to my touch, and I continued to pleasure her with bits of stinging pain from my teeth.

My hand lowered to her warmth, finding her wet and ready for me, but I wasn't ready to plunge deep inside her. Not yet. First, I wanted to taste her.

I kept my eyes on her, and with her elbows sinking into the mattress, she raised her torso, watching as I inched closer to her pelvis. The moment my tongue swiped and my mouth clasped on to her pussy, Davina screamed my name in surrender. Once I had a taste, and heard her response, I became an addict. I lapped her core, devoured her rim, and spread her with my tongue until she could no longer hold her body or my gaze. Her hand fisted the bedding as her body squirmed.

"Ilias, please." It was her pleading tone that drove me insane.

Davina's hands moved to my head, fingers pulling my hair. When it became too much, she tried pushing me away, then she would rock back, then push back with never ending pleasure sounds. She was so close, so sensitive that her cries grew louder and her body tried to wiggle from my hold. My hand pushed her back to the bed, and her hand gripped mine as the other wrapped around her bottom while I chased her release.

"Ili-as!"

My name was broken in ecstasy between her breathless weep as she let go. My dick throbbed as I watched her heaving chest, shaking body, and beautiful satisfied gaze.

Davina gently placed her hands on each side of my jaw, eyes shimmering as she looked deeply into mine. She caressed my face and moved the hair that fell over my forehead.

"Make me forget it all," she whispered.

I held her head while my body hovered over hers. Our foreheads connected, our eyes locked. "It's something you can never forget."

"Then at least for the night. Because when I'm with you, you seem to remove all the bad."

Davina was wrong. She seemed to ignore *I* was part of the bad too, underestimating what I was capable of, the selfishness that now wouldn't let her go. I trapped her into this world, and yet, as she disregarded it all, so did I.

I kissed her hard, taking her light and bathing with its shine. I took her deep and slow with unsaid promises of safety when I had no power to fulfill them.

As I rocked into her, I discovered that I would do anything to assure she would forever be mine, to always see the way her brown eyes looked at me with intensity. To always hear her call out my name, and for her skin to be the last thing I felt at the end of the day. I fucked her as if we had no future, because it was true. Our days were numbered, unless I found a way to undo it all.

And as I called for her to come with me, and her eyes shut with parted lips, I was determined to find a way.

Even if it meant vowing my soul to the underworld.

I COULDN'T KEEP MY EYES AWAY FROM DAVINA AS SHE SLEPT. The more I watched her, the more the unfamiliar feeling of attachment became hard to ignore. It was impossible not to notice how I felt, even if it was strange.

Love, for a woman.

A knock echoed into the room and a quick look at Davina deep in sleep sprung me out of bed before it could startle her awake. Picking up the towel we'd used earlier from the edge of the bed, I wrapped it around my lower half and walked across the room.

Viktor stood in the hall with a duffle bag on the floor. His hair was messy and his eyes wild. Viktor's gaze lowered to my side, and his lips twisted at the sight of my stitched wound.

He took a deep breath. "I brought you some clothes. Change and come down to the basement. Bring the clothes that need to be destroyed. Don't be long." Just as quick as he came, he left with a nod.

Not wasting any time, I did as he'd said.

I almost woke her to tell her I would be back shortly, but decided against it.

Leaving her behind, I headed to the main floor and walked deeper into the house until the basement door was in view. A digital key code hung above the lever of the door, and as I unlocked and pushed it open, screams traveled up the stairs.

I left all my decency on the second floor of this home. I left my morality with the girl with black hair and silk skin. I didn't flinch at the agony the screams released or how piercing they became the closer I got.

Even if it was from Chief Pierce.

The basement was a soundproof vast open space filled with training equipment for Lucca's soldiers. In the corner, three closed rooms were built. I'd always wondered if they weren't soundproof to assure the terror would bounce through the basement for those around.

One of the rooms was the control room, the other two were heavy duty and cold with everything needed to extort any information from those who wouldn't give it easily.

I pounded on the door to be let in, and Viktor opened it. A drop of blood slid down his cheek, and as I took him in, I noticed his bruised left knuckles.

How had I missed that before?

My eyes questioned him.

"Lo, isn't here," he replied with a shrug as he explained Arlo's absence.

It made sense. Arlo was a sick bastard that actually enjoyed exploring people's pain and limits. He called it his talent. I'd only seen a glimpse of what he did, and that was something I could shudder to.

I still didn't think it was right. Not for Viktor. Even as a made man, he still had a double life as a DEA agent to uphold, and a battered hand wasn't easy to hide.

Viktor stepped out of the way, letting me in, and that was when I met Lucca's eyes.

Leaning on the wall carelessly with rage filled eyes and sleeves rolled to his elbows, Lucca took a drag of his cigarette before putting it out with the soles of his dress shoes.

"Maybe you can give it a try?" Lucca straightened, and I followed his gaze. "What do you say, Chief?"

Pierce sat on a metal chair, hands behind his back, ankles bound, and blood dripping from his bowed head. He raised his head to acknowledge the person who'd entered the room, but as the right side of his tattered face and swollen eyes found me, he almost looked relieved.

I didn't understand why. I gave zero fucks about him when it meant I could find answers to secure Davina's safety.

"You're here," he spluttered, and the corner of his mouth slightly lifted. "Is she here?"

The room's air thickened with tension and surprise. My attention shifted to Lucca's quiet and humorless laugh.

Nothing in our world is ever a coincidence, Lucca had once said. I had hoped it would be.

"I'm the one who will be asking the questions, Chief," I sneered.

This time he didn't hide his smile. "Davina *is* he—"

My body flung forward as her name spilled from his lips. Filled with fury, I gripped his shirt, bringing his face inches away from mine.

"Don't," I seethed.

"Good. She's safe."

My hand balled, and I pulled back to deliver a blow to his temple. I wasn't here for a late-night game.

Pierce moaned, dropping his head back.

"I'll tell you everything I know. I just had to see it in your face." His head rolled to the side.

"See what?" I spat.

"That you care for her. And all the menace in your eyes is to assure she is safe."

I didn't try to explain or entertain his charade. I wanted answers.

"Then talk."

Pierce shook his head. "Only if I'm promised she will be safe."

My eyes steered to Lucca. He shook his head once. Lucca would never promise something he couldn't deliver, even if it pained us.

"Done," I blurted, feeling Lucca's eyes on me. I had no problem making promises I had every intention of keeping, especially if it could help protect her.

"Davina's my daughter." Pierce's words silenced the room, but they bounced in my skull as their blows repeatedly beat my temples. It didn't end there. "I met Diana when I was still young and foolish, flashing my badge around New York in a dive bar with others from our division," Pierce said. I wanted him to stop so my mind could catch up, but it was best to keep him talking. "We were celebrating one of the guy's birthdays. But that night was different because I was completely captivated by the bartender. She didn't even try to get anyone's attention. Diana was just ... beautiful." He laughed softly, stuck on memory lane, while I remained stuck knowing Davina's father was before my eyes. "We spent that whole weekend together. Until I never saw her again."

With a locked jaw, I waited for him to continue.

"Years passed, and as I grew in my career, so did my enemies. I guess that's what happens when the streets are filled with *mafiosos* running around. But it was just me, so I had no one to put in danger." Pierce looked past me. "Then one day I received a letter. It was worn and somehow, I knew it would change it all. Diana had sent it. She was dying. And in that letter, she mentioned Davina. Asked to please look after her once she passed, but to not contact her as she never wished to know about me." His snicker was weighted with regret. "I had a daughter who no longer needed or cared to know who I was. But I cared. So, I did the only thing I could do, assure she was safe. But the Syndicate was growing tired of me, and I transferred here, leaving my trusted friend and Chief of NYPD, Ruben, to keep an eye on her while I was away."

He was Davina's father, and no matter how many times it replayed in my head, I couldn't believe it.

"A few years later, even after I'd left to keep her safe, she became a target. All I knew was that she was admitted to the hospital after an accident, but Ruben had heard rumors that the Mafia was after her. So, I contacted her, mentioned I knew her mother and I could help her. She was desperate and soon she was in Miami."

"But once the Mafia has a target on someone, it doesn't disappear," Lucca stated Pierce's unsaid words. "What I don't understand is why Ilias?"

"I'm not some cop from butt-fuck Egypt. I'm from New York, I know how these things work. Someone on the force had to be involved, so I followed my gut. It wasn't easy, but after putting the pieces together, Ilias had the skill set and everything to lose. He was the only man for the job."

"So, you just decided to throw your daughter to an affiliated man, for what?" I roared. "A small fucking ray of hope that I would keep her safe?"

"You did." His eyes held mine without worry, and his aloof response disgusted me.

He put Davina in more danger than he would ever know because, if by some miracle we did come out of this alive, she would now be affiliated with us—with me—and that was even worse.

I shook in rage and my fist collided with his nose. I let the crunching sound of bone satisfy my thirst from taking a second swing.

Lucca placed his body in front of me. "Does anyone else know about Ilias?"

"No," Pierce uttered. "They believe he is out on personal leave."

Personal leave?

It was never a real assignment.

"Good. You are now owned by the Moretti Mafia." Lucca's words caught Pierce by surprise.

"You are not going to kill me?" Pierce said, confused, but more fearful now at the thought.

"I know." Lucca stood over him and pulled Peirce's hair back so he could see his eyes. "You know too much. But, now I know your weakness. Davina."

"No, he wouldn't." Peirce shook his head in fear.

And for the first time since stepping in here, I could feel the chill and fear in Lucca's words.

I had to trust my brother, but it became harder as he continued, "He doesn't really have a say, Chief. I mean, I could kill her. Eye for an eye, that is… If New York doesn't do it first."

My heart stilled.

"No, no. I'll do anything to keep her safe!" Pierce said in a rush.

"Great. Take a *personal leave* until your wounds heal," Lucca sneered, and before he turned, his threat was spoken. "We'll be in contact."

Viktor opened the door for Lucca, and I followed. When the door shut behind us, I whispered loud enough to not be heard from the other side.

"You can't just use her as a chess piece!"

Lucca quickly turned to face me.

"I could kill him instead, *brother*." His eyes looked down on me. "It's best that you remember who I am now, and we are *all* fucking pieces. I'm just making sure the king is not taken out, because without it, there won't be any moves left to keep the others alive."

NINETEEN
d a v i n a

I KNEW SOMETHING WAS BOTHERING ILIAS THE MOMENT I woke up finding him sitting by the chair a foot away from the bed. He was already dressed in dark jeans and a black tee. His hair was messy from running his fingers through it, his gaze centered on the bed and his eyes far away from the present.

"Hey." My voice sounded raspy from sleep, but Ilias's eyes shot up to mine.

"Hi." He smiled softly. "Sleep well?"

"I did." After everything that had happened the night before, and without Bo by my side, I was surprised at how well I'd slept. The ability to sleep through the guilt from what I'd done, as if it had never happened, sent a chill over my body. "And you?" I asked, trying to obscure my thoughts.

Ilias stayed silent, watching me. He never replied, he just gave me a short nod.

"Whenever you are ready, breakfast should be served any time now. After you eat, I thought we could go and pick up a few things you may need."

I gripped the covers closer at the possibility of facing everyone in broad daylight. But I needed clothes, and most importantly, I needed to figure out a way to get my purse that I'd left at Ilias's home. I shuddered at the thought of going back.

"Sure, let me freshen up."

After a quick trip to the bathroom, I changed into the clothes Ilias had brought last night. I hesitated leaving as I watched my reflection in the mirror.

With my fair skin, my face still held pink and puffy spots from last night's tears. The black leggings brought some comfort, that was before I stared at my scar. The short-sleeved white Henley couldn't hide even an inch with its wide neck.

Shit.

"Davina?" Ilias knocked twice before he peeked his head inside.

I took my time before facing him. When I did, he just smiled. He just fucking smiled, his clear blues raking over my body.

"Fucking gorgeous." And somehow, despite my wardrobe and puffy face, all I heard was honesty from his words.

Heat surged up my cheeks. "Thank you."

Ilias extended his hand for me to take. I did, and his arms wrapped around me.

"Come on, let's get going," he said through my hair.

"Wait." Pulling back, I looked up to him. "Are you okay?"

"Always worrying about me," he joked, but it was in his eyes. They were troubled.

I let it go. I wasn't the only one that had done an unspeakable thing yesterday. We were both working with our own demons, and mine ... mine screamed with rage in every breath.

As I followed Ilias closely through the corridors of this house, I no longer paid attention to the grand rooms or detailed décor. I was too focused in controlling my breathing to pacify the creeping anxiety that rose with each step.

Two large doors were opened with an invitation to enter the dining room. Before Ilias stepped inside, he looked back at me, pulling me next to him. I wiped my hands on my leggings, held my head high, and we walked in.

Only one other body was inside.

Lucca.

A plate with various fruits that were barely eaten rested below his hands as his phone held his attention. Lucca was dressed in yet another three-piece suit, composed, almost relaxed. That was until his eyes lifted, and I felt their burning stare on my scar.

I shifted under his scrutiny, hating myself for showing how much it bothered me.

Lucca dismissed his attention from me and turned toward Ilias. The shift was noticeable and quick. A small moment of care. How he saw Ilias as any other human would see their youngest sibling. It was strange to see Lucca any other way than a mafioso. Not even that, a boss.

I guess everyone has their weaknesses.

But how much did he really care for Ilias?

"I must let you know, within an hour, my men will be back inside the house like usual. Rumors will begin," Lucca announced. "Don't cause any more trouble."

Ilias moved over to the table and filled two plates with everything that could possibly fit on them. There was no way I could eat it all, but I remained quiet, taking a seat by the chair closest to me, and the furthest to Lucca. It wasn't hard with the size of the table, and as I waited for Ilias to sit next to me, I busied myself by counting the chairs.

There were twenty-two, and Lucca sat at the head of the table.

"Arlo?" Ilias asked.

"Hasn't been back yet." Lucca's lips twisted. "Must have been a tough clean." His eyes shifted to me.

There it was again, guilt. Remorse. The reminder of my sin.

Ilias ignored his comment. "There's a few things I need to pick up for Davina."

"No one is leaving the compound."

"Lucca."

They stared at each other.

"It's the weekend. The streets will be crowded."

"Nothing will happen," Ilias assured him.

Lucca's smirk threw me off more than his emotionless face.

Maybe we should stay.

"Ili—" I began, but Lucca cut me off.

"Fine. Viktor will accompany you, and I know where you can go."

Ilias's body tensed. "You don't trust me."

"I don't trust New York." Lucca stood, and with a nod, he left the room, leaving us in silence.

Looking down at my plate, my stomach turned. I couldn't force myself to take a bite. I was drained, not only physically, but mentally. And when I heard the distant whistles of Ugo in my head, I closed my eyes only to see *Nightmare's* wicked smile, *Tattoo's* cruelty, and Ugo's slumped and lifeless body.

THE CAR RIDE WAS SILENT. AND EVEN WITH ILIAS SITTING IN THE back of Viktor's car with me, hand resting on my thigh, I couldn't dismiss Lucca's smirk.

Something wasn't right, and the pit of my stomach only confirmed it.

"Ilias," I whispered.

His eyes slid over to me, but I also felt Viktor's gaze shifting toward the rear-view mirror.

Right now was not the time to voice my concern, I would hate to have Viktor see me with the same hatred as Arlo and Lucca. Instead, I asked something that has been concerning me. My purse.

It wasn't money or my phone that I wanted from it.

It was Martin's note that I'd kept crumbled with me. It was the bullet casing. It was the reminders.

They'd kept me sane for this long and now, more than ever, I needed them as the paranoia and anxiety drowned me in fear of what was to come.

"What is it?" Ilias's brows furrowed.

"I'd left my purse in your house. Do you think—"

"Don't worry about it. Arlo will most likely bring it if he finds it."

Most likely?

"They should be ready for us. Lucca called when we left," Viktor said as he rolled past a small boutique and parked the car by the back entrance.

"This is all not necessary—" I began.

"Davina, we'll be fine. Just a quick stop, and we'll head back." Ilias squeezed my thigh before exiting the car, taking my hand to follow.

"I'll wait here," Viktor's unconcerned voice said before Ilias shut the door.

There were two people waiting for us when we stepped inside the shop. A heavy-set older man, with a smile I didn't trust the longer I saw it. His hair was thinning at the edges showing his age. Next to him was a thin blonde-haired woman. Her lips were too full to be natural, and her jawline was heavily pronounced by the amount of make-up that tried to hide her age. Although, her smile was able to put me at ease compared to the man's, and I took a second to relax.

"Ilias! It's been a long time, how have you been—and who is this beautiful woman?" His accent was a thick mix of Italian and Cuban, and his smile only grew more.

Ilias took a step closer to me. "Thank you for closing the shop, Roberto. We'll only be a few minutes."

I noticed how he didn't explain or say anything about me. It didn't bother me. On the contrary, I was able to breathe easily.

"Of course, take what you need. We'll give you some space." Roberto waved his hand further into the shop, and with the smile that never left, he stepped out of the way and toward the far corner, along with the woman whose name I'd not learned.

"Anything specific?" Ilias asked, but his attention was still on the couple.

"Something warm?"

"Figures." He chuckled.

After a few minutes inside, the clothes I had in my hands cost more money than I ever owned in New York. Just one pair of jeans could've bought me food for a week.

"Here, I'll take them to the dressing room," Ilias offered.

With a small smile, I shook my head. "I don't need to try on everything, just the jeans. Here, hold these instead." He reached out while I placed the tops and sweaters on his arms as I kept the bottoms. "I'll be a sec."

Leaving Ilias behind, I headed toward the dressing room, and Roberto surprised me as his voice drowned the light background music of the shop. "Use the one on the right, *bambina!*"

I acknowledged him with a nod but stopped when Ilias asked, "Why?"

"The light bulb is out on the other," Roberto explained.

A quick glance to my left confirmed it. Behind the curtain, only darkness spilled through the lit hall.

Opening the curtain to the dressing room on the right, I made sure the material was secured to the corner. Then, I felt it again.

The looming presence of death.

"It's the paranoia, Davina," I whispered, bringing the denim closer to my chest. My eyes couldn't leave the white shiny floors and dread-filled goosebumps covered my skin in a rush.

When my eyes lifted to the mirror, I saw him. Index finger pressed over his faint tilted smile, knife rolling through his fingers close to his side, and eyes that terrified my vocal cords to attempt the slightest sound.

Nightmare.

My hands balled underneath the jeans, trying to hide the tremors, the memories, the pain.

I couldn't remove my eyes from the mirror, from him.

It wasn't a vision, it wasn't my mind or my paranoia.

He was here, in the same room I was, and yet, I just stood frozen in fear.

He dropped his finger from his mouth and stretched his palm out for me not to make a move, a warning. But I already knew how quick *Nightmare* was to react without remorse or second thought.

This was it.

I was going to die today. Instead of red staining the white snow with my blood, it would be the hard, white sparkling floor below.

His eyes lowered from my face to my scar. Not one trace of emotion passed through his dark eyes when they returned to mine.

He took a step closer, and I reacted, taking a step back as I spun to face him. He didn't appreciate the movement as his head craned to the side with puckered lips.

Two steps later, and I stood petrified at his proximity.

My heart drummed inside its cage, faster, heavier. His clean and faint cologne swirled around, and my lips couldn't hold the shaky breath that escaped between us.

Nightmare leaned forward and his breath brushed my ear as he said, "We match." His white teeth peeked through his smile as he winked with the eye that held the thick old scar over his brow.

Time now held its own clock, hanging all of its power over me as I stood at its mercy and brink of existence. It was as if I had no control over my own body. As if I was a vessel, and my soul had exited along with my will the moment I saw his face.

"This will be fast," he murmured, the same blade that had once pierced my neck now pressing into my ribcage. "Don't talk. Don't move," he warned, but it wasn't needed. The sharp edge of the blade had already pricked through my thin shirt and into my skin.

One slight movement, and *Nightmare* would drive the knife deep into my side and through my ribcage. I knew the way his knife could slice and dig without effort.

Then I felt his touch on my hips, shocking me. The little movement I'd made was enough to feel the tip of the knife breaking skin.

I locked my jaw, keeping a hiss from coming out, and halted any further movements while the knife continued to sting. His hand stilled for a second as his eyes watched me carefully before he continued to move his hand lower.

But his touch wasn't sexual.

His touch searched the places where pockets could hold things; he was looking for something.

It didn't calm or help my body from feeling uncomfortable, from hoping his hands would stop running over my body, or the reminder that it wasn't an option as the knife threatened cooperation.

"*Fuck*." *Nightmare's* agitation wasn't lost, his low curse bouncing around us. He removed his hand, then the knife.

"Everything okay?" Ilias's voice carried from where I'd left him. Across the shop.

Nightmare quickly raised the knife to his lips. Traces of blood was smeared on its tip, and my body shook with threatening tears. Each step he took backward, the more my chest bounced and my lips quivered.

Then with one swipe of his hand, he held the far end of the curtain from the opposite side where I'd come in, and slipped out of the room. He was gone along with his shadow as if he'd never been here. But the sting of his knife had left yet another reminder.

Tears pooled in my eyes, my teeth trapped my trembling lips, and my body wobbled as the tears finally spilled out of my broken soul.

ILIAS

ROBERTO KEPT SWAYING SIDE TO SIDE SINCE HE'D GIVEN US SOME space, his smile never left. The beads of sweat that formed over his shiny head were new after I'd asked why couldn't Davina go into the other dressing room.

I kept my eyes on him, watching his every move as his body screamed for me to take notice.

The longer Davina tried on clothes, the more the blown light bulb bothered me.

As upscale as this shop should be, the more it didn't make sense. Shouldn't they be working on it?

"Everything okay?" I said, knowing Davina would be able to hear me, but when I took a step away from the wall, Roberto's swaying sped.

Davina didn't answer.

Quickly, I pulled my phone out of my pocket, typing *vnutri* to Viktor, Russian for inside, as I rushed to the dressing room. One word was all he needed. Before I made it to the beige curtain that Davina hid behind, I realized I'd failed.

I reached behind my waistline, gripping my concealed gun and pulling back the curtains.

Davina was leaning against the wall, her dark hair covering her face and the pants she should've been trying on were still folded on her arms as she squeezed them tightly up to her chest.

"Davina?" I murmured, but she wouldn't look my way.

My eyes quickly took her in. A small patch of deep red stained her side. My stomach dropped, and as much as I wished to rush to her, my mind ordered me to search.

My gun was ready between my hands as I stepped out of the dressing room. I kept my attention far into the hall, my eyes shifting behind me in case Roberto tried to come up behind me. It was a terrible position to be. I didn't trust moving too far away from Davina's room, as it left her unguarded.

Evening my breathing, I walked closer to the end of the hall, turned both ways and found no one in sight.

The back door shot open, and I aimed my gun at the body.

Viktor's eyes landed on my gun, then to me, and I lowered my firearm. Viktor didn't say a word, quickly reaching for his firearm. I motioned to the doors I'd not been through yet. He headed for the one on his right first. I stayed alert, watching my back and Davina's room. Viktor didn't take long to come out and quickly moved to the last door on the left.

When Viktor returned, he flipped the lock to the back door and waited for information.

"There's another dressing room with a blown bulb. Double check to see it's safe, and watch over Roberto and his wife. It was a trap." Viktor's features hardened as he listened carefully. "I need to check on Davina and get her out of here."

"I'll take care of it."

"Do you think Luc—" I couldn't say the words out loud. There was no reason to ask when I knew the answer.

Lucca had to know something, and it bothered me. No, not bother, it angered me. How could he?

"I'm sure there's—" Viktor began, but my eyes cut him off.

I'd left Viktor behind, trying to sway the feeling of distrust out of my mind, but as I met Davina in her dressing room, it only heightened.

"Davina," I whispered, placing my gun back in its hidden holster.

She didn't look up to me and her tears were now dry. Gently, my palm touched her jaw, and it wasn't until she leaned into it that I was able to relax my shoulders. Her big and round brown eyes lifted, spent, and broken before her body leaned forward, her head resting on my torso. With my hand on the back of her hair, I kissed the top of her head. I held her close for a moment to remind myself she was alive. Her warmth and beating heart bounced between our bodies, easing my dread.

I couldn't dwell on how quick it all happened, and how it should have never happened. It was a hard task to do, and I was the one who didn't keep her safe.

Shifting my head, I glanced down to her side. The blood stain on the shirt hadn't grown, and the bleeding had stopped. But it wasn't enough, I had to know the damage. To know she was really okay. I lifted the thin white material high enough to see from this angle.

Another scar would mark her body, but one that would heal and fade to a thin line with time. Yet, any time she would see it, she would remember today.

And I would remember the day I'd failed her.

TWENTY
ilias

THE CAR RIDE WAS FILLED WITH TENSION AS NEITHER ONE of us spoke. We'd waited for one of Lucca's men to arrive. He'd walked in, explaining he had orders and that we were free to go.

Just like that.

It'd only added more resentment toward Lucca, added more confusion. And the anger I felt only increased the closer Viktor drove back to the house.

"Davina?" I looked for her acknowledgement, or an indication of her mental state.

Her face was stripped of emotion aside from her alarmed eyes as she tried to lie. "I'm fine, Novak." She called me by my last name, the alarm I'd thought was really fury.

I didn't press her, not when we couldn't speak freely. I twisted back into my seat as the gates of Lucca's home were in view. My mind raced as I thought of Davina, the shop, and the possibility of Lucca having a part in what transpired.

I could've lost Davina today, during my own watch, only a few feet apart from her.

As soon as the car stopped, I let the door open for Davina, but she didn't wait for me to shut it, she was already heading toward the front doors of the home. Viktor's eyes slid over to mine in question when I stood watching in confusion, but soon, I was following behind.

The soldiers' eyes were on me as I walked through the heavy doors, mine were on the distance between Davina and me. She wasn't heading upstairs. She was leading the way straight into Lucca's study.

Fuck.

While I quickened my steps, her hand was already on the door. The man standing steps away from the doorway tried stopping her, but she pushed through, ignoring him. His gaze turned to me in shock and unsure of what to do. As I walked inside the room, Davina's interruption boomed within the walls, and the doors closed behind me as I heard Arlo's voice.

"I guess you really do have a death wish." He stood in his spot, shoulders crossed, body leaning over the built-in bookcase in the far corner. His smile was far off from kind as he spoke the words directed to her.

My fists balled as I badly held my temper.

Davina stopped in the middle of the floor, her gaze lowered to the floor. Her chest shook with each breath as it sped, and my attention shifted to Lucca.

With Davina inside the room, my eldest brother was nowhere to be found. All I saw was Lucca Moretti, the King of Miami's underworld. The man who people feared, even before he took the seat. The man whose strike was calculating and quick, no time between earth and hell. A man that could wipe feelings away with a wink. And now, Lucca's eyes stayed solely on Davina as he dropped his whiskey glass to the desk.

I wanted to see the side of my brother he only let us see, the side that could remind us to never question our trust.

"Did you know?" I gritted through my teeth.

"What exactly was I supposed to know, Ilias?"

"Don't, Lucca." Our eyes met, and it was his silence that spoke the loudest. "You put me in a trap?"

"What makes you think I did?"

I wasn't surprised by his response, if anything, it irritated me as he kept asking questions rather than answering mine.

"You smirked," Davina said, surprising me. Her gaze lifted to him, filled with hatred. "After Ilias pushed for us to leave for a few things, you caved. But it was your smirk that gave it away." Lucca's attention was now fully on her. "Whether you were trying to prove a point of the danger of us leaving, or your hope I'm no longer alive to cause you problems..." She took one step closer, and her lip curled. "Play with my life for all I care, you are not the only one, but not with others. Not *his*."

"You're observant, but it looks like you only see the small picture." He scoffed. "Think bigger, Davina." His gaze dismissed her with annoyance and turned to me. "I don't need to explain myself, brother. But as I see the mistrust in your eyes, you are clearly not thinking straight."

"Just answer me, Lucca. Did you know?"

"I needed to make sure Roberto was loyal to me. I had to find out. Now, I'm taking care of it."

"So, what were we? A fucking experiment?"

"Ilias," Arlo warned.

"In theory." Lucca's matter-of-fact reply baffled me. "But it answered things that were necessary to understand the little information I had. If you remember, I'm trying to undo your downfall."

"By endangering me? Her? Viktor?"

DAVINA

"VIKTOR KNEW OF THE POSSIBILITY OF ROBERTO PLAYING ON THE fence with two families. He couldn't be trusted. You wouldn't take no for an answer and gave me the perfect opportunity. I had men close by, and now thanks to you, and your... Davina, I have one less man to worry about betraying me."

Lucca was poised with each word that uttered with no effort. In the corner of my eye, Ilias struggled for composure. Lucca's gaze moved from Ilias and centered on my blood-stained shirt. His lips moved slightly before he looked up to me.

"Now, let's think of the bigger picture, shall we? Sit."

As I inched closer to the chair near me, the knock on the door kept me on my feet.

"I don't fucking knock, open the door!" was heard from the other side. The door opened, and Viktor walked in. Behind him, an older man followed. The fedora over his head covered most of his balding head, but nothing hid the deep dark circles around his eyes, the pronounced hollowness of his cheeks, or the way his skin tone reminded me of my mother's last months.

The faded color that cancer carried.

My heart squeezed as I saw this man's frail body walking in, but even in his state of sickness, each step he took held power. By the time he reached the leather chair that matched mine, his breath was labored. Before taking a seat, he took his time to adjust the collar of his dress shirt over his sleeveless sweater. Once settled, he let out a huff and spoke with the richest Italian accent.

"This meeting couldn't have taken place in my room, Lucca?"

"Some exercise may do you good," Lucca replied. "Plus, you're still around and needed."

Ilias shook his head, and his eyes turned away from everyone and out the window.

The man noticed Ilias's gesture. "Still young, I see," he uttered.

"And still not made," Ilias jabbed.

"*Yet.*"

Ilias quickly faced the older man, confused. It seemed the whole room tensed by the one word.

"What does that mean?"

The man ignored his question, and said, "Oh, to be young and clueless." Then his attention wandered to me. "You must be Davina. Quite the mess you've made."

He knew of me, and I had no clue who he was. And the last thing I wanted was to seem like the clueless woman in this room filled by men.

"Delirium is often a side effect caused by the medication you take, and me causing a mess is not one of them," I said, thinking it would keep us even.

The room grew silent.

A small grin hid in the corner of his face. "Has anyone told you that you're observant?"

"Very recently," I replied, and his smile grew.

"It can be a great weapon, until you mix it with emotion. Sometimes it is best to keep those observations quiet" he coughed, "because now I've learned more about you with the only sentence you've spoken to me." My heart hammered at the realization of how much I'd offered without intention. "You were able to know about me with just a glance which means, you've lost someone you've loved due to this illness. Probably cared for them up until they died. For you to have fled New York without help, says I speak the truth."

I closed my eyes to compose the feelings he'd brought back, the pain I'd lived through those last years I had to see my mother fade into nothing but a memory. Despite my efforts to keep it all in, the tears threatening behind my closed lids, the tightness of my chest and my constricting throat, I was still capable of grasping who he was.

He, too, had said too much. I'd pieced it all together. It was the way he'd walked in as if this was his second home, the familiarity to the men in this room, his thick accent, the way he and Lucca spoke as equals, and the way he spoke to me as if he's been trying to teach me instead childing me.

And the only way to be sure was by saying his name out loud. I'd heard it once on the night I'd killed Ugo. The night I'd met Arlo, and though he'd spoken in Russian, a few names stood out.

"Noted, *Sal*."

This caused his smile to fully reach his eyes. "You learn quick," he praised, but made a tsk sound of disapproval and added, "Now, you got to work on not showing it."

It was my turn to try to hide my smile.

He shrugged toward Lucca. "I like her."

I peered over Ilias, but his eyes were already on me. All of a sudden, I wanted to be closer to him. With all the ups and downs of today, I needed his strength. I needed to stare into his blue eyes and let them pull me away from it all.

Soon. His lips said silently, and his shoulders relaxed as we stared at each other.

"Are you finished with your lecture?" Lucca asked, getting only a slight wave from Sal. Quickly the tension returned, and my eyes lowered to escape the feeling. "As I had mentioned, men were scattered around the perimeter of the shop." Lucca's tone brought my attention back to him. "I was able to find who was in the shop, waiting for *you*." His brown eyes held mine.

This got Ilias's attention, as it did my heart. Just when I thought I had some courage by barging inside this room with the idea to stand up for myself, it quickly vanished.

All it took was the thought of *him*.

Lucca pulled his phone out and pushed it across the desk for my eyes to see. "Now, why would one of New York's *principe's* be in my streets, and not just a soldier looking for you?"

My eyes fell to the phone.

Nightmare's picture lit the screen.

"*Principe?*" I whispered, and my eyes couldn't stray away from the picture. My mind screamed at the chaos inside as I tried to understand what Lucca had said. It screamed for me to run from this life I was now wrapped in. But what would happen to Ilias?

I was scared, terrified, but even then, I knew I couldn't leave without him.

"Second in line to New York's throne," Sal explained, but it was the end that troubled me as he continued, "And my god-son." *What?* "Don't worry, his family and I are far from close." He finished as if it'd left a sour taste in his mouth.

"I'd made some calls after I found out who was under my roof." It was now Lucca who'd spoken, but I couldn't look at him. It was too much, so instead, I found Ilias. "As much as we detest the Yankees, we are still a family, and oftentimes, if one falls, it opens the doors for the rest of the families to be exposed. So, when we got word that a woman was a threat to our Organization, we started looking for *you*."

Finally, I faced Lucca.

"And last night, during one of those calls, I found out just how much you were worth, especially when you are wanted alive."

I shook my head in denial. "They don't care about me."

"You are right about that." Sal shifted in his chair. "So, it only means you have something they want."

"Now you need to answer me two questions," Lucca's voice deepened, tired of explanations. "What did Leo Vitelli say to you?"

I could finally put a name to the face of the man who'd tortured my dreams and life. Even then, knowing his name didn't make him more human from the nightmare he was.

"Davina?" Ilias questioned for me to say anything. He too wondered what had happened in that dressing room. I could see the guilt in his eyes, the way he blamed himself, and if I said too much, it would only cause him pain.

"He didn't say anything," I said, keeping my eyes on Lucca. He didn't look pleased, and I continued by affirming Sal's words. "He searched my pockets, and when he didn't find what he was looking for, he left."

"What was he looking for, Davina?" Ilias probed.

I couldn't look at him. "I don't know."

206

Arlo's scoff wasn't lost by anyone, but it was the truth.

I had an idea of what possibly *Nightmare*—Leo—searched for. The only thing I'd taken from that bleak and icy night.

The bullet casing.

The one that was fired by his gun, and the one I held tightly to.

I wasn't ready to give that information, not when I didn't know how much power it had. Until I found a way to use it to remove Ilias's target and mine, I would keep it to myself. But first, I needed to get my hands on it again.

I needed my purse.

"Fine." Lucca took a sip of his glass, and I knew he wasn't done. He wouldn't stop until he had the answers he wanted. "You know, usually we have a way of getting information out of people."

"You wouldn't," Ilias said through gritted teeth.

"Matter of fact, Ilias did just that last night with the chief." My brows furrowed. Lucca smiled. Why hadn't he'd said anything about it this morning? What else was he hiding? "I thought you knew, but my point is not to threaten you, *right now*. It's to tell you how gracious I've been by taking you in without knowing anything."

That was a lie. Lucca didn't seem the type to be gracious for another human. He had to know something, and now he was trying to put it together.

"Listen, *bambina*." My attention shifted to Sal. "We need to at least know what you witnessed that night. Your life is not the only one at stake now." His head bounced to Ilias.

"I never told anyone, and it wasn't because I feared for myself. Saying it aloud would be a death wish for whoever heard about it." I trapped my bottom lip, wondering if they could understand as an outsider looking in. "I may not understand the way of this life, nor do I intend to, but everyone knows the rumors of the Cosa Nostra."

"What did you see, Davina?" Lucca's sharp tone demanded this time.

My chest tightened, and the room spun with the pressure to retell— no—to *relive* that night. Maybe I was wrong all along I wasn't trying to protect others, maybe I was just trying to protect myself.

My eyes wandered around the room. I was way over my head.

I couldn't outsmart the cunning or the years of scheming it'd taken to see these men before me. A room filled with power held by fear, money, and blood.

Lucca had an empire, and each brother had a position of power within this family. From the crooked cop I'd fallen for, to a dirty DEA agent. Their looks and accent were far from Italian to even be affiliated with him. They blended right in with Miami's pool of immigrants. Then you had his right hand, the muscle and fear inflictor by just one look. It left him in the position of trust he needed as a boss. If they've managed to keep it in the dark, it meant he had control deeper inside. He ruled this city and the underworld, but how far did his dominance go?

"It was the struggles and begging that had made my feet stop in the middle of the sidewalk." That girl was no longer me, and I retold the story as if it'd happened to someone else. I let out a breath, detached, and continued, "It was late, cold, and a snow storm warning had been issued before my boss told me to leave early and walk home. I tried not to watch and tune out the inevitable as I hid behind metal cans in the alley. I was quiet."

I shot a glance at Ilias. His lips had formed a thin line as his brows pinched together, and with arms crossed, he waited for my next words.

"And so was the gun when it was fired by *Leo's* hands." Lucca's small bow let me continue, "Then, I made a sound, and another man found me. I followed him deeper into the alley until I stood inches away from the lifeless body. That's when Leo had a hold of me with his knife on my neck."

"*Fuck,*" Ilias uttered as his hands ran through his hair continuously. He walked past Lucca toward the window and looked out. But I knew I was all he was paying attention to.

"They asked who I was, but nothing would come out, and when the knife stung me with a threat. I reacted in surprise, so did Leo. They took the body next to me, and left me for dead."

"What did the other man look like?" Lucca asked.

"Tall, dark-haired, tattoos covered his hands, and he walked with precision. He didn't say much, and when he did, it was with authority." The longer I described Tattoo, the more it seemed as if I was describing Lucca.

Quickly, Lucca swiped the phone from the table. His fingers moved rapidly, and when a dark grin appeared on his face, he slid the phone back to me.

"Was this him?"

Tattoo had replaced Leo's picture on the screen. Even with the picture highlighting his profile with brightness, he still looked just as dangerous as he did that night.

"Yes." I cleared my throat, lifting my eyes to Lucca.

His grin was filled with longing malice, and I wished he could share the brewing trouble he was planning. "I guess Viktor's contacts were right. You could be New York's downfall by hurting their hierarchy."

"What does that even mean?"

"It means you are safe," Sal explained.

"For now," Lucca added. "First, I need to find a way to get you both out of this alive before the charity gala I'm hosting."

"With the amount of people under this roof, you can't expect it to be a good idea!" Ilias exclaimed, troubled with the thought.

"And yet, it's something we can't undo. It's been confirmed months in advance, Ilias," Arlo spoke up.

"New York will be here." The room silenced with Lucca's admission, and my heart faltered of the danger not just I, but we would all be under.

Soon, my fate would be in the hands of men, and I had no control over Death's call.

TWENTY ONE

ilias

D AVINA WALKED BEFORE ME AS WE ENTERED OUR ROOM
upstairs. She hadn't said a word, but with so many men inside
Lucca's home, it was expected. Though, when the door closed
behind us in a loud click, she remained quiet.

Her footfalls were silent as she reached the balcony doors. The sun's
leftover rays spilled over her frame as she looked out to its radiance. The
blood stain on her shirt was dry, but she didn't make a move to change it
or acknowledge her cut.

Davina was deep in thought as she crossed her arms. I wanted to give
her time to think. I, too, needed a minute to collect my thoughts and place
everything I'd learned from today.

I understood Lucca's move of using us as bait. It'd brought us more
information that could give us a way to win in this chaos. Still, I was

annoyed to be blindsided by him. Being the only one out of this Syndicate, it's always been this way.

Sal's words bounced in my head, *"yet."*

I knew it was true.

Even if we found a way to get Davina out of this mess, it still left me with one of New York's made-man dead by my hands.

They had all kept me from knowing too much, it was the only way. But now, not knowing was dangerous for her. For us.

Deep down, I knew what had to be done to survive.

"What happened to Chief Pierce?" Her voice was low, and her hair furled as she faced me.

"I can't explain that to you."

"Is he even alive?"

I tried not to show how much her question stung. "He's fine," I said between my teeth, taking a step closer. "Now, what is it that you are hiding?"

"Me?" Placing her hand to her chest, she moved away from the patio door. "I learned just days ago who your family really is, and today, you keep things that would matter to me. You kept them to yourself."

"Please, I didn't know a thing about you. You didn't ask, and neither did I. So, *we* didn't share." I stopped walking once her gaze reached mine. "The real question is, Davina," I held her neck while staring into her large eyes, "Are you okay with it?" My hand stayed to keep her from looking away, and the other gripped her hip, bringing her closer to me. "Because it seems it'll only get darker, *kroshka.*" My thumb caressed over her hipline, moving under her shirt to feel her skin.

Davina's eyes fluttered with my touch. Her mouth parted, letting our breath mix. I stopped moving to see her reaction, to know where we stood.

"Why did you stop?" she asked.

My head dipped to her neck. My lips crossed over her scar as my scruff scratched its way to her ear. "Because I need you to answer. I need to hear the words I so desperately want to know." When I pulled back, her eyes looked away from me.

My hand slipped away from her neck and to the back of her hair, pulling it by the roots to get her dark eyes back on me.

They snapped quickly to me as her chest rose.

"Yes."

"Yes, what?"

DAVINA

I WANTED TO SAY YES TO EVERYTHING, ANYTHING HE COULD offer, but my mind reminded me what it would be agreeing to a life filled with blood and secrets that were best kept unknown. A life of always looking over my shoulder for danger because there would always be a target by being affiliated to Ilias. To any of them.

Would they ever let me go? After everything I'd learned?

Most importantly, could I ever go back to living a normal life? No. I couldn't. Not if Ilias wasn't next to me. He made me feel protected, cared for, and strong. Something I hadn't found or felt years before my mother's passing.

Ilias had given me the strength I needed to feel the way I did today. He made me realize I could be fierce and stand up for myself.

How could I even think I was better than any of them? I, too, had killed. I'd lied, and kept secrets for my own gain, our gain.

Love could be blind, but as I stared into his bright blue eyes, love could also be vibrant to those who found it.

And now that I'd faced death and lived to tell the story more than once, I would take my chances of happiness while I could.

His grip around my hair tightened as he demanded my response. But all it did was add more desire and craving for him.

"To us," I rasped.

Ilias pushed me back against the French patio door before pressing his body to mine, and I could feel his longing for me. Keeping my head pushed with his tight grip on my hair, he took my lips in a carnal kiss that was insatiable.

His large and heavy palms held me at his mercy, and I was needy by just their touch, their strength and fervor as they held my body. My legs squirmed with the passion only his kiss could bring.

I needed to touch him, to feel more of him. My hands clung to his chest, and I felt his warm body through his shirt. His throat made a pleasing sound as my nails scratched their path up to his hair. Soon, my lungs gasped for air as his force picked me up. My legs quickly found his hips, but Ilias bounced my core to his hard, jean-covered bulge.

Another gasp expelled from my lips, and I wanted more. My desire pled for more, for friction, for his carnal need for me.

His mouth pulled away, and his scruff burned a trail up my cheek. His teeth nipped the sensitive spot behind my ear, and his voice was rough as he promised, "To us."

Ilias twisted away from the door with me wrapped around his body. His steps weren't hurried, and as we ventured away from the bed. I pulled his head back in question. He shook my hand off his head and continued walking until my back was pressed onto the built-in bookcase.

Wood shelves dug on my back, but it didn't matter, not when the sting created a sweet pain with his touch on me. Ilias shuffled my body and placed his knee between my legs to keep my feet from touching the floor. With one swift move of his hands, my shirt was thrown to the side.

His eyes watched my chest hungrily. His head dipped to my neck, and his tongue and lips took each nipple into his mouth. I rocked on his knee to ease the ache but came up short as it wasn't enough.

I wanted more.

As if he'd read my thoughts, Ilias's arms bulged with strength as he lifted me, pulling my leggings down and freeing my bottom. With a swipe of his hand, the books were gone and replaced by my ass.

Too far gone to care about the sturdiness of the shelf, I let him place my body as he wished. And with my ass halfway sitting, he removed the rest of my clothes.

He parted my legs, and placed his hand over my chest to hold me from falling as his head lowered.

He didn't waste time. Ilias's mouth took my pussy in hunger.

His tongue was restless and his mouth devoured, making it impossible to catch my breath as I panted through the assault. Each time he sucked, the closer I got to my release. The wild pleasure he brought was something I didn't want to end. But it also made me greedy. My hands held his head as mine rolled backward. It was bliss, and my body was ready to let go. Ilias's fingers rubbed, and with his mouth on me, his fingers dipped inside me. They stretched, and curled, and quickly, I let go.

"Ili—" I whimpered, fisting his hair in ecstasy.

"I know, *kroshka*," he rasped between my legs.

My body squirmed with sensitivity. I couldn't take it anymore. No matter how much I pushed, Ilias didn't stop until his tongue trapped my tremors. I continued taking breaths to calm my racing heart, and when I looked down, his eyes were on my bouncing chest. Ilias's lips were swollen, and his eyes were wild as he rose from below.

High from release, I stared at the man that had rendered me speechless. Any small imperfections were overlooked by his eyes, and any past or future events were swiped to the side with just the thought of *us*.

As long as I could have this man's eyes on me for as long as death allowed, I would do anything to keep them. The bullet between us would soon be brought to light, leaving nothing to stand in our way.

Ilias held my head, his eyes boring inside of me. "Fucking gorgeous." His thumb ran over my lips before he stole another taste. "Now, I need to fuck you until my name spills breathlessly from those swollen lips."

His lips lifted at the corners as he watched the way his words affected me. Ilias let my legs fall to the ground, they faltered but his strong hands held me until the shakes subsided.

The sound of his belt buckle, the zipper of his pants, and the flop of his jeans falling urged fire through my body. My gaze watched, captivated by his build. And when he removed the last piece of clothing and stood inches from my touch, I smiled.

Always managing to surprise me, Ilias flipped my body around. Books were now my sight, but he still held my undivided attention as both hands took my hips away from the bookcase and out toward him.

I bit my lip with each second that stretched as it did my impatience and greed.

His touch wasn't gentle, and my skin crawled when his hand ran from my curled ass and up my spine, taunting me from what was to come. I wiggled desperately, trying to find some comfort to the building ache between my legs.

His hand tangled my hair, lowering to the nape of my neck. With the other hand on my hip, my cheek pressed against the shelf, and I couldn't contain the whimper of imagining how we looked in such a position.

I didn't get to recover from the first orgasm before Ilias had me begging for more.

To have not his mouth on me, or fingers inside me, but to have *him* deep inside.

To be one.

"*Bozhe moy, kroshka.*" Ilias's Russian tongue was my breaking point.

"Novak, *please!*"

"Please, what?" he baited.

Damn him for making me so needy, so needy to have me say it out loud, and to always ask to elaborate.

But I wasn't shy, not with him. Not while I was bare and ready for my partner to take me. If this wasn't the time to voice out my body's wants, when? And he knew it.

"Stop talking, and take me alr—ahh!" my eyes closed shut, while I tried to hold on to anything, but all I had was the seam of the shelf when he buried himself deep inside of me.

It was too much, yet not enough.

The sting eased as he moved, only to drive back, bringing my hips to meet him.

"Ilias," I whimpered.

My head lifted but his hand quickly brought it back to the wood as he pounded inside me. My body tensed from the position as I stood on my tiptoes to take all of him. Each time he drove inside me wasn't gentle, it was erotic. Books fell from his force, scattering around the floor, and the sounds of our bodies meeting provoked a part of me that'd been deprived until I met him.

Now, I wanted it all.

His throat quipped sounds, and our bodies heated as he continued to own me with each pounding thrust. The hand that gripped my hip tightened while the other pulled my head upwards and brought me to his chest. He took two steps back with me trapped by his hands, falling backward onto the plush chair near. My pussy sank on him with the momentum, driving his dick deep inside.

My scream was loud, and the more he continued to fuck me without restraint, the closer I was to my next orgasm. Ilias's hand snaked over my throat once my legs gave out.

I felt his need, smelt his sea breeze scent as it mixed with mine when he whispered in my ear, "Come, *kroshka*,"

Completely his, with my neck in the palm of his hand, adding to the pleasure, my body bowed on his lap. Giving him what'd asked, and what I'd so desperately craved to give him. Myself.

ILIAS

I'D LEFT DAVINA IN THE TUB TO SOAK AND RELAX HER MUSCLES. Before I'd left, I had stolen a kiss from her satisfied mouth. She tried pulling me back into the tub, and as much as I wanted to, I knew I wouldn't be able to keep my hands off her. I would give her an hour before devouring her again.

Just the thought of having another taste had me hard as I picked up the mess we'd made. Every fucking book I placed back on the shelf was worth it.

I ran my hand over my face as a smile broke at the fresh memory.

A knock on the door had me readjusting my dick as I made my way toward the sound.

Viktor stood at the door, his eyes taking in my bare chest, the angry gash on my abdomen. My attention quickly shifted.

"*Boris,*" I cooed, like a fucking pussy.

Bo quickly met my hands, and my fingers were already scratching his head. His paw slapped my feet happily.

"Miss you too, asshole," I replied after he whined.

"How's the pain?" Viktor asked.

Confused, I met his gaze that were trained on my wound.

"What pain?" I replied, causing him to look displeased.

"Figures." He scoffed. "Bo is all yours now. Lucca is aware he's in the house. Watch out with Vino and Wex, never know when those two will be inside."

"I trained them, Vik. I can handle all three in the same room."

"As long as it's not me." Viktor chuckled, and I joined. "One more thing," he added, reaching behind him and pulling out a 40mm Glock. He released the full magazine, cocked the gun to assure the chamber was empty, and put it back together before holding it by the nose of the gun and handing it for me to take.

I couldn't say I was surprised after today's events. After all, I did point an issued police firearm while on *personal leave*, inside a known mafioso-ran shop, ready to be fired without a thought of consequences.

"If you do go back to the precinct after this is over, use yours. But while you are out with the famiglia… don't you dare pull that out again," Viktor warned. "Use this instead, and here's an extra magazine."

I took the magazine with my other hand. "You will never stop childing me, will you?" I joked.

"Last time I checked, I'm still the oldest," he quipped. "Stay safe, brat. I'll see you around, *da?*"

"*Da, brat,*" *yeah, brother,* I replied, knowing next time I would see him either this would be over, or…

We stood facing each other. Words weren't necessary to know he would rather stay until I was safe than go back to his agency.

He was reluctant to leave me, but neither of us knew exactly what was next. A hug? A pat on the shoulder? An awkward *I love you*? Neither one of us did such things. There were other ways to express our bond to one another, and between us, it was never needed.

"I know, me too," I said with a nod.

With a small chuckle, he said, "Night, *bratik*."

I watched as he walked away until he was no longer in sight before ushering Bo inside the room. As I closed the door behind me, I heard Davina through the bathroom door.

"Ilias?" she asked.

"Yeah, it's me. Viktor brought a surprise."

Bo stood by my legs, waiting patiently, but as soon as the bathroom's door opened, it was clear who was his favorite as he ran toward her.

Davina's excitement said it all, and her towel-covered body lowered to meet him.

As I watched them in happiness, all I could think was of Viktor.

He'd said, "If I did go back to the precinct."

If.

I guess I wasn't the only one who thought what my best move would be.

TWENTY TWO
d a v i n a

MY EYES OPENED TO THE COMPLETE DARKNESS OF OUR room. With a slight turn toward the nightstand, I was able to read the time.

Fifteen past twelve. Midnight.

Under the covers and in between both of the men in my life, I'd awakened due to their warmth. Hot and thirsty. My mouth felt like sandpaper, and even as I tried to go back asleep, I couldn't.

Slowly, I shifted away from Ilias's hold.

Boris's head poked awake to watch me as his ears shifted in confusion.

Ilias brought me back to his chest in one swift move. His eyes stayed closed as he mumbled, "Where are you going?" *Looks like I woke them both.*

"I'm thirsty," I whispered. He opened one eye with a sly smile making me chuckle against his chest. "For water."

His chest bounced, and his eyes closed once again. "I'll grab you a bottle."

"Don't bother, I'll be quick." I placed a small kiss on his jawline. "Plus, you mentioned earlier everyone is stationed outside at night."

His only answer was his arm lifting off me so I could slip away.

"I'll bring you one too."

Boris watched me as I stood and looked for one of Ilias's hoodies he had in a duffle bag. There may not have been any of Lucca's men inside the house, but I couldn't risk walking around in a home that wasn't mine in a thin white tee.

Pulling the hoodie over my head, my skin tugged on the unnecessary Band-Aid Ilias had placed on my side. I ripped it off to let the small cut breathe. Shaking my head with a grin, I placed the used bandage in the trash and headed toward the door. Boris beat me to it, and with a pat on his head, I motioned for him to wait and slipped out the room.

The hall lighting was dimmed with corner lamps guiding my steps to the large staircase. I looked up the stairs once I'd made it to the main floor, wondering if I should head back to the safety of Ilias's arms. The house was quiet, my heart raced, and I took a step forward.

I kept my head straight ahead, not caring for any of the detailed accents of the home I would've appreciated any other time.

Get the water and go to your room, replayed in my head.

If what Ilias had said was true, it should only be us and Lucca inside the house tonight. I'd learned Sal also lived here, but in a guest home that you could see from afar. I couldn't even consider it a guest home; it was a full-sized two-story house.

The deeper I walked into the hall, the more my anxiety creeped in, but unlike the rest of the low-lit home, the kitchen spilled light into the hall, and so did the smell of freshly brewed coffee.

Three steps away from the doorway, I saw him.

Lucca stood with his back facing me, leaning on the island between us. A steaming white coffee mug rested on the counter top, untouched.

"Can't sleep?" he asked.

I guess no one could sneak up on him. He turned, still wearing the same attire from earlier. The only difference was his sleeves. They were rolled up to his forearms and showcased the ink that stained his skin.

"Just looking for a water bottle."

Lucca's eyes bore into mine as I stood by the entrance. He nodded toward the large stainless-steel refrigerator and returned his gaze to the window.

I rushed over to the fridge, and when I opened the door, the back window-paned door echoed. A tall older woman with kind eyes and caramel hair walked in.

"Mr. Moretti," she greeted, grabbing the coffee that was left on the counter and leaving just as quickly as she came in.

Confused, I held two water bottles to my side as I watched through one of the door's windows, her retreating body heading back to Sal's home.

Lucca made his way to the door, locked it, and walked past me to leave the kitchen.

I was left puzzled as to who she was. Sal's wife? No, the tone she used was filled with respect in the same way she would speak to someone higher or of a boss. If so, why had he had a coffee who I thought was for him ready?

It shouldn't matter, and it wasn't my business to have cared, but as always, I absorbed any information given.

"Lucca," I said before regretting to get his attention. Knowing I didn't have any options left, and truly believing he cared for Ilias, Lucca was my last hope.

Lucca stopped mid-stride until his attention and body faced me. He lifted his brow, acknowledging me without a word.

"Can you promise you will do everything to assure Ilias comes out of this alive?"

"I'm trying, but not everything is in my hands, Davina." It wasn't the reply I was looking for, but it was better than nothing. "It's not your fault." His head shook slightly. "I see your guilt-ridden eyes, and as much as I would love to blame it on you, it's not."

"I believe otherwise." My lips twisted.

"Do you really believe it was a coincidence that out of any city or state in this country, you ended up in Miami? And it just happened to be a man affiliated to me, protecting you?"

"Then—"

"Don't search for answers until you are ready for them, Davina. They may cut deeper than you were looking for."

Whether he spoke the truth or just wanted to fuck with my head, I listened because my concern wasn't the past. It was our future.

"That night, I'd thought it was my last." I tucked my hair behind my ear at the admission and vulnerability as I spoke further in detail to him. "And you know, I was okay with that." I chuckled with no humor, only realization. "I was alone and no one would miss me. I struggled everyday with my mother's passing and the pain that lived in my head. In a way, I was ready for the possibility of mental freedom." His features remained impassive. "And no, I wasn't suicidal, I just believe once we leave earth, there's an afterlife where things are better. It brought me peace for a short moment. And during those cold minutes wrapped around the pain that was inflicted by Leo's knife, I saw it. A glimmer of the casing that had taken his life." Lucca straightened as I carried on, "In the brink of unconsciousness, my hand slid over the blood and snow until I held the cool metal between my fingers. Then, they took him and left me to be claimed to the harsh streets."

Lucca took a minute before dipping his hand inside the front pocket of his dress pants. When he pulled it out, a small Ziploc bag I'd only seen before in documentaries or pictures where drugs were usually kept, was a single casing.

"You've found it."

"Arlo did, along with the remaining contents of your purse. But this one stood out." He held the bullet between his fingers. "Somehow, I knew this was it, I just needed for you to confirm it."

"So, this afternoon?" I questioned, understanding what he'd done, the questioning.

Lucca nodded.

"It wasn't a lie when I said you could be New York's downfall. But with this, it would mean their end."

"So, we can take them down?" I asked with too much hope.

"Careful," he warned. "My reasons for disliking New York are personal, but we are still a *famiglia*. The only reason they left you alive this long was to see if you had this. Eventually they would've given up and taken you out, but this casing filled with your finger prints links the murder of a very powerful politician. The evidence they've already collected from his computer all lead to New York. But, it's not strong enough without this, or you."

If I'd gone to the authorities, my statement would have proved my story, and without it would've been too weak to bring such an operation down. The casing was a threat, and so was I. They needed to have both to make it all disappear.

"Why are you telling me all this? I'm sure this is something I shouldn't know."

"The same reason you didn't say anything after you witnessed someone being shot dead before your eyes. You knew the danger of speaking about it out loud," he shrugged, "and you weren't wrong not to. You could have spoken to the wrong official, maybe the wrong FBI agent, and it would've made it that much easier to get rid of you."

"But you still don't trust me." It wasn't a question.

"Don't take it personal, Davina. In this world, only few have that." Lucca placed the bag back inside his pants pockets. "It's late, you should rest."

Lucca walked away, and the soles of his shoes echoed with each passing second.

I didn't gain anything by my confession. Just the question of whether Lucca was on our side or if I was sleeping under the roof of the man who I should've been running from.

When I finally made it back to my room, Bo was there at attention. Only when I closed the door behind me did his stance relax, but Bo wasn't the only one waiting for me. Ilias's blond hair stood messily over his head, dressed in black jeans, and fixing the shirt he'd just put on.

Ilias's shoulders straightened as he watched me. His eyes filled with questions and unease. "Talk to me."

I'd made my way to him, and once his arms held me, I did. I told him everything. From what happened that night, to Martin, to hiding and now the conversation I had with Lucca. I said it all in his arms, not leaving anything between us, not even a bullet.

TWENTY THREE

ilias

WITH ONLY TWO DAYS AWAY FROM THE CHARITY event Lucca was hosting, the house became filled by strangers. Not another word had been spoken about New York since then. We couldn't risk someone listening, and the only room that stayed safe from ears or listening devices was Lucca's office. But Lucca, too, didn't touch the subject. Davina had mentioned her concern about Lucca, what he would do with the information she'd given him. But I knew my brother. He was a quiet person for a reason, and only said what he chose for someone to know. He planned and mastered the way to always come out victorious at the end. And often, he was trapped by his own mind and thoughts.

Davina had given him an advantage and knowledge of the situation, even if she didn't see it in such a way. Soon, I would need to make a move as well.

The soft knocks on the door sprung me onto my feet. With a quick glance, I made sure Davina had dressed from her shower and ushered Bo to yield.

Since Boris had been back, I'd noticed a change in him, clinginess toward her. I didn't mind, but it was becoming an issue as he became anxious when she wasn't around. With time, he would feel more at ease, and I would work with him to get him back to that.

When I opened the door, I was greeted by short, dirty-blonde hair and a timid smile, but her blue eyes were fucking wicked.

Anna.

By the large rolling rack filled with dresses, she didn't come here for Lucca's attention. She was sent to work.

"Lucca mentioned a woman needed a dress for the charity event." Her dark stained lips puckered. "So, here I am."

Great.

Anna's mother, Mrs. Greco, was the head staff in Lucca's home. She often came to pick up her mother on her days off. Other days, Anna would be found leaving Lucca's office with an unrespectable appearance. I doubt she'd seen more of the house than his office and kitchen. Yet, here she was, and I didn't like it.

"Thank you, you can leave now."

"Ouch." She winced, but I wasn't convinced she cared. "But, no can do. I'm supposed to find the—"

"I said you can leave now."

Anna met my eyes and shrugged. "Fine." She looked over my shoulder, and her eyes took in Davina from head to toe.

I seriously wondered what the fuck was Lucca fucking with?

A Mafia groupie?

A queen want-to-be?

There was not one hair on her body that had class. It didn't matter if she managed to pull off becoming a small well-known designer at her age, her attitude and ego would forever hold her back.

With a shrug, she walked away, clicking her heels and bouncing her hips more than necessary.

I brought the cart inside and shut the door.

Davina's eyes were wide from the interaction, or was it the amount of clothes, shoes, and accessories that were piled in the cart?

"Who was *that?*"

Of course, it couldn't be about the clothing.

"Honestly... *no one.*"

Her mouth twitched as she tried to contain a smile, but she couldn't hold it, and she chuckled.

"Don't tell me, her," she pointed toward the closed door, "and," her pointed finger moved to the floor.

Fuck if she wasn't too intuitive.

"Then don't ask."

This made her lose it, and her laughter bounced round the room. It was contagious, and I joined her.

DAVINA

I'D TRIED ON MORE THAN SEVEN DRESSES. NOT ONE FIT. NOT IN THE way I wanted them to. Maybe I had the wrong idea that a dress could speak the way I wanted to be perceived as. The skimpy material wasn't it. They reminded me how my body couldn't fill in the curves, and how, even in high heels, they didn't end where they were meant to. They reminded me of the amount of weight I'd lost over the past couple of months and all they have managed was to make myself look closer in the mirror to see all the things I didn't have.

I hated it.

"*Kroshka*, just try one last one. If it doesn't fit like I think it will, we'll try again tomorrow."

How could I say no to him?

I stuck my hand out the bathroom door, grabbed the dress, and closed it back.

"As if I haven't seen and explored all of you," Ilias muttered on the other side.

I smiled at images running through my head while I gazed down to the dress in my hands.

Immediately, I liked the color. It wasn't bright like the previous ones, and it held a touch of darkness in its deep green hue. I slipped inside the dress, adjusted the back, buttoning one of the few buttons that met the low V, and took a look in the mirror.

It was stunning.

The front A-line complimented my shape perfectly, and with the off-shoulder style, it left my shoulder and neckline exposed. It was elegant, and it's back had a piece of danger.

It left my scar visible, but it was time I wore it proudly.

To show them I still walked among them.

This was it.

Unable to remove the smile from my face, I carefully took off the dress.

"Do you like it?" Ilias asked.

"It's per—"

The door was ripped open with Ilias' searching eyes. "Wait, what are you doing? You are not going to show me?" His hands waved at the dress I kept from touching the floor.

"No."

"Just like that."

"Uh-huh." I shrugged. He could wait until I could put the heels on and fixed my hair to my vision. Today was not that day. "I'll make sure not to ruin it, and I'll find a way to make sure I pay her for letting me rent it."

"Rent it?"

My eyes widen. "I can't let Lucca or her pay for it."

"Lucca?" He laughed. "I'm not poor, you know."

I laughed. "I never thought you were." Not with the house he owned or the polished car he drove. Then it hit me. "*Thank you.*"

"Thankful enough to show it to me?" he baited.

"Nice try."

WE NEED TO TALK, ILIAS HAD SAID.

He wouldn't specify, and I hated each minute we walked in silence around the outskirts of Lucca's place. We'd left through the back door, while madness continued to brew inside the home as the staff prepared and guided contractors for the last day before the charity event. My anxiety was already crawling through my veins like venom and spreading, knowing that within less than twenty-four hours, I would face *Nightmare* and *Tattoo* again. Lucca wasn't the only one who didn't trust, because as he held the power of both of our lives, it made me not trust him. Maybe we should've ran a long time ago. But it would've been stolen time, and Ilias would've never ran from unfinished business.

We came across a large man-made forest. Rows and rows of tall trees strategically planted to obscure the house from view.

"A bit much?" I murmured, when two guys in all black casually stood at the start of the tree lines.

"You'll understand shortly," Ilias snickered as we made our way around the forest.

The more I took in the pines, I found them odd to be in south Florida's soil. But as a private dock and beach came to view, Ilias was right, I understood.

"People are surprised at how far a bullet can travel. Even a small caliber handgun bullet can travel for a mile, some up to more depending on many factors." He turned back to the trees. "They don't just hide his home, they protect it better than a fence would." His body twisted, taking my hand and guiding me closer to the water.

My body calmed at the view. It wasn't as open as a beach. It was a narrow inlet that I was sure connected to the rest of the ocean after a few minutes with a small sized boat. But it was private, and the sun reflected off the water, while under our feet, sand marked our steps.

"After you opened up about Martin and your mother, I thought you would appreciate this."

Emotion welled inside, and I bit my teeth, trying to hold on to his thoughtful way of easing the darkness that continued to threaten.

"I love it, thank you." I looked up, falling deeply into his eyes. Outside, his eyes always cleared and brightened with the light. That perfect color that I searched for every morning, Ilias had it. And I no longer needed to wait for the morning to find it.

My feet raised as my mouth searched for his lips. He didn't hesitate to take them, and just like every kiss Ilias gave, it was never enough. His lips were smooth and tender, but they also toyed, and his tongue teased. Ilias held my face in his hands, and I lost myself in his lips.

A small breeze swept around us, and my lungs filled with his scent, taking away my senses. I tugged his shirt as he deepened our kiss.

Too soon, he pulled back, leaving only our heads connected as we slowed our breathing. Ilias kept his eyes on me. They were loudly shining in a deep and vast emotion of care.

My palm lifted to his cheek, and his scruff lightly pricked my skin, but I loved its feel. It always heightened the touch it left behind.

"Talk to me," I whispered.

"I don't think you'll like what I have to say."

"I can adjust."

"What if you can't?"

I took a step back and placed my palm on his chest. "Talk to me," I repeated.

Ilias's eyes lowered, his tongue ran across his bottom lip, and he took a deep breath. As much as I found it sexy and wished his tongue was on me instead, this was different. Ilias looked nervous.

"You've given Lucca an advantage with the bullet casing and information you've shared." His eyes lifted. "And it's time I own up to what I need to do."

"And you are worried about how I will take it." I scoffed. "Please, Ilias, you've met and seen my worst. What could you possibly do that I would even—"

"Becoming part of the same family that had been hunting you. Becoming one of them."

My heart staggered. He couldn't mean New York, no, Miami's. But they were *Cosa Nostra*, and if Ilias had been a made man before he met me, things might've been different. Because he would've known about me.

I tried not to dwell on the thought. I couldn't continue to live in the past or in a different lifetime that was not now. I had already come to peace with a life with him and the danger it would mean.

Why would I let that change?

"Is it done?" I asked as tears pooled in my eyes.

But they didn't threaten to fall over my own sadness, they threatened to fall for him. Ilias wouldn't be in such a position if it wasn't for me.

"I haven't spoken to Lucca yet." He cleared his throat, and his foot twitched to take a step, but stopped before it had the chance.

"I can't risk being in the dark anymore. It's not safe, not knowing what's brewing in the streets, and yet walking among them." The more he explained, the more his demeanor darkened. "I've kept thinking of a way I could make it out of this alive and next to you. I always led to this." His head shook slightly. "But I have you now, and I need to know if it would change this — *us*."

"The Cosa Nostra won't define you in my eyes, you've already done that by who *you* are." Unable to stand our distance anymore, I grabbed him by his shirt, bringing him closer to me. My hand slid over his shoulder and to the back of his neck gently while our eyes stayed captivated with one another.

"We all live on borrowed time, Ilias. I choose to spend it with you."

He took my chin between his fingers, his jaw locked as his gaze fell on my lips before he promised, "I'll make sure you can treasure every minute."

My fucking heart swelled. It cartwheeled inside and cheered my body to euphoria. A smile broke from my lips with a chuckle of joy. And now that we were both on the same frequency, I wanted to enjoy us while we had one last day of freedom.

I was going to live today as if it were my last and, in a way, it could be.

232

And what best way than to spend it wickedly and filled with pleasure.

"Davina…" Ilias's head leaned to the side, feeling the change of energy.

ILIAS

I'D CREATED A MONSTER.

Davina's fuck-me eyes shone while she watched me, and my dick quickly reacted. I checked our surroundings, and I hated risking exposing her skin or pleasure ridden face to anyone. It was only for me and my eyes to see.

"Come," I ordered with my palm stretched for her to take.

She didn't.

"It's too far."

"Davina," I warned, but her hand gripped my hard dick over my pants. *Fuck.* Before she had the chance to slide her fingers under my jeans, I picked her up. Her hair swirled with the quick movement, and her throat released a loud shriek.

With her hips and legs wrapped around me, I took a step further into the tree line. With each stride the more painful it became having my cock constricted by the material. Davina's body wiggled, driving me mad with want.

"Ilias?" I heard my name from a distance.

Recognizing Cesario's voice, one of the soldiers who guarded this area, I stopped.

"Everything is fine. Head back to your post." I tried to sound composed but Davina's smirk made it difficult.

Knowing how close he had to be to have heard her, I needed to keep her quiet.

I rasped in her ear as I pushed her back onto a tree branch. "Shh. This won't take long."

Davina bit her bottom lip. "You sound so confident."

"Is that a challenge, *kroshka*?"

Without hesitation, my hand slid down her pants. She let a small gasp escape, but when my fingers dipped inside finding her wet, she moaned loudly.

This definitely wouldn't take long. Not as her core spasmed with my fingers deeply inside.

With her juices on my fingers, I left her warmth only to coat her center with it. Running my fingers slowly around every inch of her pussy until I was satisfied, I flicked her clit, over and over, letting her whimpers and cries satisfy me for now. But the longer I continued, the louder they became, and I wasn't even inside her yet.

One of her legs fell as the other stayed hooked on me, and my hand covered her mouth, trapping her vocals. Her bite and noises her throat made were just as good. Davina moved her hips, or at least she tried as I'd caged her against the rough branch. I was driving her desperate, but she was stubborn as she tried holding her release, a game she couldn't win.

"Come on, baby, I know you want to," I rasped while her eyes shut. "Give in." She wouldn't. "Fucking stubborn, but I always get what I want, and I'll give your body what you are trying to keep." And I dipped my fingers inside, pumping, and making her whimper loudly even with my hand pressed over her mouth. Her muscles squeezed my fingers eagerly, and I pressed my palm to her sensitive clit, rubbing with the same movements as my fingers.

"Ilias!" Her muffled scream let my smile spread, and my face fell on the crook of her neck as her legs tensed and her body tremored.

I took a minute to breathe her in. Her faint flower smell was mixed with sex, and dear God, it was breathtaking.

The moment she finished coating my hand with her release and her muscles continued to spaz, I unbuttoned my jeans. I hooked her legs back to my hips, held both of her hands tightly over her head while the other stayed on her mouth, and watched her wild eyes as I pounded deep inside her.

She was going to take it hard and fast for questioning me. But it wasn't a punishment, not when she was enjoying the way my dick hammered her and the only way to keep her from falling were my thrusts.

I tested taking my hand off her mouth, but her cries were blaring with pleasure. I kissed her deep, taking her swollen lips, devoured them just as my body did.

A slight shift of my hips, and our kiss broke with her moan. She couldn't be trusted to stay quiet, and the other would come to inspect the sound, so I cupped her mouth shut.

Davina's head lifted as her eyes looked up to the clear sky while my cock smashed her harder onto the tree. Her teeth ground my palm, and the pain it brought made my balls tighten while her pussy quivered.

My dick pulsed as I felt her walls claim and release her pleasure, and I spilled my cum inside her, not stopping until she milked every drop. Dropping my head to her shoulder, I evened my breathing. She did the same while our bodies remained connected. I took the chance to remove my hand off her lips, and she gasped deeply for air.

Crashing my lips for one more taste, I pulled out of her heat. Her legs fell to the ground. While I tucked myself in and buttoned my pants, I watched as our cum ran down her legs. I could never get tired of staining her skin with my release. Next time, I would cum over her body after claiming her.

Without anything to clean her, I took a step to her spent body and pulled her pants up with a smile, knowing she would walk back to the house with my cum between her legs.

I pinched her chin, held her gaze, and smirked. "Try questioning me again, *kroshka*."

She wet her dry lips with her tongue. "It'll be a must."

I'd indeed created a monster, awoken a sex daredevil, and she was mine. I was one fucking lucky bastard.

As we made our way back to the house, a tall frame rested near the backdoor entrance. It was too far to tell who it was, but his stance was familiar. The closer we got, Davina's body tensed, but I could tell it was Arlo.

"I'll meet you upstairs shortly," I said, stopping us a few feet away from him.

Davina's eyes looked over to him, and they hesitated before falling back to mine. "I would wish you good luck, but..."

"It's not needed." I winked, and my hand lowered to her back, ushering her ahead of me.

With a quick nod, she walked past Arlo and stepped inside the home. My eyes stayed on her body through the glass until she wasn't in sight.

We stood in silence as the chaos of scraping chairs, tables, and voices carried out the doors. I knew what I needed to do, who I needed to speak to, but I had trouble with voicing it to my brother.

"I haven't seen Lucca much lately," I began. "I need a word with him."

Arlo nodded. "I figured after Sal's comment, your mind would put the pieces together." He ran his hands over his dark hair and exhaled heavily. "Viktor is going to hate this."

I thought so too. "He'll understand."

Arlo scoffed, unconvinced. "Lucca is in his study now. But within an hour, he'll be gone for the rest of the day. I suggest you go in now."

"Thank you."

"Oh, and Ilias." I turned to face him, and with a wicked smile playing on his lips, he said, "It's much more fun on this side."

There had been times I'd questioned Arlo's sanity, and this moment was one of them.

Leave it to him to remind me that even if I were surrounded by blood thirsty fuckers, I would have the trust of at least three. The more I understood Lucca.

As I made my way inside, I tried to tune out the chaos. I wanted a clear mind before walking inside Lucca's space. It was the sense of a set of eyes watching me that made my feet falter, and my attention to shift.

I found Esmeralda's brown eyes, red rimmed from dried tears. Her dark brown waves were the messiest I'd ever seen, and her appearance screamed fear and concern. It had been so long since I'd seen her as I hardly went to Malvagio's. She was one of the four aerial dancers of Lucca's upscale club.

My brows pinched. The question wasn't how she got inside, it was what was she doing here and in such condition.

My body turned away from my path and to her, but my head quickly snapped to my left as I watched Arlo making his way toward her. He, too, seemed confused but mostly troubled as his eyes roamed over her body. Her eyes left mine, finding Arlo's, and her chest began to bounce from nerves. Although, her eyes softened while they filled with tears.

Arlo's jaw locked, and his head craned to the side the closer he got. Once he reached Esmeralda, he held her elbow and took her away with him, away from view.

What the fuck just happened?

Something had to have happened to her while working. Arlo was in charge of, not only *Malvagio's* dancers, but of *Peccato's* too, the strip club that too often had handsy, drunk men get thrown out of. It made sense for her to look for him. Yet, *Malvagio's* aerial dancers were never close to the crowd and hardly had any issues inside the club.

Knowing Arlo would take care of it, I made my way to Lucca's. Two knocks later, I pushed the heavy wooden door open.

My back straightened as I stood alone with Lucca inside his office. Even with his attention on the conversation he had on his phone, his eyes shifted to me. With a nod, he asked for me to sit.

I did, and as I lowered onto the chair, I felt the shift. It was a shift that had to happen. Lucca was not only going to be my brother, but my boss. I'd never disrespected him. On the contrary, I always saw him as most young brothers saw their older siblings. But I'd always spoken to him without filter, without worry of retribution, even before Sal left Miami's empire to him.

Lucca ended his call with a deep inhale. His crisp white dress shirt stretched as he pinched the bridge of his nose. I waited in silence.

"I can find another way," Lucca said mostly to himself before his gaze slid to me.

"In less than twenty-four-hours?"

"It may not even be enough, Ilias," his tone warned. "Are you willing to take the oath even knowing it may change your outcome but not hers? And that's still a big maybe."

"I am. Because if I'm not who you are worried about anymore, it means the attention to her outcome will now be first."

"It's not that simple."

"Then simplify it."

Lucca chuckled darkly.

"New York doesn't trust us. How can they when we have Davina? The one thing that can take away not only Leo, but Enzo's throne by locking them up for life. The two Vitelli *principes*."

"I know Davina, she wouldn't."

"Tell that to New York, Ilias!" he exclaimed, waving his arm outwards. "Without trust, those are just words. They don't mean shit in this world. It's best you learn that quickly."

"It's all we fucking have, and we have the upper hand by me taking the oath and having Davina by our side—"

Lucca's head shook. "Listen to me carefully, Ilias. Tomorrow, they'll be here. Enzo is composed and careful, while Leo is a loose cannon. He will try to play his games as he's known for, but he *cannot* harm one of us tomorrow night. Not without the rest of the families' vote. But it doesn't include Davina, and you need to keep your emotions in control because a war can start the moment they leave this house."

It doesn't include Davina.

Just the thought of Davina being fair game already had my emotions high and my blood pumping with rage.

"But nothing will happen to her tomorrow, just her course of fate will be known."

"Do you even hear yourself?" I scoffed.

"Do you? Because to me, it sounds like you are not seeing the fucking big picture." Lucca stared calmly. Detached, and cold. "No one does. So just follow my orders." He stood, grabbed the black blazer from the back of his chair, and adjusted it over his body. "We need to have your oath tonight. Be ready." Without another word, Lucca walked out of the room, leaving me with my mind in chaos and my heart in turmoil.

There was never a straight answer in this world. The more control I thought I had, the faster it slipped off my fingers. Even in childhood, I always had rules to follow, strict orders to obey in the life I was placed, and with time, orders and rules were the only thing I understood. That was until I met *her*.

And while I had to pledge my life with an oath to the famiglia, Davina would always come first.

The line would never be blurred, but my life would always be.

TWENTY FOUR

ilias

I DIDN'T WANT TO SCARE DAVINA, BUT I ALSO DIDN'T WANT to lie to her. I stood quiet, ignoring the growing tension since the moment I'd walked inside the bedroom. We'd hardly spoken. She, too, seemed out of it, trapped inside her mind as she continuously ran her hand over Bo's shiny coat.

She watched my every move in silence. Her gaze followed me when I stepped inside the bathroom, then out after I'd freshly showered.

I'd changed into dark clothing with the feel of her eyes on me.

After Lucca had left, Arlo walked inside the office. He'd given me a specific time to be ready, and the clock on the nightstand warned the few minutes I had left before meeting him.

"Are you nervous?" Davina's soft voice carried over to me with care. My lips lifted at the corner as I finished buttoning my pants.

Shifting my gaze to her, I found hers trained on Bo.

I thought about her question, and I felt many things. Nerves were not one of them. I'd always been between worlds, and in the end, the underworld always had a claim on me. To some degree, I'd been ready for this day.

I was too stained to be anyone's hero and, in the darkness, I could punish without remorse. The danger of such life was higher, but at least I had *her*. My grounding stone.

"Why would I be?"

Her eyes captured mine as questions swirled around her dark irises.

I hadn't mentioned where I was going, and I preferred keeping it that way. There were certain things I would lock inside me to assure I could never let her light flicker. She'd already been through so much, seen and done things I wished she never had to experience.

This was my way of keeping her safe.

"Will you be long?" she asked, ignoring my question.

"I'll be back before you know it," I said, making my way toward the bed. "Meanwhile, try to rest. Tomorrow is going to be…" I couldn't find the right word to explain tomorrow. *Draining? Stressful?*

What could I possibly say when a war could spark our lives to flames? Nothing.

Instead, I kissed her head and left before I said too much.

THE MOON WAS HIDDEN WITH NEVER-ENDING CLOUDS, MAKING the night murky. Dew spread in the distance, obscuring the surroundings of a warehouse I'd never been to. The ground was soft underneath my boots as I walked next to Arlo toward the large metal building. Arlo's side grin seemed permanent with a skip in his steps.

"Is anyone here?" I asked, looking around. Not one car was parked aside from Arlo's a few yards away.

He didn't reply, and we stood in front of a metal side door. Arlo faced me. His smile was gone and his posture straightened, transforming back to the man who was incapable of guilt.

"The atmosphere inside will be tense, and whatever you hear, don't engage."

"I need more than that," I replied.

His eyes shifted to the door, then back to me. "Lucca has slowly molded the rules of Miami's Cosa Nostra. Only our eldest generation isn't too... *content* with the changes. Being a boss without a wife, and now letting another non-Italian into the Organization only adds more voices with the whispers."

Huh.

"How many non-Italian are there?"

"You will be the second." We stared at one another.

Viktor was the first.

"Like I said, ignore the whispers. It's all they are. No one will actually speak up about it, and with time they'll see the other changes as the cash flow only grows, making their greedy hands happy and loyal."

"Understood." I nodded.

"Good. Come on." He ushered, and with his fist, he knocked.

Before we stepped inside, obscured within the mist, a shadow acknowledged me.

I was aware only the higher positions would be here, like the capos and above. For me to believe we were alone was foolish. Protection was always a priority.

With a dip of my chin, I returned the gesture and followed Arlo inside.

Our footfalls echoed the deeper we walked inside the dim warehouse. Crates scattered the place along with heavy machinery. The smell of rust and wet soil crowded my senses as the whispers grew louder the closer we got to the center of the building. I couldn't find who they belonged to or where they were coming from.

Lucca stood in the middle, relaxed and under the lone industrial hanging light. Sal stood a few feet away from Lucca. Acting as *consigliere* and former boss, it spoke volumes to have his presence to those who thought of questioning my future place within the Syndicate. Like Lucca, Sal wore a three piece all black suit. His fedora sat low over his head, hiding most of his features. Even with his posture, Sal looked worn, sick, and in need of rest. But for me, he stood tall.

I stopped before them while Arlo took his position next to Lucca's right side.

The whispers stopped the moment Lucca raised his hand. That's when I noticed the shadows around the square balcony, giving their attention and respect to their boss.

My body stood still as I watched Lucca's lips move as he spoke with power.

"Ilias Novak has been working undercover for us since his first day in Miami's Beach precinct. Not only has he been first on a scene, covering some of your soldier's asses, but yours too as they respond to you. Represent *you*."

His eyes moved away from mine as his head lifted higher. As he continued to speak, he slowly acknowledged everyone. "He's tipped us many times when the heat was close, and kept us from being in the constant radar of our local police." The more he said, the more agreeing sounds echoed.

"He's been valuable to our Cosa Nostra without being one of us. And I believe it's now time for him to walk among us and become a soldier of The Moretti Famiglia."

Taking a deep breath, I waited, knowing Lucca's next words held importance the second he paused and the murmurs stopped with a deadly silence thickening the stale air.

"This is the only time I will allow anyone to speak their mind. Do so now, openly."

The room stilled with its silence, and as I watched Lucca open his arms outwards, waiting, Arlo's jaw locked. Something told me this was new, but Lucca never did anything without reason, and I had to trust the outcome.

"Anyone?" Lucca asked once more. "Then—"

"Did he kill Ugo?" The voice was loud without the need to yell his pain.

I looked up to the older man who had taken a step closer to the rail. I couldn't recognize him with the lighting, but Sal's expression wasn't surprised. He almost seemed pleased.

"He did not, Anthony. But you and I both know your *son* betrayed me by going against my orders. Therefore, betraying *our* famiglia." Lucca's voice was stern.

Another man leaned over Anthony's ear and placed their hand on his shoulder before retreating back to their spot next to him.

"Perdonatemi per averi fatto perdere tempo," Forgive for wasting *your time*, Anthony said with a shake of his head. His tone was displeased and tired.

I couldn't shake Ugo's father's voice as Lucca continued speaking. It didn't sound like a man who looked out for retribution. Only pure disappointment.

I had to control the smile that wanted to break free as I understood Lucca's actions. He knew Anthony would speak up from the pain of losing his son, just as Sal knew. But it gave Lucca the opportunity to crush the rumors that could rise to hunt for trouble within his Syndicate by voicing out Ugo's betrayal. In this life, it meant death. There were many people who had protection from La Famiglia, I was one of those without asking for it. For Ugo to come into my home, he'd gone against the rules. No one would no longer care what had happened to him because in their mind, Ugo was now a traitor and deserved what was handed to him.

And Lucca had taken out one of Davina's targets by doing so.

The Moretti Famiglia.

My attention was no longer on Lucca's words or the voices that voted in the distance as they mimicked each other in an echoing. *"Aye."*

I pledge my loyalty, blood, and life to the Mafia. Each sentence I recited after Lucca stripped a part of me as I sold my soul to the underworld.

It wasn't until I was sitting in the passenger seat of Arlo's car, staring at the handgun in my hands, that the events of the night finally cleared and for time to slow to its usual pace. Sal had handed it to me, the last thing done before everyone made their way downstairs to welcome me. There were too many faces and voices to put together and learn in such a short amount of time. Everyone spoke Italian, and thankfully, I understood every word, but my speech needed to improve if I wanted to gain their respect.

"It's a lot to take in," Arlo's voice brought my attention to him. "If it makes you feel better, I hardly remember mine." He continued talking as he drove through the dark streets. "The thing I recall the most, is how I almost pissed myself in a room filled by mafiosos." He chuckled darkly.

"How old were you?"

"Seventeen."

TWENTY FIVE

d a v i n a

I WOKE STARTLED AND GASPING FOR AIR AS I TRIED TO ESCAPE from the lurid and vivid nightmare Ugo had trapped me in. He now inhabited a piece of my conscience with no sight of disappearing. A constant penance for my sin.

Quickly, my gaze fell to my hands, expecting to find his blood running and sweeping into the living world. But as I stared at my trembling hands, I was the one brought to existence.

Today, my fate will be sealed.

TWENTY SIX

ilias

TWO HOURS LEFT BEFORE THE CHARITY GALA WOULD start, and the tension inside the house continued to rise with each passing minute. Maybe I was the only one who noticed because as the staff quickly walked from one end of the home to the next, adding the final touches, they were clueless of the other side.

The side that walked into the light, but only knew of the shadows. The ones who really held power in this world.

My neck ached from the tension and the constant watch I'd kept on everyone around the house.

With each minute that passed, the sun descended, and soon, I wouldn't be able to see the outskirts beyond the house with my naked eyes. Lucca said New York would not cause trouble tonight, but I highly doubted it would be that easy. La *Cosa Nostra* may be divided between families and territories with a said bond, but how together were they?

It was clear Miami and New York had bad blood years before Lucca even stepped in as boss, and with the current situation only adding to its weak bond, one wrong move could fracture the peace between the families.

My phone vibrated inside my jean's pocket. Stepping outside the front door, I checked the caller ID as I made my way down the steps and away from listening ears.

"*Brat*." *Brother*, I answered.

The line stayed quiet, causing the corner of my lips to twist the longer I waited.

"I should be there." Viktor's tone made it hard to recognize his mood, and yet I understood his troubles.

"It's for the best."

"I heard—" Viktor stopped talking, cleared his throat and continued, "that congrats are in order." This time his annoyance spoke clear through the line. "But in the end, I was naïve to believe I could keep you away from it."

"What do you mean?"

"Nothing. Welcome to the family."

"That doesn't sound too sincere."

"It wasn't meant to."

"Vik…"

"I got to go. But please, don't do anything stupid tonight."

"Define stupid," I replied, trying to ease his mind. It didn't.

"Fuck off, Ilias," Viktor said before the call disconnected.

With a light chuckle, I placed my phone back in my pocket.

"Ilias."

I heard Lucca's voice calling my name. Turning around, he stood at the end of the steps, and I made my way toward him.

"You should go and spend the remaining time left with Davina and get ready. Come back down with her in your arms ten minutes after nine," he instructed.

I didn't question him. "See you then." And I left to meet the girl that not only turned my life upside down but the underworld's too.

"ARE YOU SURE WE HAVE TO GO?"

I watched Davina's large eyes as they filled with concern.

Unable to keep my touch away, I pulled her body toward mine. My hand cupped her neck as my thumb ran over her jawline. Heat rushed to her cheeks as they pinked, and her mouth parted from the feel of my hands on her.

The room still held the floral fragrance from her bath, and the deeper I inhaled, the richer her scent became, clearing my mind.

"Did I mention you look stunning?" I asked, taking a step back and letting my eyes roam down her body.

The deep green dress complimented her fair skin and dipped in all the right places, making it difficult to steer my eyes away from her. Her hair was up in a soft twist, and only a few strands had fallen from the updo, taunting as they kissed her bare collar bone. I was surprised when I noticed her scar sitting proudly and unhidden, but more than surprised, it rendered me speechless.

She was going to walk into a den with the same man that almost took her life, without showing how it's affected her. She was going to walk with her head raised high and with the spirit only a survivor of pain ever could.

She was my woman, and fuck did her strength only add more to the ways my heart beat for her.

Returning my gaze to her, her long lashes fluttered, and her make up highlighted her features in a delicate taste. Her lips had a chocolate touch of color, and I ran my thumb against them to test how resistant the stain was on her plump lips.

When not a smudge was visible, I wondered how long it would take to change their color to a deep fuck-me red with just my mouth and tongue.

"After this is over, I will ravish your body," my lips whispered inches away from her eager mouth.

"Why not now?" she whispered, dampening her lips with her tongue.

Fuck me. Davina had me hard and thinking of ways I could release the tension that kept climbing just minutes before we needed to go.

"*Kroshka*," I warned.

"Yeah?" she taunted, using her teeth to nip my bottom lip.

She was distracting me, and I struggled to focus on the reason why we had to leave.

"You said *we* had to make our way downstairs at nine-ten." Her palm slid over my white shirt as her nails scratched through the material, firing my need. "There's still ten minutes left," she baited.

"Ten minutes is not enough." I closed my eyes, taking a deep breath and a step away.

The small distance I'd taken was erased as she leaned forward, trapping my lips to hers. The kiss was slow and gentle. Something we rarely did as our hunger and desire always won with intensity.

Her lips fell away from mine as they trailed down my neck. My dick twitched as her lips toyed my skin. But when her body fell to the ground, knees on the hard floors, fuck-eyes peering up at me, and hands quickly working my belt buckle, I had no restraint or will to walk away.

She freed my cock from my jeans and wet her lips, watching as she took the base with her hands.

"Ten minutes is enough for me." Her eyes flickered up before returning to my dick. "At least for now." Then her wet mouth took me in with a long pull, and I surrendered.

My head fell back as a deep sound fled my throat.

Davina was right, I wasn't going to last. Not with the way she dragged my hard dick with no restraint. With one hand on the base pumping what she couldn't take, the other snaked down my balls. My skin heated with the ecstasy of pleasure. My hands shot to the back of her head, and I tried to mind her hair, the time she'd spent placing every lock where she meant, but Davina was making this fucking difficult, never the less keeping my mind thinking straight.

The need to watch as she savored me let my jaw fall and my eyes to take in the striking sight of her, and her stained chocolate-colored lips sliding in and out.

It was then when I figured the best way to test her stained puckers lips. All I had to do was last enough to see the color I favored the most.

I took over the speed, and she didn't mind it one bit, if anything, it seemed she wanted my direction, and I was glad to give it.

With one hand on her head and the other on her jaw, her head bobbed faster until her movements became sloppy. The wetness of her mouth spilled and coated her lips, and her breathing labored.

It was enough to leave me at the edge as my balls pleaded for release.

"Davina," I warned, the tightness spreading over my body.

She didn't stop. She continued the same speed and gave her tongue permission to circle as I pulled back.

I had no warning left as I gave in to the need, filling her mouth with my release.

Her mouth didn't slow until my dick's last twitch.

A quick look to the clock, and I was late for my first order. I took my time bringing her back to my arms.

Davina's eyes were wild as I tucked her hair back in place, my attention was on her lips, searching for the raw red color. I swiped any left-over wetness with my thumb and kissed away anything I'd missed while nipping her bottom lip and gripping her ass to bring her body flush to mine.

"Forget ravishing your body tonight, I will eat every inch of you until you beg for me to stop. And even then, I won't stop until I fill you with my cum."

Her bottom wiggled, and her eyes lit. "Ilias."

"Soon," I said between her lips. "And trust me, the wait will only enhance your need."

"Then we best go, as you have a promise to fulfill."

Closing my eyes, I rested my head on hers before letting her go.

DAVINA

I'D DISTRACTED THE TENSION ILIAS HELD THE MOMENT HE'D walked inside the room, as well as mine. But as we stepped outside the bedroom, each footfall that echoed around the hall brought it back.

I raised my head high, squared my shoulders, and focused on Ilias's hand as it rested on my bare back.

The commotion downstairs from the gathering got louder the closer we got to the stairs, but before we were in view, I allowed my hesitation to falter my steps. I needed one last moment to breathe, to compose and remind myself I was strong.

"Let's go," I said with a small nod.

Four steps later, and Arlo stood at the bottom of the staircase.

Annoyed.

As Arlo fixed the cuffs of his suit jacket, waiting impatiently as we made our way down the curved staircase, my eyes shifted around the home. The large chandelier twinkled lights all over, and the open terrace that sat in the middle of the home let the moon shine through and fresh air to flow with the doors open for people to freely move around. Over in the corner, where the large piano stood, a violinist accompanied the soft tunes of the pianist, creating an elegant and classy melody. Expensive suits and even more expensive evening dresses shone all around, screaming influence and power. Large white rose bouquets were scattered about the terrace, and waiters swerved between bodies with empty and full cut-crystal glasses.

"I never asked, what's the charity this gala is for?" I asked Ilias the moment we stepped on the main ground.

Arlo replied, "For Miami's orphanages and group homes." My eyes shot to his, understanding, while his fled to Ilias. "You are both late." Heat rushed over my body, and Arlo's gaze returned to me.

"Are they here?" Ilias asked.

My eyes searched for any unwanted familiar faces.

"Yes, Enzo and Leo arrived minutes ago, along with a woman who held onto Enzo's arm."

"Anyone else?"

"Just those three inside."

I'd heard Arlo's response the same second I found it for myself.

Leo Vitelli stood under a shadow, alone in all black. His wicked smile directed at me while his eyes watched us from afar. I tried hiding my reaction, not showing how my heart raced or how my mind had taken me back to the feel of his knife. I held his gaze unable to let it go. Even in the distance, I saw the snicker he tried to contain as his teeth trapped his bottom lip. Leo tipped his head and slipped from view.

The spot where he'd stood seconds before sat empty, allowing fear to creep in. I didn't know where he'd hidden.

"Don't allow him to make a mess inside your head, Davina," Ilias whispered in my ear.

Turning my head, I glanced up to Ilias and smiled.

My smile was big, it was fake, and he knew it too.

"You should both go and mingle, and for the love of God, behave," Arlo said the last part to Ilias, but Ilias didn't acknowledge his brother. He ushered me forward, leaving Arlo behind while his strong hand guided me away.

The voices and laughter blended along with the melody of the room the stronger my heart beat. My heels clicked softly, and I returned any polite smiles as we walked, not caring to remember the faces of the strangers.

"Miss, would you like a glass?"

Taken aback, I twisted toward the voice. A slender young man smiled with a tray on his hand.

I didn't get the chance to reply before Ilias raised his left hand, the other guiding me forward.

"No, thank you," he replied as he passed by the waiter.

It wasn't until we stopped in front of a bar that matched the rest of the house, even if it didn't belong inside, that Ilias moved next to me.

"Care for a drink?" he asked, and my brows pinched.

"Did you just want to offer me a drink? Or is there a reason."

"We don't drink anything unless it's poured from one of ours," Ilias murmured. "Even then," he raised his hand to catch the attention from the guy behind the bar, "you watch it carefully." Ilias was warning me, teaching me, and in a way, molding me for a life by his side. Though, all I could replay in my head was the way he'd said, *"we"* and *"one of ours."*

I'd already known this would happen. I hadn't asked any questions from the night before, and now, they weren't needed.

Ilias was one of them.

A mafioso.

As I looked at his side features, his strong jaw line and generous lips while his attention remained ahead, nothing had changed.

He was still Ilias.

He was still mine.

"You are staring." His lips lifted at the corner.

"Am I?"

Ilias's head turned, and his icy blues warmed before turning his attention back to the man who approached. "Aberto," he acknowledged with a dip of his head. "Just a glass for Davina, please."

"Of course." Aberto smiled and stepped away.

"Nothing for you?" I asked.

"I want to keep my hands free." He shrugged. "Plus, you've been fidgeting your fingers since we stopped moving. You need something to keep them busy and your mind distracted."

My gaze fell, realizing I was indeed playing with my fingers.

"Ilias," Lucca's deep voice made my skin jump, startled from his sudden appearance. His dark eyes moved toward me. "Davina," he said, acknowledging me.

I gave him a small smile as my drink was lowered to the bar. My hands glued to the bubbly glass flute as Ilias and I turned toward him.

"In an hour, the event will be over. As I give a thank you speech, head over to my study," Lucca instructed casually, too casually with a smile I'd never seen.

A quick look at Ilias, and I noticed how he, too, had changed his posture. It didn't take me long to understand, Lucca had mastered the illusion of having an easy and pleasant conversation. When in reality, he was giving an order for us to wait for the danger.

In the corner of my eye, Arlo stood a few feet away, facing the crowd but watching us. Me in particular. His brows raised and his head moved slightly before he crossed his eyes. I couldn't help the chuckle of surprise that escaped to see Arlo do such a thing.

"Good, you're learning," Lucca commented with his white teeth showing without his smile fully reaching his eyes.

Comprehending what Arlo had done, I looked past Lucca in search of him again. With a nod, I thanked him. All his face showed was annoyance before shaking his head and looking away.

"Will we be the firsts there?" Ilias asked.

"Yes. Now, if you both excuse me, I have a few more loose ends to tie." With a grin, Lucca lifted his glass before taking a sip and leaving us behind as he made his way through the crowd.

I knew we'd stepped down to the gala hours after it had started, but being aware of only having less than an hour before I would face *Tattoo* and *Nightmare* together again, it all seemed too quick.

My mind couldn't fool my body from letting the rising anxiety spread. My fingertips prickled, and the tight grip of the flute's stem didn't help keep my hand stable.

"Davina," I heard my name as it fell from Ilias's lips, but it'd blurred into a small whisper as the conversations around grew louder, and the laughs, the whispers, and the music suffocated my mind as it began to crack into the depths of my darkest thoughts. "Davina." Ilias strong tone stopped the cracks from continuing, and when his touch stroked my chin, pulling my gaze to his eyes, I gasped for air. He pulled me out of the pit my anxiety was ready to throw me into.

Ilias grabbed my elbow, guiding me away until the voices were only a distant noise and fresh air filled my lungs. My gaze moved around, finding us alone as the backdoor stayed open and the bright light of the kitchen spilled into the dark night.

Ilias turned my head to face him, his eyes were intense and careful, and as his jaw clenched, he said through his teeth, "I need you *here*. I need you to remember what you've been through, but most importantly, where you are now. Here, with me."

"I thought I could do this." My voice broke, and his throat made a gruff sound.

"Because you can!" Ilias held me between his hands. "You were fucking afraid of every creak a house made, terrified as you walked in the dark for necessities. Sleep wasn't your friend, and you'd lost your appetite from the trauma you'd been through as you lived stuck in the past. But *this* is the present, and your future. I need you to come back to me and remind yourself who you fucking are."

I'm not weak.

I'm a survivor with scars that told the tale.

I've outrun death, and the depths of my conscience.

I was Davina Cohen, a girl from New York who now walked in a man's world.

And I was strong.

"Now, *kroshka*," Ilias breath whispered through my hair as his head lowered toward my ear. "Remember who you are. Remember you are mine, and who you've become."

I took a step back to look up to him, but as the feel of the grainy brick scratched against my bare back, I was taken back to the cold winter night in the streets of New York, trying to hide.

I wouldn't hide. Not tonight. Not ever again.

I pulled away from the rough wall, squared my shoulder for the last time, and looked up to Ilias's wild blues.

"Thank you," I managed to say.

His lips stole a kiss that spoke more than what he could have said. It was unapologetic and accepting to all of who I was. I tugged his arms as I tried to take strength from him. His kiss deepened before stopping abruptly.

Ilias pulled away while keeping his hands on my neck.

Then I heard it too, Lucca's voice inside as he thanked the attendees and spoke about the charity.

It was time to go, and I was ready.

I'd cheated death twice, what was once more?

TWENTY SEVEN
d a v i n a

A S WE WALKED THROUGH THE HOUSE, MY STEPS MATCHED
Ilias's while his arm wrapped around my back. The crowd was
silent as Lucca's voice echoed inside, keeping hold of their
attention as we moved swiftly on the outskirts, taking longer to get to his
grand office.

I didn't see *Tattoo* or *Nightmare* in the crowd, but somehow, I knew
they were somewhere, watching.

Then I felt the sensation of a pair of eyes on me, and my gaze snapped,
expecting to find either of them. It wasn't but a tall, beautiful woman with
sleek, chestnut hair and large eyes watching me curiously at the other end
of the room. She wasn't hiding in the dim lighting, or hiding her gaze,
she just stood there, polished and comfortable in a luxurious, long, deep-
red dress. So deep, it had a tint of purple. She looked regal and never
wavered her eyes away.

"Come," Ilias ushered, missing my interest in the woman.

But it didn't matter, not now. Maybe even never.

"Baldo," Ilias said, bringing me before him.

I looked up to the large man named Baldo as he stood next to Lucca's door. He didn't glance at me, only directing his attention to Ilias before opening the door for us to slip inside.

The smell of books and whiskey replaced the multiple mixed perfumes from the gathering, and I welcomed the utter silence the room gifted us.

I took a few steps deeper into the room, unsure of where to wait, and watched how there were two more chairs facing the middle of the room.

The door flew open, and I quickly turned to find Lucca walking inside as Arlo followed behind. In quick strides, Lucca reached for an empty glass, poured, and drank. After he took a deep breath, he faced the room and walked toward his desk.

"Davina, take a seat there." Lucca's eyes landed on the chair that stood at the corner of his desk. I had a clear view of the door and him as I sank into the leather. "You two, stand on each side of the door." He pointed at Ilias and Arlo. "Once they come inside, you can move behind her or next to her if you wish," Lucca added, resting his elbows on the header of his plush chair.

"Remember New York is famiglia, not an enemy we can take care of even if I wished. There are rules I follow outside of Miami, and the last thing I need until our Syndicate settles is a war," Lucca spoke clear as he looked toward the door. "Our goal is to assure they won't come after you." His eyes moved to Ilias.

My lips twitched with relief knowing Ilias would be safe, but he didn't take it the same as I did.

"What about Davina?" Ilias's veins popped in his neck, and the muscles of his jaw pushed his mouth shut.

Lucca's mouth readied to respond but paused as a knock vibrated through the door.

I closed my eyes briefly when I caught his motion for Arlo to open the door. As the small creak trembled from the door hinges, the atmosphere of the room turned dangerous and sinful. My eyes flew to the door, and my eyes fixated on the male's hand with the ink mark of NYS.

I couldn't find the will to raise my gaze to the man who'd ordered for me to bleed to death as white snow fell over my limp body. But as another set of pants stood inches behind him, I couldn't ignore the screams in my mind as it yelled for me to look. To watch them as they both saw me sitting in the same room they now were. Alive.

But they had names, Enzo and Leo. Their faces were no longer a memory, and they were no longer unknown to me.

Enzo took another step inside, and our eyes locked. The same dark eyes that had found me were now the eyes that led to where I am now. And I wouldn't retreat my gaze. I wasn't going to show the same fear I once had.

I should've never doubted my strength. Even if fear crept nearby, I could let go of the pain.

"I've always said, bedding a mafioso was the best way for protection," Leo said through his smirk, exploding the tension like a bomb within the walls.

It all moved so fast, and before the chaos began, my hands gripped the chair's arms and my eyes widened. Ilias reacted to Leo's words, and being the first time he'd ever seen the man who's knife had carved my skin twice, his anger had gotten the best of him.

Ilias pushed forward until his fists gripped Leo's shirt. With one abrupt move, he had him against the wall, and as he pulled back his right fist, my heart skipped. With all his force, he struck Leo's jaw.

It wasn't until Leo reached behind his back that I responded. I shot up from my chair before Leo's knife opened in his hands, aiming for Ilias's side.

The unique sound of a gun cocking as it shifted a bullet onto the chamber, ready to be fired, petrified my soul. All our eyes slid to Arlo, who had his gun-holding hand stretched out in front of him.

"Don't," Arlo spat as his finger arched around the trigger, the barrel pointing straight for Leo's head.

Ilias and Leo stood face to face, neither backing out.

With blood staining his teeth, Leo craned his head as he chuckled without a care for the gun that threatened his life.

Lucca and Enzo, still facing each other a few feet apart, waited, unamused to the scene unfolding. They must've seen this coming as their features stayed indifferent.

With his smile still present, Leo wiggled his hand, returning his knife back into its guard while blood spilled from his lips.

ILIAS

IT TOOK ALL OF ME TO TRY TO REASON, WHEN ALL I REALLY wanted was to spill Leo's blood just as he had Davina's. The only difference, I would make sure I watched every drop drain from his body until death claimed him.

The sick fuck thought this was a game, a joke, as if her life didn't mean anything.

It meant something to me, and as much as I wanted to continue pounding his face into a pulp, Davina was my priority now.

"Enzo," Lucca greeted, and Enzo did the same before Lucca asked, "Drink?"

"No, thank you. I'm hoping to leave Miami as soon as this meeting is over."

I stared at Leo for a minute longer, watching as his blood spewed from his mouth, and as much as rage consumed me, it had to be enough. For now. My chest bounced with leftover adrenaline and drive for blood, and I let go of Leo and retreated until I was standing next to Davina.

"Would you both like a seat?" Lucca asked smoothly. Ultimately, I too let my gaze slide off Leo and toward Lucca as his hand waved toward the empty chairs for them.

Enzo's head dipped as he lowered on the chair. Lucca did the same, but Leo didn't move, he stood right where I left him by the door.

"It seems like we've crossed some lines, Lucca."

"It may seem that way."

Enzo chuckled dryly. "If your brother wasn't in the line, you wouldn't have given it a second thought."

Lucca's eyes warned me to calm down. I couldn't disrespect Enzo, but I also knew the truth to his words. If I wasn't in the middle of it all, Lucca would've just handed Davina over without remorse or guilt in his heart.

The Famiglia is always first.

"But he is," Lucca replied.

"You are willing to speak freely with a woman here?"

"You see, Enzo, I know for a fact Davina won't speak a word that comes out of this room. Not from trust, but I cover my tracks to assure the best for Miami's interest."

Ugo's dead body, and the murder weapon Lucca had ordered retrieved.

Davina's body winced at the sound of her name, and she wasn't the only one who reacted. Enzo's lips twisted with the jab Lucca had just given.

"You know I've heard the rumors of how you've been trying to change some old ways, and how many aren't too kind to such changes."

"Funny," Lucca smiled, "I heard a few whispers myself. They all say how much she's worth the future of New York's hierarchy. How one *woman* holds the power to bring your father's Syndicate to the ground with no Vitelli left to takeover."

Enzo leaned forward. "Are you threatening me?"

Lucca's eyes signaled for me to reply.

"He's not, we would actually like to offer an agreement." I walked closer to the desk, hating each step I took farther away from her.

"*You* want *me* to listen to an agreement when you've killed one of mine?" Enzo stood from the chair. Lines creased his features as he spoke, "You are lucky to still be breathing, let alone in the same room I am."

"Your man entered a home whose house is protected by the Moretti Famiglia." Lucca's voice held his composure with a deadly edge.

"You know that wouldn't even make it to a vote, Lucca." Enzo huffed.

"He's a made man now, and it will." Lucca's confidence quieted the room.

I continued, "We have the casing your brother searched so... impatiently for." Enzo's head snapped my way with poison swirling in the depth of his eyes.

"And I don't want to waste time with the troubles it would cause the rest of the families or mine if it resurfaced," Lucca added.

"She lives," I stated, and searched for her fair skin.

"For your life?" he asked.

Davina flinched, and her striking eyes dimmed with terror. Sweet Davina only had one care for tonight's outcome, and that was for me to stay alive. While all I cared for was her safety.

"No," Lucca responded. "For you to have a Syndicate to rule."

"All in what?" he asked incredulously, "On the good faith and trust of one mere girl."

"You have my word, and Miami's," Lucca swore.

"And yet you know it's not enough."

"I know there's no trust, leaving the reason why I would keep the casing in assurance. If she dies, the casing may just find its way somewhere we all wish it hadn't."

Enzo shook his head. "You wouldn't threaten the Cosa Nostra."

Lucca didn't reply. He wouldn't say such a thing, and deep down, I knew he wouldn't harm *La Cosa Nostra*. He would just find another way because Lucca believed in honor and loyalty. He was Mafia.

"I never spoke to anyone about what I'd seen."

Time stilled as Davina's soft voice bounced loudly as she spoke between a conversation with a mob boss and New York's soon-to-be boss. My caged heart beat furiously as my eyes took in Arlo's rigid muscles as they bounced.

"*Cazzo*." *Fuck*, Leo murmured, amused.

Lucca's body stilled as Enzo took a moment.

But even as observant as Davina was to read a room and people, it didn't stop her, and she didn't give me a chance to try stopping her as she continued, "That night took away my innocence, my humanity." Her head lowered to her hands—they didn't fidget—and the few fallen hair strands swiftly moved around her delicate features when she raised her eyes to meet Enzo's. "I never planned on telling anybody about that night. That was until Ilias's life was on the line because of me." Davina dampened her lips. "I'm not here to cause trouble, and it seems I'm now deeper into a treacherous world since the day I opened my eyes in a hospital bed. The last thing I would do is speak about it again, knowing I would put his life in danger and the whole Italian Mafia against me." With her scar on full display, along with her strength, she stated, "I would win *nothing* and lose it all if I said a word about *just* a lucid memory, Mr. Vitelli."

I couldn't read Enzo as he just watched her.

"I do admire your sincerity, and oddly, I believe the honesty in your words. But in this *treacherous* world, that's all they are, Ms. Cohen." He paused with a head shake. "The risks are too high, and finding out your father was who placed you deeper into it, a chief nonetheless, causes a concerning issue for *my* Organization."

I couldn't close my eyes, even for a brief moment, after he'd shared the only piece I'd waited to share with her.

Guilt snuck into my eyes as I watched her perplexed expression.

"But by the look in your eyes, you weren't aware of it," Enzo said to Davina, surprised. He turned to face Lucca. "But of course, you were." He scoffed.

It was then Davina's eyes shifted to mine. They held a hint of hurt, but it quickly disappeared with a small smile directed to me.

Kroshka.

As if she had heard my thoughts, she gave me a slight head nod.

"You know, Lucca, your reputation wasn't wrong. You hold all the cards, and play them all. Assuring you aren't blinded by any moves." Enzo shifted, smirked and said, "Even if I place my trust in you and let her live, it still leaves him. And we both want to keep this from going further tonight." He meant a vote from all families. Lucca wouldn't risk having my life in the hands of others, and Enzo couldn't be seen weak in their eyes, even if it wasn't his mistake to clean but his brother's—he was here for Leo. "And I listened to your reputation, knowing this wouldn't be easy. You asked for an agreement. I have one. You can take it or leave it."

The hidden risk of Enzo's admission chilled my bones as I worried about the wager coming into play.

Lucca would take it if it benefited him, and me. If it benefited his Syndicate.

"There's been tension between our families for quite some time." Lucca didn't give anything away as he listened to Enzo. "For me to fully trust this would work, I need something that ties both of our families together."

When Enzo motioned his hand, and Leo moved toward the door, I hurried over to Davina's side, keeping her seated with my hand on her shoulder as the door creaked open.

We knew danger wouldn't be able to penetrate Lucca's home let alone his study unless all his men were dead, but it was my chance to feel her presence near me, touch her warm skin as the next minutes could be the end of it all.

But when a woman walked through the door with such a regal presence with every step, I was taken aback. Her footfalls didn't stop and her dark red dress shifted fluidly until she stood next to Enzo. Her long brown hair was pushed to her back and her green eyes settled on Lucca.

"A marriage," Enzo proposed.

For the first time with others around, I noticed the small cracks of Lucca's composure trying to slip as his eyes held fury. It was a small slip. His eyes roamed over her, and with a scoff, he smiled.

"Katia Vitelli," Lucca said as if it were a joke. "I thought you were a myth. Guess they just kept you well hidden."

"They did, for years in the old country. That is until you are needed to *fulfill* your duty."

No one missed the way she almost spat her last words.

Lucca chuckled as if this all amused him. "Does your *boss* know about this?" he asked Enzo without removing his gaze from Katia.

"My orders were to fix the problem and solidify the family. I am just following orders. I don't make them *yet*."

Davina's hand slipped over mine, comprehending how this woman was offered like a pawn, and sadly, for *principessa's* like Katia, high in power and regal blood, it meant wedlock for someone as powerful for the best of the Famiglia. Love and care was a luxury in this world.

Lucca's smile widened, and I was sure he had his reasons. "Deal."

Katia closed her eyes briefly but otherwise remained composed, appearing unbothered.

"One last thing," Enzo expressed while fixing his cuff and turning our way. "I advise never returning to New York," his tone warned Davina. "You nor your father."

"I won't. Miami is home now," Davina replied, unaffected to know she would never step foot in the city she was born and raised.

"Then it's settled." Enzo took a hold of Katia's elbow announcing their exit, but she didn't remove her eyes from Lucca right away.

It was only a few seconds, but enough for everyone to notice how she wanted to say more. Instead, she remained quiet until breaking the eye contact she held to her future husband as she turned her body toward her brother. Enzo looked down to Katia, his lips twitched slightly and said to Lucca, "We'll be in contact with the arrangements."

Lucca nodded and raised his palm outwards, motioning the door.

When the door closed, I felt the air return to its normal pressure even when the shock of this turn of events lingered in a vow.

And now, nothing stood in the way.

DAVINA

MY FEELINGS RAN CHAOTICALLY IN MY MIND. SHOCK AND disbelief to have witnessed an arranged marriage in this day and age. As a woman, it infuriated me. Katia had no voice and no say to speak her thoughts. But as she stood in the middle of the room, with the same confidence and assurance for herself as she did in the gala, something told me if it wasn't Lucca, it would've been someone else. She knew when she stepped inside the home why she was here, and instead of showing any weakness or displeasure, Katia remained a true princess who'd been molded in the life of crime and royalty.

It was hard to ignore the relief that warmed my body, knowing it was over. New York would remove the target on Ilias's and my head. Enzo didn't have many options but to trust. Since he couldn't, he chose the Famiglia instead of his own blood.

A foreign thought, but a rude awakening to understand how organized and how far they would go in, all for the name of *Cosa Nostra*.

"Davina," Lucca's voice pulled me away from my thoughts. "I can't express how stupid it was for you to speak at the time you did, and although I believe it benefited us... I'm going to ask you once. Don't do it again. It's not a threat," he added. "It's a warning. Men in this life have different views, and I hate to go through all this trouble for nothing."

Leave it to Lucca to sound concerned for a mere second before taking it and adding more to his trouble. But I didn't care, I found it funny that he at least tried to remind me of the views of the underworld.

I hid my chuckle with a smile. "It won't. Because it won't be needed again."

I wouldn't have to, just for the simple reason that Ilias's life was no longer on the line. I wasn't naive to the fact that danger would always stalk him, he was one of them, but whoever dared harm him would meet their fate. It also came down to the terrifying circumstance that anything could take him away. One thing I knew for sure, I would be by his side and live our present as if every day was our last.

It was the only way to cherish every breath I would take.

"Good. Now, I need a minute with Arlo."

As soon as he finished his sentence, I was up on my feet and ready to leave this room with Ilias.

He followed behind, his hand never leaving my lower back as he opened the door.

The gala was over, and only a few people remained as they cleaned as quickly as possible. The pianist and violinist were also here, taking a break and leaving me wondering why have they stayed even if the event was over.

The question didn't bother me to find an answer, I just wanted to flee to the room so I could finally let go in his arms.

I took the first step up the staircase, but his hand stopped me. With the force of momentum, I spun around until we were on eye level.

"Wait, I just..." Ilias tried finding the right words. His eyes apologized instead as his thumb and index finger held my chin. "About your father."

"Don't." I shook my head. "It would be pathetic if I believed you hid it in spite. After everything we've gone through, all you've risked for me, I don't need an explanation, especially when I'm sure you were just as surprised as I was."

"I wanted to tell you after all this was over."

"I don't know him," I stated, and it was true. I'd only spoken to Chief Pierce a few times. The conversations were short and impersonal. I had never cared about my father enough to find out his name or who he was. It had always been mom and me, and after she passed, I couldn't find the courage to find him. "But I can't be mad, when in the end, he's the reason I found you."

"*Kroshka,*" Ilias growled, making me chuckle as he didn't know the right way to take my feelings. He looked around the room, and when his captivating irises held mine, he asked, "Would you like to dance?"

My brows pinched. "Now?"

"*Da.*" *Yes*, he'd said bringing me down the step.

"Here?" My lips twitched.

"No one is watching."

"Without music?"

"*Do you want to dance?*" He stressed again.

This time with a smile, I replied, "*Da.*"

Ilias took my hand, pulling me as he walked backward into the open space. His hand lifted and my body spun before he brought me to him.

A soft tune began to play from afar. My palms rested on his chest, feeling his beating heart against them. Emotion welled as I couldn't fathom how this could be possible.

How did I cheat death again and get him, too?

"Is it really over?" I whispered. My voice cracked with doubt, knowing I didn't have to run anymore. It cracked with the pain and trauma I could let go of with time.

"Hey." Ilias brought my eyes to the depths of his blues. With his hand on my neck possessively, he whispered, "Nothing will get between us."

My throat tightened and my chest constricted to his words. It was the strength and certainty of *us* in his voice that tugged my heart. The small smile that tried to calm the raging war inside of me, and it did. He did. Now the uncertainty was gone after a deep breath as I kept my eyes on him. My reality.

EPILOGUE

d a v i n a

MIAMI'S SUN HID UNDER THE ROLLING STORM CLOUDS, darkening the skies. The loud cracking from above stole my attention as thunder and rain poured heavily from above.

A midsummer day in this city should have a clear sky and tourists walking around as they take in the scenery, enjoying a hot and sunny day.

But of course, not today.

Not on Lucca's wedding day.

As I waited at the entrance of our condominium, I rushed beneath the carpool, waiting to be picked up. It wasn't far, but I hoped I would make it to the church in time before the crowd of guests arrived.

Running my fingers over my formal dress, my mind raced through today's events and how today would seal the deal of the arrangement that had taken motion months ago.

The arrangement that tied trust, families, and the life of Ilias and me.

"Davina!"

My head shot up at the sound of my name, but it wasn't Ilias's car that waited for me. It was James's black SUV.

I don't think I could ever call him Father or Dad, and James never asked for such a thing. He understood those years were lost. He understood it was hard to build a relationship when we were still strangers in a way, and since I knew it bothered him when I'd referred to him as Chief Pierce or just Pierce, calling him by his first name fit us.

I rushed to his cracked window while remaining dry under the building canopy.

"Where's Ilias?" I asked.

"He's fine, but couldn't make it in time. He called for me to get you, hop in before the seat gets soaked."

Lately, Ilias has been more careful with my safety, and the only other person he trusted me with, aside from his siblings, was James, even if he wasn't a fan of him.

I slid across the leather seat and turned to my father. His peppered hair was turning gray around his temples since the first time I'd met him. It was awkward, and we never spoke again of the day when we'd sat in the café without anything to say, just a month after I'd found out his secret. Me.

"Do you know anything?" I asked.

"You need to be more specific." He chuckled as he drove deeper into the heavy rain.

"Do you know why there is always a guard at the door of my place or following me? Or why are you always taking me places when he can't?"

"Have you asked him?"

"He said safety is important."

"Isn't it?" he asked.

"Yeah, but..." I stopped mid-sentence. James may be my father, but I couldn't just give information that may harm Ilias. So, I kept how Ilias had said it was *temporary,* for now. "Never mind, I'm just over thinking."

James nodded. "He just wants you to be safe. Can't blame him."

Since I didn't know what to reply or what I needed to say next, I remained quiet for the rest of the drive. It didn't upset him, somehow we always fell into a comfortable silence.

"There he is," James whispered.

Indeed, he was.

Ilias stood over a small tent under the church's side entrance dressed in a full black suit. When he noticed me inside the car, he smiled under an opened umbrella and walked the distance of those few feet away that kept us apart.

He opened the car door as I tried holding the skirt of my dress higher.

"Thank you, James," Ilias said once I was out of the car and in his arms.

"Any time."

Ilias closed the door, and I gave James a wave before he drove off.

Once we were both under the protection of the church, I was able to look up to him, and let my eyes get captivated by him.

"*Kroshka*," he murmured, not leaving any space between us.

My hand ran over his hair gently before caressing his jawline as his scruff pricked my skin.

"Ilias," I replied.

"Have I mentioned how stunning you are?" His lips lifting at the corners.

"Not since I woke up with your body over mine."

Ilias chuckled with eyes that ran over my body before they shot up to my mouth. His thumb traced my bottom lip and the air thickened, making it difficult to breathe evenly.

"That was hours ago."

"Mhm," I managed to reply.

"What's a few more when we can end the day the same way we started it?"

Now it was my time to chuckle.

"We should take our seats. I've been counting the minutes for this arrangement to fulfill." His eyes held a touch of alarm but it was overthrown with the sound of relief in his tone. The promise that granted us the freedom to live.

"I need to do something before I walk inside," I murmured, gazing over the side church door.

He didn't respond, and when I shifted my attention back to him, Ilias watched me carefully.

"Out here?" he asked.

The rain had died, leaving behind humidity and quietness.

I nodded.

His brow raised. "Fine, I'll be right inside. Don't be long."

As I pulled away from him, his arm resisted bringing me back. Ilias held my jaw captive, bringing our mouths to collide in a haste kiss. My hand balled his tuxedo, savoring the feel of his lips possessively taking mine. He stopped abruptly, giving our mouths a few inches of distance.

"Fucking stunning." He shook his head, unable to wait the few hours he'd spoken short minutes ago. "Now go, before I change my mind." Ilias ushered as he gave my hips a tight grip before he entered the church.

His back was visible through the stained glass window, waiting. I bit my smile with a small head shake and walked a few steps deeper into the quaint courtyard.

Looking up, the clouds parted, letting small rays of sunshine to slip through the sky, bringing their light into the world.

I closed my eyes and took a deep breath to the smell of petrichor that lingered in serenity, and now was the right time to gather the courage to do one last thing I'd been thinking since the day after the charity gala.

I fished for the note inside my small clutch, and once my fingers caught the paper, I pulled it out and opened it, tracing every crease with my thumb.

With the note in one hand and my phone in the other, I dialed and waited.

The phone line wasn't disconnected. It worked, and I was sent straight to voicemail.

I waited until the tone rang.

"Hey, it's me," I said with a dim smile. "I've waited till this day to talk to you in the only way I could." My eyes fell back to the note. My chest constricted as sorrow moistened my eyes. "I just wanted to tell you, I got your note, and I did run." Tears fell freely, remembering how I left his lifeless green eyes behind. "You would've been a great doctor. You would've made a woman lucky to call her your fiancé one day," I gasped, "I'm sorry." My heart ached in grief for his life, and I tried to regain my composure as I continued, "In the note, you asked for me to call when I was safe ... I'm safe Martin. See you in the afterlife."

THE END

*"The Vitelli's had taken something from me ...
Now, I was taking her."*

COMING SOON

A War Around Us
(The Moretti Crime Family Book 2)
Lucca & Katia

Add *A War Around Us* to your Goodreads TBR.
https://www.goodreads.com/book/show/57795524-a-war-around-us

NOTE FROM AUTHOR

Surreal, that's how I feel after publishing *A Bullet Between Us*, my first dark romance novel, mafia romance at that. I've always read and kept up with this genre while falling in love with everything that comes within. The angst, the plot twist, the world building and research. I could only dream to be able to do such a thing.

Then it all came rushing, from beginning to end. And I knew I could too.

Now it's out in the world, and read by you.

And for that I am thankful.

Thank you, for taking a chance with my words, and remember, fear lives within all of us, but we are strong.

You got this.

Oh, and one more thing, every relationship starts with a stranger. Treasure those relationships, time is never guaranteed.

If you enjoyed Davina & Ilias's story, don't be shy, leave a review. I would be thrilled to read your thoughts and emotions you've experienced while reading their love story.

Stay dangerous, gorgeous.

Hugs,
K Dosal

THANK YOU

Someone close to me once told me, "Real life is not within the books you write." I knew that, but it's still a world I love. A world that has brought me so many people I am thankful for. A world where I get to dream and let others in. My words create emotions that sweep into the real world, and this time, I have some people to thank for helping me to do so with this book.

First, my readers. Your kind words, messages, reviews, and love is something I'll forever cherish.

To my Street Team & ARC Team. I mean seriously, what you guys do to help my books be where they are by your honest reviews, shares, stories, posts, and overall support, *insert mind blown emoji* thank you. You ladies make me smile every day with all your love.

Nicole, you have the power to make me laugh at the stupidest shit. You lift me, cheer me, listen and understand my frustrations, and crush any doubts I may encounter. Having you along in this journey knowing I have you on my side as my friend is truly beautiful. Cheers to corny lines and growing together while living our dreams. Love you, Niks. If you would like check out some beautiful written masterpieces you can check out Nicole Fiorina at, nicolefiorina.com

Justin, I did it, babe. You said, "Write what you want, what's stopping you?" With your support, how could I not? You never let fear limit us, and for that, I know our boys will always be brave. I love you, and our two mini us.

Mitch, I can't believe how lucky I was to find you. I'm still in awe of how you were able to understand my vision based on my rambles. You captured the beautiful, dark, broken, and romance edge I wished to portray for this cover with your art. Thank you is not enough. You are the best. If you would like to check out his art work or poetry you can go to radpublishing.com

Amy S, street team leader, late night messenger, Netflix recs swapper, and overall badass, I am so, so thankful to have you. Thank you for your kindness, your support, and always being there for me.

To my editor, Amy Briggs, thank you for your flexibility and answering my many questions.

For those who always keep me sane, Mia K., my family, friends, readers, and the never-ending video scrolling TikTok strangers, thank you.

Love,
Kassandra

JOIN A BOOK CLUB

If you would like to join us each month for a themed romance book read & be part of a great gang of ladies, we would love to have you.

Find us on Facebook:

https://facebook.com/groups/littlemissobsessivebookclub

ABOUT THE AUTHOR

K. Dosal is a hopeless romance author, with work ranging from Contemporary, Young Adult, to Mafia. She lives on the Gulf Coast with her Amazing husband, who is always supportive of her wild dreams, and their two energetic boys. When she's not writing or reading, you can find her at the beach with her family, going on boat rides, binge watching, or taking a bike ride.

K started writing on a spiral notebook after reading a book that made her ask herself, *why not me?* After falling in love with the first pages she wrote, she continued until there was no paper left, then switched to her laptop. Since then, she's been making her dreams come true and living on the *why not me?*

Music lover, kitchen dancer, poker player, and beach lover, K is always looking forward to book-talk and watching where her mind will take her with the stories that inhabit within.

I love to hear from readers.

Feel free to contact me on social media:
@ k d o s a l b o o k s

K D O S A L . C O M
SWEET & DANGEROUS ROMANCE

Printed in Great Britain
by Amazon